# THE RIVER

# THE RIVER

## Rumer Godden

CHIVERS LARGE PRINT
BATH

British Library Cataloguing in Publication Data available

This Large Print edition published by Chivers Press, Bath, 1998

Published by arrangement with Robert Hale Limited

U.K. Hardcover ISBN 0 7540 3409 7
U.K. Softcover  ISBN 0 7540 3410 0

*To*
**R.** DE **L.P.**
*in perpetual thanks*

# THE RIVER

The river was in Bengal, India, but for the purpose of this book, these thoughts, it might as easily have been a river in America, in Europe, in England, France, New Zealand or Timbuctoo, though they do not of course have rivers in Timbuctoo. Its flavour would be different in each; Bogey's cobra would, of course, have been something else and the flavour of the people who lived by the river would be different.

That is what makes a family, the flavour, the family flavour, and no one outside the family, however loved and intimate, can share it. Three people had the same flavour as the child, Harriet, who lived in this garden; were her contemporaries, her kin; Bea was one, the others were Bogey and Victoria. They lived in their house beside the river, in a jute-pressing works near a little Indian town; they had not been sent away out of the tropics because there was a war; this war, the last war, any war, it does not matter which war.

It is strange that almost the first words you have to learn in Latin should be 'love' and 'war'.

| Bellum | Amo |
|--------|------|
| Bellum | Amas |
| Bellum | Amat |

| Belli | Amamus |
|-------|--------|
| Bello | Amatis |
| Bello | Amant |

'I can't learn them,' said Harriet. 'Do help me, Bea. Let's take one each and say them aloud, both at once.'

'Very well. Which will you have?'

'You had better have love,' said Harriet.

In the heat they both had their hair tied up on top of their heads in topknots, but Bea wore a cerise ribbon; the effect of it on her topknot gave her a geisha look that was interesting and becoming. Her eyebrows, as she studied this Latin that it was decreed that they should learn, were like fine aloof question marks.

'Do you *like* Latin, Bea?'

'No, of course I don't, but if I have to learn it,' said Bea, 'it is better to learn it quickly.' She glanced across at Harriet. 'You are always trying to stop things happening, Harriet, and you can't.'

But Harriet still thought, privately, that she could.

It was the doldrums of the afternoon and Bea and Harriet, the older children, had to do their homework, opposite one another, at the dining-room table. It was hot. Outside the garden was filled with hot, heavy, sleepy sun; there was a smell of leaves and grass and of sun on the house stone. Beyond the garden was the sound of the river and from far away came a whoop from

2

Bogey. 'I wonder what Bogey has found now,' thought Harriet, and wriggled. The fan blew on her forehead, but it only blew hot air, the polish of the table was sticky and held the skin of her arms, there was a dusty dry feeling of dust between her toes. 'You will get hookworm, Harriet, if you go barefoot,' Nan told her. 'Why do you? Bea doesn't.' Harriet looked now under the table to see. No, Bea's feet were gracefully crossed in their correct sandals.

'You had better get on, Harry,' said Bea. 'You have algebra to do as well, and music, and you haven't learnt your Bible verses yet. Better hurry, Harriet.'

Harriet sighed. Latin, and algebra, and music and other things: eating liver, having an injection, seeing a mad paidog—how did Bea manage to take them all so quietly? How? Harriet sighed. She could not, nowadays, aspire to Bea.

'Nan, why is Bea so different?'

'She always was,' said Nan.

'No, she is changing.'

'She is growing up,' said Nan. 'We all have to, willy-nilly.' Harriet did not much like the sound of that expression, 'willy-nilly.'

'Oh, well!' she said, and sighed again and her mind went off on a rapid Harriet canter of its own, too rapid for stops. 'Will-I-get-hookworm-you - get - all - kinds - of - worms - in - India - and - diseases - too - there - is - a - leper - in - the

3

- bazaar - no - nose - and - his - fingers - dropping - off - him - if - I - had - no - fingers - I - couldn't - learn - music - could - I - no - March - of - the - Men-of-Harlech.' She looked at her own fingers, brown and small and whole, except that one had a nail broken where Bogey had banged it, and one had a scratch new that morning, and two were stained bright yellow from the dye she had been making from the yellow flower of a bush that grew beside the cook-house.

The middle finger of Harriet's right hand had a lump on the side of it; that was her writing lump; she had it because she wrote so much, because she was a writer. 'I am going to be a poet when I grow up,' said Harriet; and she added, after another thought, 'Willy-nilly.' She kept a private diary and a poem book hidden in an old box that also did as a desk in an alcove under the side-stairs, her Secret Hole, though it was not secret at all and there was no need to hide her book because she could not resist reading her poems to everyone who would listen. Sometimes she carried her book pouched in her dress. She was writing a poem now, and, as she began to think of it, her eyes grew misty and comfortable.

*'Saw roses there that comforted her heart*
*And saw their crimson petals plop apart.'*

'*Plop* apart?' asked Bea, her eyebrows more

4

clear and more surprised and Harriet blushed. She had not known she had spoken aloud.

'*Do* get on, Harry.'

'Yes, Bea—*Amo. Amas. Amat . . . Bellum . . . Belli . . . Bello. . . .*'

War and love. 'How many children,' wondered Harriet, yawning, 'had had to learn those since'—she cast round in her mind for someone prominent who could have learnt them—'since Julius Cæsar, say, or Pontius Pilate (they must have learnt them, they were Romans) or even Jesus—perhaps-if-Jesus-went-to-school.' She yawned again and reached for the Outline of History. 'Loves-and-Wars-' she thought, flipping over the pages. 'Xerxes - Alexander - Gothsand Huns - Arthur - and - Guinevere - RichardtheLionheart - Marlborough-Kitchener. Love and war, love and hate all muddled up together.' She remembered she had no history to prepare; it was Bible verses and she shut up the book and opened Father's old Bible that they used for lessons. 'Ever-since-AdamandEve,' cantered off Harriet, 'Cain-Abel-Jacob LeahandRachel-the-Children of Israeland-all-the-rest-of-them. Even in stories, even in plays,' and she looked at Bea's elbow holding down the edges of the Shakespeare's flimsy pages that blew up under the fan. 'Shylock and Portia-and-RomeoandJuliet-and-Cleopatra.' She liked Cleopatra best, but even thinking of Cleopatra

5

she wondered that no one ever grew tired of it, of all this love and all this war. 'Or if they do,' she thought, 'someone starts it all over again. It is as much life as living,' thought Harriet. 'You are born, you are a he or a she, and you live until you die... Willy-nilly. Yes. Nan is right. It all *is* willy-nilly, though I think you could live very well without a war ... and I suppose without being loved. But I hope I am loved,' thought Harriet, 'as much as Cleopatra,' and she thought, 'I wish I were not so young ... children don't have loves or wars.' She drew circles on her algebra. 'Or do they?' wondered Harriet. 'Do they ... of their kind?'

A drum began to beat softly in the village behind the house. Harriet sat up. 'Bea. To-night is Diwali.'

'I know. But if you haven't done your homework,' Bea pointed out, 'you won't be allowed to go.'

Bea loved Diwali night as much as Harriet did, but when she was excited, she managed to contain her excitement as she contained her likes and dislikes. How? Harriet gave her another long look and sank back baffled. 'I thought you had forgotten,' she said.

'How could I forget?' said Bea. 'Listen to the drums.'

All day the drummers had been going round the town and the villages that lay around it. Diwali was the Hindu festival of the Feast of

Lights.

There are ritual festivals in every religion throughout the year, and every family keeps those it needs, the Chinese and the Roman Catholics being perhaps the most elaborate in theirs, though the old Russians and the Hindus come close and Tibet has charming holidays of its own. Diwali was a curious festival to find in the keeping of a European family, but in Harriet's, as in every large household in India, there was always someone who had to keep some one of the different festivals as they occurred: Nan was a Catholic; Abdullah, the old butler, was a Mohammedan, and so was Gaffura his assistant; Maila, the bearer, was a Buddhist from the State of Sikkim; the gardeners were Hindu Brahmins, Heaven Born; the sweeper and the Ayah were Hindu Untouchables and Ram Prasad Singh, the gateman, the children's friend, was of the separate sect of Sikh. Now the gardeners were away in the bazaar, buying the little saucer earthenware festival lamps and the wicks and oil to float in them, while Abdullah and Maila were not interested. The children kept Diwali because it is an irresistible festival and no one could live in the country in which it is held and not be touched by it.

'To-night when it is dark,' thought Harriet, her eyes anywhere but on her work, 'Ram Prasad will have bought for us a hundred or two hundred lamps. They are made of earthenware,

7

shaped like hearts or tarts or leaves, and they cost two pies each' (a pie is a third of a farthing), 'and in each we shall put oil and float a wick; then we shall set them all along the roof and at the windows and in rows on the steps and at the gate and over the gate; and we shall light them. Everywhere, on every house, there will be lights, and on the river the boats will have them burning and we shall see them go past, and other lights on rafts will be floated down and the rich Hindus will give feasts and feed the poor and let off fireworks and we shall stay up to dinner to see.'

Diwali, to the children, was also the official opening of the winter. The greenfly came, millions of insects that flew around the lights at dusk. The gardeners began to plant out vegetables and flower seeds. There was a coolness in the mornings and evenings, a thicker dew, more mosquitoes. Then Diwali came, and it was winter. 'Winter, the cold weather. That is the best time of all,' thought Harriet with relish. It seemed to her, as she looked forward to it, a pageant of pleasantness. 'Soon we shall have fires,' thought Harriet, 'and sweet peas. I wonder what we shall do this winter? What will happen?' And as people far wiser than Harriet have thought, she answered herself. 'Nothing. Nothing at all. Nothing ever happens here.' And then she asked Bea, across the table, 'Bea. Is Captain John coming tonight?'

Bea raised her head. 'I suppose he is,' said Bea, and she added uncertainly, 'Bother.'

'Yes. Bother,' said Harriet. 'Bother! Bother! Bother!'

★　　★　　★

'We must have a quiet winter this year,' Mother had said. 'The world is too unhappy for anything else. There are hurt men and women, and children dying of hunger. . . .'

'Oh, Mother!' said Harriet, wriggling.

'Yes,' said Mother firmly, 'think of Captain John.'

'I don't want to think of Captain John,' said Harriet with a feeling of fixed hard naughtiness. 'Why should there be a Captain John?' she asked angrily. 'Or if there must be, why should he want to come here?'

Captain John had come because he had to try to pick up again the threads of living and of earning his living. He had been a prisoner of war and escaped, only to go for more than a year to hospital. He had been tortured in the prison camp, and he was wounded before he went there. He was a young man, or had been a young man, but now his stiff grey face was any age; he had a stiff body, one leg was amputated at the hip, and he had a heavy artificial one that made him more jerky still. The children were warned to be careful of what they said to him. He

9

eschewed grown-ups, but he seemed to like to come into the nursery. 'Why does he?' wondered Harriet. 'What does he want?' He seemed to want something. To be hungry. For what? At first he liked Victoria best, and this was surprising to Harriet because Victoria treated him in a matter-of-fact, off-hand way, that was shocking.

'You mustn't, Victoria,' Harriet told her. 'Captain John was *so* brave. He stayed there in the battle until his leg was shot off.'

Victoria's brown eyes rested thoughtfully on Captain John. 'Why didn't he stay until the other leg was shot off?' she asked.

But he still seemed to like Victoria best.

'Did Victoria ask him to come to-night?' said Harriet now. 'Or did Mother?'

There was a silence, and then: 'No one asked him,' said Bea. 'He asked me.'

'*Asked* you?' said Harriet. 'But. . . .' She had thought that grown-up people did not ask for things.

'He seemed to want to come,' said Bea.

Harriet stared across the table, but all she could see of Bea's face was her forehead and the withdrawn sealed look of her lids as she studied her book. The shadow of her ribbon made a mark of shadow, like a moth, on her cheek. She had withdrawn even further into herself than usual.

*     *     *

Harriet's river was a great slowly flowing mile-wide river between banks of mud and white sand, with fields flat to the horizon, jute-fields and rice-fields under a blue weight of sky. 'If there is any space in me,' Harriet said, when she was grown up, 'it is from that sky.'

The river emptied itself, through the delta, into the Bay of Bengal, its final sea. There was life in and over its flowing; an indigenous life of fish, of crocodiles and of porpoises that somersaulted in and out of the water, their hides grey and bronze and bubble-blue in the sun; rafts of water-hyacinths floated on it and flowered in the spring. There was a traffic life on the river; there were black-funnelled, paddle-wheeled mail steamers that sent waves against the bank and other steamers towing flat jute barges; there were country boats, wicker on wooden hulls, that had eyes painted on their prows and sets of tattered sails to put up in the wind; there were fishing boats, crescents lying in the water, and there were fishermen with baskets, wading in the shallows on skinny black legs, throwing fine small nets that brought up finger-length fishes shining in the mesh. The fish were part of the traffic, and each part was animated by a purpose of its own, and the river bore them all down on its flow.

The small town was sunk in the even tenor of

11

Bengali life, surrounded by fields and villages and this slow river. It had mango groves and water tanks, and one main street with a bazaar, a mosque with a white dome and a temple with pillars and a silver roof, the silver made of hammered-out kerosene tins.

Harriet and the children knew the bazaar intimately; they knew the kite shop where they bought paper kites and sheets of thin exquisite bright paper; they knew the shops where a curious mixture was sold of Indian cigarettes and betel nut, pān, done up in leaf bundles, and coloured pyjama strings and soda water; they knew the grain shops and the spice shops and the sweet shops with their smell of cooking sugar and ghee, and the bangle shops, and the cloth shop where bolts of cloth showed inviting patterns of feather and scallop prints, and the children's dresses, pressed flat like paper dresses, hung and swung from the shop fronts.

There was only one road. It was built high among the fields so that the monsoon floods would not cover it; it went through villages and sprawling bazaars, and over hump-backed bridges, past bullock carts and walking people and an occasional car. It stretched across country, with the flat Bengal plain rolling to the horizon and clumps of villages, built up like the road, in mounds of mango, banana and coconut trees. Soon the bauhinia trees would bud along the road, their flowers white and curved like

12

shells. Now the fields were dry, but each side of the road was water left from the flood that covered the plain in the rains; it showed under the floating patches of water-hyacinth, and kingfishers, with a flash of brilliant blue, whirred up and settled on the telegraph wires, showing their russet breasts.

The river came into view from the road, its width showing only a line of the further bank, its near bank broken with buildings and patches of bazaar and high walls and corrugated-iron warehouses and mill chimneys. Small boats, covered in wicker-work cowls, put out from one bank to ferry across to the other. In boats like that the children went fishing for pearls. The pearls were sunset river pearls, but it was the divers, not the children, who found them; the children could not get their hooks to go deep enough; the divers dived naked to the river-bed.

The children lived in the Big House of the Works. The Works were spread away from the bazaar along the river with the firm's houses and gardens on the further side. The life of every family is conditioned by the work of its elders; think of a doctor's house, or a writer's, a musician's or a missionary's. It is necessary for the whole family to live in the conditions that such work brings; for these children it was jute.

The jute grew in the fields; they knew all its processes: from the seed which their father germinated and experimented with at the

13

Government Farm, through its young growth, when they could not ride their ponies across country, to the reaping and steeping in the water along the road, in dykes along the fields, when its stench would hang over the whole land. They saw it come in on country boats, on bullock carts, into the Works and the piles of it lying in the sheds for carding and cleaning and grading, while the great presses went up and down and the bales were tumbled out of them, silky and flaxen with a strong jute smell. They saw it go away to the steamers; the steamers and flats were piled high with it and took it down the river to the mills of Calcutta.

The sound of the Works came over the wall: the noise of trucks running on their tracks, wagons pushed by hand by brown, sweating coolies, of the presses working and of machinery and the sound of bellows and iron on iron from the foundry, and the clang of the weighing points, the shouting of the tally clerks, the bumping down of the bales and always the regular puff of escaping steam, puff-wait-puff; it was like a pulse in the background of the children's lives. In the inner dimness of the press-rooms was the sheen of the press-tubes, of brass locks, going down with the pale shining heaps of jute that came up again as bales. There was a smell there of jute dust and coal, steam and hot oil and human sweat, that was one of the accompanying smells of their childhood, like the

14

smell of cess and incense and frying ghee in the bazaar and of honey from the mustard and radish flowers when they were out in the fields, and in season, the stench of steeping jute. There were thousands of coolies in the Works, though they were as impersonal as ants to the children. (Bogey used to eat ants to make him wise.) In the concrete-built, double-floored offices there were scores of clerks, babus, in white muslin shirts and dhoties; the children used sometimes to go with their mother to visit the babus' wives and they were given coconut shredded with sugar and 'sandesh,' a toffee stuck with silver paper. The firm had its own fleet of launches, called after Indian birds: the 'Osprey', the 'Hoopoe', the 'Oriole', the 'Cormorant', the 'Snipe'; each had its own crew. There were porters or peons, with yellow turbans and staves to guard the gates.

Beyond the Works was the White House, where the Senior Assistant lived, and the Red House where the Junior Assistants all lived together, and the Little House where the Engineer lived. They stood in their own gardens beside the Big House garden.

Other firms were scattered up and down the river and to them assistants came, young men from England and Scotland, usually from Scotland, even from Greece, who came out raw and young to learn the trade and ended up as magnates. Later on, they married, and too often, Father said, their wives ended up as magnums.

There were a few other Europeans in the town: a Deputy Commissioner, Mr Marshall, and a doctor, Dr Paget. Once there had been a cantonment, but now all that was left of it was a row of graves in the small European cemetery, where grew trees with flowers like mimosa balls. One grave was of a boy, Piper John Fox, who died nearly two hundred years ago when he was fourteen years old.

Perhaps the place and the life were alien, circumscribed, dull to the grown-ups who lived there; for the children it was their world of home. They lived in the Big House in a big garden on the river with the tall flowering cork tree by their front steps. It was their world, complete. Up to this winter it had been completely happy.

*       *       *

Half of Harriet wanted to stay as a child; half wanted to be a grown-up. She often asked, 'What shall I do when I am? What will it be like?' She often asked the others, 'What shall you be when you are grown up?' It was always Harriet who started these discussions. No one else really liked them except Victoria, who was too young to know what she was, even now.

'I shall be a cross red nurse when I grow up,'

16

said Victoria.

'She means a Red Cross Nurse,' said Nan.

'What shall I be?' thought Harriet, fascinated. There seemed to her to be infinite possibilities. 'I might be a nun,' she said, 'or a missionary perhaps, then I could help people. Or a doctor. It would be wonderful to be a doctor, to save people's lives, and give your own life up.' The vista was exciting. 'Wonderful,' said Harriet. 'Wouldn't you like that, Bea?'

'No,' said Bea. 'I want my life for myself.'

Harriet was too truthful to deny that she did too, and she tore herself away from the thought of being a doctor. 'So many grown-up people seem to be nothing very much,' she said. She was thinking of the people she knew, of Nan and Father and Mother and Dr Paget and Captain John. 'They are nothing important,' thought Harriet, wondering. 'Why?' They did not seem to mind. 'But I want to be important. I will be.' 'Perhaps I shall be a great dancer,' she said aloud, 'or a politician and make speeches.'

'I thought you were going to be a poet,' said Bea.

'Well ... I am a poet,' said Harriet.

'You will be what you are. You will have to be,' said Nan, who was unconcernedly darning. 'In the end everyone is what they are.'

'But how shall I know?' cried Harriet, chafing.

'You will find out as you grow,' said Nan,

17

running her needle in and out of the sock stretched on her hand. That seemed altogether too slow for Harriet.

'Bea, what will you be? An actress? Or a hospital nurse? Or a doctor? A great doctor? When you are grown up, what will you be?'

'How can I tell till I get there?' asked Bea.

'But say. You must say. You must be something.'

'I shall wait till I am,' said Bea, tolerantly, 'and then be it.'

'That is a funny sort of answer,' said Harriet, disgusted.

'It is rather a good one,' said Nan.

Harriet found her family maddening. Father was too busy, in a general family and office way, to have any special time to spare for Harriet, or for any of them; Mother was busy, too, with the house, the family, the servants, notes and letters and lessons and accounts; and besides, she was having another baby soon and had not to be disturbed. Nan? Well, Nan was Nan, and to Harriet that was like bread, too everyday and too necessary to be regarded, though she was the staff of life. There used to be Bea, but now Bea was different; she had withdrawn from Harriet; she was quiet, altogether elderly and distant, and she had new predilections; for instance, she had made friends with Valerie from across the river, a big, hard girl, whom Harriet disliked and feared, and who switched Bea away with

18

secrets and happenings in which Harriet had no part. She was no longer sure of Bea. Harriet would have liked to play with Bogey. Though he was much younger, she was young, too, in streaks, but Bogey played in his own Bogey way that was not at all Harriet's. Harriet could never leave anything alone, and Bogey liked things to be alive and behave themselves in their own way. For instance, he played with lizards and grass snakes; he played armies with insects. He did not like toy soldiers. 'They are all tin,' he said. 'I play soldiers with n'insecks.'

'But can't you pretend, Boge?' asked Harriet.

'No, I can't,' said Bogey. 'I like live n'insecks best.'

He was a very thin little boy, with thin arms and legs; his hair was cut short and his forehead showed sensitive and lumpy, while his eyes were small and brown and quick and live. He was absorbed in a completely happy and private life of his own, and though he occasionally needed Harriet, it was seldom for long. His best game was 'going - round - the - garden - without - being - seen,' and that hid him even from her. He was always being stung or bruised or bitten, but he managed to contain his wounds as Bea did her difficulties. 'You will get into trouble one of these days,' said jealous, discontented Harriet, but he only smiled and she sensed that he preferred to get into his own trouble himself. It was no good. It was just not possible to play

19

with Bogey.

In her loneliness, Harriet was driven to adopt places; there was her cubbyhole under the stairs, and there was a place on the end of the jetty, the landing-stage by the house. Harriet liked to sit on the end of it, her legs hanging down, her back warmed with sun, her ears filled with the cool gurgling of the water against the jetty poles.

'How is it a Secret Hole when it isn't a secret and it isn't a hole?' Valerie asked about the Secret Hole, but it still felt secret to Harriet, though she used the jetty for her more open thoughts. The flowing water helped her thoughts to flow. She had also, though she did not yet understand about this, an affinity with the cork tree. It was her tree, as the brilliant jacaranda trees, the bamboos and the lace tangles of bridal creeper in the garden, belonged to Bea, and the tight Maréchal-Niel rosebuds were Victoria's. Why? She did not know, but she liked to go to the cork tree, she liked to look up into it and if she really wanted to hear the river, she went to listen to it there. There it was not too loud, too near, drawing Harriet, drawing her away as it did on the jetty. Under the cork tree, she could hear it running steadily, calmly and with it, always, the puff-steam-puff from the Works.

'It goes on, goes on,' said Harriet, her head against the cork tree. 'I wonder what is going to happen to us?' And by that she meant, of course, 'What is going to happen to me?'

There were ways of telling. Nan used sometimes to play charms with them. She dropped pieces of lead tinfoil into a saucepan of boiling water, and, when they were softened, she lifted them out with a spoon on to a cold plate where they hardened. Whatever shapes they made told your future.

They played this one Sunday morning some three weeks after Diwali when Valerie had come to spend the day. Captain John, too, had limped up the drive after breakfast, and was there, sitting by Nan, his stick propped by his chair.

'He is always here, always,' thought Harriet crossly. 'And so is Valerie. Why should they be? Haven't they homes of their own?'

She noticed now that, when Captain John was alone with them, some of the stiffness went out of his face. Sometimes he laughed and his eyes were not unlike Bogey's, except that Bogey's were quick and his had often a curious emptiness; but they were gentle too. 'Yes, he has nice eyes,' Harriet admitted, 'but I wish he were not so jerky.' 'Why is he so jerky?' she had asked Mother irritably. 'Because he was hurt so badly,' said Mother. 'Unbearably hurt.'

Looking at Captain John now in the light of this soft warm morning, as he bent his head down by Victoria's, as Victoria leant against his knee, it was difficult to think of him as being

21

unbearably hurt. 'Unbearably?' questioned Harriet, wrinkling her forehead. 'What is unbearable? When I caught my nail in the railway carriage door I went mad with pain. Mad. Then why isn't he mad? Why didn't he die? What is it that made him live and not go mad?' 'He must be stronger than we think,' said Harriet, looking at Captain John.

She considered him, as he put Victoria carefully away and took the saucepan from Nan, to let Nan have a change and rest. His hands were steady now, and his face had colour from the warmth of the fire. He looked big, yes, almost strong among the children, and his hair, that was dark, patched with white, was attractive. 'Like a magpie,' thought Harriet. 'Why, he is very good-looking,' thought Harriet in surprise.

She knew Nan admired him. 'He is like a young prince,' said Nan.

'A funny kind of a prince!' Harriet had said. 'And he isn't young, Nan.'

'He is, poor boy.'

'Oh, Nan!' said Harriet impatiently. 'And why does he come all the time—all the time?'

'Perhaps—we have something he needs,' said Nan.

'What?'

'I don't know. We must pray for him. He will go on when he is ready,' said Nan.

'Go on? Where?' asked Harriet, but Nan did

22

not say. Instead, she added in her admonitory seeing-through-Harriet voice, 'Now you are not to go saying anything to him, Harriet.'

'As if I would,' said Harriet indignantly, but she knew that Nan was right and that probably her curiosity would get the better of her. 'A young prince,' thought Harriet now. She was not quite so sure that Nan was wrong.

'Captain John,' said Valerie, 'will you drop a charm for me?' Valerie, by courtesy of the family to her place as visitor, had been given the first turn. Why then should she have another so soon?

'It is Harriet's turn,' said Captain John crisply, and Harriet heard him, and she knew, warmly, in an instant as she heard this crispness in his voice, that he did not like Valerie either, and did not approve of her. Harriet came closer.

The smell of live charcoal from the brazier filled the verandah with the smell of hot lead from the charms and the smell of warmth in the starch of Nan's apron. Ram Prasad, who was always with the children in all their games, blew up the fire as Captain John dropped a charm for Harriet. The lead melted, ran wide, and he caught it in the spoon and lifted it and dropped it again on the plate, but curiously, the pellet ran together, sizzling, again, and formed itself into a round ball.

'It is round,' said Bogey, 'like a marble.'

'It is a world,' said Victoria. They did not

23

understand her until Nan reminded them of the globe of the world on Father's desk.

'It *is* a world,' said Harriet, taking it in her hand now it had cooled. On its rough surface she imagined she saw seas and lands. 'I wonder what it means?'

'Well, Harriet, are you satisfied? Now you have the whole world?' said Valerie.

Harriet gave her a long straight look.

'It is your turn, Captain John,' she said, wanting to reciprocate. 'Let us make a charm for you. Let us see what you are going to be.'

Valerie nudged her sharply. 'What a silly you are!' she whispered down Harriet's neck. 'You will make him feel awful. How can *he* be anything?'

'But—he has to be,' thought Harriet. 'Of course he has to be. He didn't die.'

'What do you want to be?' asked the little Victoria, putting her head back to look at him. 'What could you be?'

There was a long silence. No one had any suggestion to make. 'Oh well,' said Victoria, 'I think you had better just stay here with us.'

'Make a charm for Bea,' said Nan.

Bea had a loop, a circle, that made a rough little ring. 'That means you will be loved and married,' said Nan.

Bea took the ring and looked at it by the verandah rail, turning it over and over in her fingers. After Captain John gave the saucepan

24

back to Nan, he stood up and stretched, and limped over to Bea.

'What is the name of those flowers?' he asked Bea, presently.

'Poinsettias,' said Bea, politely.

'They make me realize I am in India,' said Captain John. 'They look so hot and red, even in the rain. And those, those little low pale blue ones on the bushes?'

'Plumbago,' said Bea.

'This is a lovely garden,' he said.

'Why,' thought Harriet, 'does he talk to Bea so—earnestly?' He was not talking to Bea as if she were a child, but as if she were grown-up. 'Bea is a little girl,' thought Harriet, 'and why is Bea so polite? There is no need to be so polite to him.'

'I am glad you like it,' said Bea.

'I think it is the most beautiful garden I have ever seen,' said Captain John, earnestly.

It was a beautiful garden. The poinsettias grew round the plinth of the house, huge scarlet-fingered flowers with milk sap in their stems. The house was large, square, of grey stucco, with verandahs along its double floors and tiers of great green shuttered windows. It had a flat roof, with a parapet where the children played, and the parapet was carved with huge stone daisies. Can a house, a serious house, be carved with daisies? This was.

Below the poinsettias was the plumbago; it

25

made hedges of nursery pale blue and the flowerbeds it bordered would later be full of the pansies and verbena and mignonette that were now in seed pans in a seed-table made of bamboo. Along the paths were ranged pots of violets that held the dew. Other pots of chrysanthemums were on the verandah and in a double phalanx down the steps. These chrysanthemums had mammoth heads of flowers that were white and yellow and bronze and pink; some of them were larger than the children's heads. Later, in their place, there would be potted petunias.

The lawns rolled away to the river under the trees, but there were flowers, bougainvillæas, that spread themselves into clumps and up the trees, orange, purple, magenta and cerise, like Bea's hair ribbon; there were Maréchal-Niel turrets with their small lemon-yellow roses, and other roses in the rose-garden, and bushes of the small white Bengali roses tinged with pink. There were standard hibiscus that were out already in pinks, and creams and yellows and reds, and morning glory and other creepers, on the house, over the porch, along screens, up trees: jasmine and orange-keyed begonias, passion flowers and quisqualis that would flower in January and the spring; now there was only the pink-and-white sandwich creeper out and Bea's bridal creeper over the gate. There were squirrels and lizards in the garden and birds:

bulbuls and kingfishers and doves and the magpie robin and sunbirds and tree pies and wagtails and hawks. Birds are little live landmarks and more truthful than flowers; they cannot be transplanted, nor grafted, nor turned blue and pink. The birds were in the flavour of that garden, as the white paddy birds and the vultures were part of the flavour of the fields, and the circling kites and the kingfishers of the river; the garden was full of swallow-tail butterflies bigger than the sunbirds and of Bogey's insects and Bogey's ants; no one really knew the insects except Bogey. At night there were sometimes jackals on the lawn and fireflies, and there was a bush that used to fill the whole house with its scent in the darkness, a bush called Lady-of-the-Night.

Harriet's cork tree stood on the edge of the drive, directly in front of the steps. It was as high as the house. Soon it would bud, then be covered in blossom, and the flowers, when they fell at the end of the winter, would make a circle deep in flowers on the grass. Woodpeckers lived in the cork tree and in season it had Japanese lilies round its foot.

Now Captain John was looking at it. 'And that is a most beautiful tree,' he said.

'It is Harriet's,' Bea told him.

'Harriet's?' He said it as if he were surprised, and Harriet was suddenly oddly shy, and oddly pleased.

'At least, she says it is hers, though I don't know why,' said Bea.

Harriet felt his look bent on herself for a moment, but when she brought herself to look up, she saw that he had forgotten her; he was looking down at Bea and she had a sudden remembrance of him on Diwali night. She had felt him looking at something then, or someone, and she had followed his look and found it on Bea. Why? Why did he look at Bea again with that same extreme gentleness and interest. Then Bea, too, looked up and back at him.

'Let me see your ring,' he said.

Bea gave him a curiously startled glance and dropped the ring into his hand from above and walked away to the others.

Nan had made a charm for Victoria. It was scoop shape.

'It is a bucket,' said Victoria.

'Or a thimble,' said Nan.

Nan and Victoria could not have appeared more different. Victoria was very plump, very blonde, built into a beautiful heavy pink and pearl fleshed body with dimples at the joints and fat bracelets at the joins; especially inviting were the backs of her legs and thighs. She shone by contrast with Nan, the old Anglo-Indian, who was thin, small, very dark, with a fine brown skin that was slack and tired now and showed bluish shadows and pouches under her eyes. Her hands were small and thin and busy, and

28

her fingers were wrinkled and pricked at the tips with a lifetime of washing and sewing. Her hair was black and dry and thin and held, each side of her head, by tortoiseshell combs. She wore a striped dress and an apron that had a convent thinness and cleanness. Her eyes were like Victoria's, brown and clear; as her body receded it seemed to leave all her life in her eyes.

Besides their eyes, Nan and Victoria were alike in that, at the moment, they were both perfect. Victoria had reached the stage of completed babyhood; little girls, especially, sometimes linger in this stage for three or four months, and during that time they are quite unconsciously perfect. Victoria had no troubles, she did not trouble anyone, and nor did Nan. Nan had completed her hard womanhood, and she had managed to shed her troubles. She had reclaimed, through living and service, what Victoria had not yet lost.

Then Nan made Bogey's charm.

Sometimes the charms did not act, and now Bogey's refused to coagulate. It ran and spread on the plate and took no shape at all.

'What is the matter with it?' said Harriet. 'How can we tell what it means?'

'It won't tell,' said Nan.

'Put it back and try again, Nan.'

'No,' said Nan. 'If it won't tell, it won't. I am sorry, Bogey.'

'I don't mind,' said Bogey cheerfully. He

29

picked up the still soft lead and rolled it into a ball like Harriet's and began to play marbles with it.

Harriet left the others and went away. It was Valerie's turn for another charm and she did not want to see Valerie's turn. She went on to the drive and under the cork tree, and looked up at it, thinking of how Captain John had admired it. She herself did not think it was as beautiful as the jacaranda trees, for instance, or even as the peepul tree in the wall by Ram Prasad's house that stood at the gate. 'But I like it,' said Harriet aloud.

She saw a crevice in the trunk low enough for her to reach. Stepping over the lilies, she fitted her charm neatly into it, and the ball rolled down and lay in the five-inch hollow at the bottom. She could reach it with her fingers, but she left it there. 'That is a safe place,' thought Harriet. 'Now I can find it again.' Bogey might play marbles with his charm, but she was sure that hers was an omen.

★    ★    ★

Each year there were nests in the garden. There was always a sunbird's nest in the bougainvillæa that grew up the house wall; a long untidy tear-shaped nest made of fibres and dried leaves with the sunbirds shimmering in and out. Now there was a dove's nest in the creeper above the verandah; you could see her sitting on her nest; she would sit there quiet for hours; her breast was grey, flecked with brown.

'What is she doing?' asked Victoria.

'Brooding,' said Captain John. He spoke often, and very kindly, to Victoria.

He was staying in the house. Mother had made him come over from the Red House so that she and Nan could look after him, because the wound in his good leg had opened and was discharging.

'It can't be very good then,' said Harriet.

'It isn't, but it is the best I have,' said Captain John.

'He shouldn't work here, in this climate,' Harriet heard Father say. 'It is cruelty,' but Captain John managed to work, though he looked ill and frayed and stiff and worn, and he managed to speak kindly to Victoria, though he did lose his temper with the rest of them.

'Brooding?' said Victoria, looking up at the nest. 'Is that brooding?' she said. 'She looks . . . happy.'

'I think she is,' said Captain John, seriously. 'She sits on her nest and she feels the whole world going round her, and she takes everything she wants from the world and puts it into her eggs.'

'You shouldn't tell Victoria things like that,' said Bea. 'She thinks they are true.'

'But they are true,' said Captain John.

'How queer you are,' said Bea. 'You say such

queer things,' and Captain John's thin cheek suddenly burnt and he put up his hand to smooth his hair, which was a trick he had to hide his stiffness. His hand was shaking again. 'Why does he *mind* Bea?' thought Harriet. She knew, then, that it was too tiring for him to speak as he wanted to do, to Bea. It was much more restful for him to bark, as he barked to Harriet, 'Blast you, Harry. Take your great hand off my leg. You hurt me.' He would never say that to Bea. 'And he isn't queer,' said Harriet. 'That about the dove was nice.'

'Are we in eggs?' asked Victoria.

'You are,' said Harriet, teasing her. 'Father says you are still in the egg, Victoria.'

It was funny to think that she, Harriet, who was still a child herself, could remember a time when Victoria, standing so large and solid on the verandah beside them, was not. Then there was no Victoria. 'And there was no gap before,' thought Harriet, puzzled. 'There was no empty place and yet we fitted her in.' It was funny, and notable, that families always did fit the babies in. Then she remembered, what she was supposed to know and had been told and still could not yet realize, that soon, in a month or two, or three or was it four, they, the family, were to have another baby themselves.

'Did you know that?' she asked Captain John.

'Know what?'

'How do you expect people to understand

32

what you are talking of, if you go thinking in between?' said Valerie. Bea did not defend Harriet, but looked at her severely too.

Harriet left them.

'Are we in eggs?' Victoria had asked. 'Fancy asking that,' thought Harriet, wandering away, 'but it would be funny if we were.' As she said it, she was frightened. She had too often this feeling of being enclosed, shut in a small shape like a dome, and, if it were an egg, she had no beak to break it. 'How can I get out? I never can get out,' she was just going to say in a panic, and then she remembered that, if she were in an egg, just like the chick, she would grow too big for it and break it. 'The thing is to grow very quickly,' said Harriet to herself, and she said aloud, 'Nan says we change our skin seven times in our lives. Perhaps this is the same idea.'

'That is snakes, not people,' said Bogey. 'Harry, Ram Prasad says there is a cobra under the peepul tree, but you are not to tell. We are going to watch it. Perhaps we shall see it change its skin,' said Bogey.

'Ugh!' said Harriet. She had none of Bogey's freemasonry with insects and reptiles, but in fascinated horror she went with him to the peepul tree. The garden wall was built each side into its trunk, so that it formed part of the wall and half of it was in the garden and half in the road outside. Harriet knew why the cobra, if there was a cobra, had come there. It was

33

because the front part of the tree in the road was a shrine with a whitewashed plinth and the villagers used to put saucers of milk on it with offerings of rice and burnt sugar and curd. Snakes like milk, and Harriet guessed it had come there for that.

She and Bogey squatted on their heels, watching the roots, but nothing stirred. At any moment Harriet expected the horrid bronze-grey lengths of the snake to come flowing out, over, and under, the roots. 'Ugh!' shuddered Harriet, and when at last she tired and stood up, her hands and the backs of her knees where she had folded them were wet. 'I don't want to see it,' she said. 'Bogey. You know I am sure we ought to tell. We are supposed to tell if we see a snake in the garden.'

Bogey had not heard. He was still squatting, still waiting, the whole of him intent on the snake hole. It was not that Bogey was disobedient as much as blithely unaware he had been told. 'Oh well,' said Harriet, 'we haven't seen it yet, and it isn't really in the garden. It is in the peepul tree.'

She went back to the house, and on her way she passed Victoria with her doll. 'I play so beautifully with my baby,' she said to Harriet as Harriet passed. 'She was born again yesterday.'

'You are always having her born,' said Harriet scornfully.

'Why not?' asked Victoria. 'You can be born

34

again and again, can't you?'

It was puzzling. Every time Harriet examined somebody's silly remark, it seemed not to be so silly. 'I don't understand it,' she said, and she wondered who could explain it to her; its surface silliness was such that she doubted if she would find anyone to whom she could make clear what she wanted to ask. Then she made up her mind; she would risk a chance and ask Captain John.

'He may swear at me,' thought Harriet. 'He likes Bea, but never mind, he can talk to me for once,' thought Harriet. 'If he laughs at me, he laughs at me. Never mind.' And she wavered no more, but went to look for him.

He was leaning on the verandah rail, idling, looking at the sun and the flowers, quiet and dreaming.

'Captain John,' said Harriet, interrupting him, 'I just want to talk to you.'

'Must you?' he said lazily.

'Yes, I must; about being born.'

He still did not seem willing. 'Can't you talk to Bea or Nan about that, Harriet? I can't talk about being born.'

'Oh but you can,' said Harriet, putting a compelling hand on him. 'I don't want to be told anything. I want to talk.'

He looked down at her, his face lazy, not at all stiff.

'Do you know, your eyes have speckles in them, flecks?' he said.

35

'Like the dove's breast?' asked Harriet.

He looked at her more particularly. 'What dove?'

'The dove on her nest. I liked that—that you said.'

'Did you?' he said, and he seemed pleased. Talking to Harriet he had not changed his lounging, dreaming attitude, and he forgot to smooth his hair and pull his tie straight. He looked down into her eyes lazily without thinking of himself.

'Listen,' said Harriet, and leaning on the rail beside him, she told him of what she was thinking, puzzling over, and it came in words that were unusually clear, almost crystalline. She told him of Victoria's remark and of how it was silly and yet it rang true; of his own remark that Bea said was queer and yet was true too. 'Is everything a bit true then?' asked Harriet.

She could see the peepul tree over the bamboo clumps that hid its lower half, and she wondered idly if the cobra had come out. 'Ugh!' said Harriet again, and moved her shoulders in a shudder while she waited for Captain John to speak.

'My idea,' said Captain John, 'isn't very different from Victoria's, though she didn't mean hers in this way. I have an idea,' said Captain John, his eyes looking now, not at Harriet, but across the rail to the garden, 'that we go on being born again and again because we

36

have to, with each thing that happens to us, each new episode.'

'What is an episode?'

'It really means an incident ... between two acts.'

'I don't understand.'

'Call it an incident, a happening. With each new happening, perhaps with each person we meet if they are important to us, we must either be born again, or die a little bit; big deaths and little ones, big and little births.'

'I should think it would be better to go on being born, than to die all the time,' said Harriet.

'If we can,' said Captain John, 'but it takes a bit of doing. It is called growing, Harriet, and it is often painful and difficult. On the whole, it is very much easier to die.'

'But you didn't,' said Harriet.

'I just managed not to, but I am no criterion,' said Captain John.

'What is a criterion?' asked Harriet, and before he could answer, she asked, 'Who is it who is important to you, Captain John?'

'Never you mind,' and he stood up and stretched himself. 'Do you think you could leave me alone now like a good girl?'

Harriet went along to the jetty and sat down in her usual place. 'I *wish* he had told me,' she said. She hung her feet down above the water; they were still bare, and she had still, so far, not had hookworm. Wriggling her toes to feel the dust between them, she wondered, all at once, how she, Harriet, appeared to Captain John. Then she wondered more truthfully, if he ever saw her at all. 'But he said that about my eyes,' argued Harriet. 'Yes, he said they had flecks in them,' but if that were in derision or admiration she did not know. She thought again of the way she had seen him looking at Bea when they lit the lamps for Diwali. They had been on the roof, in the darkness, and the point of light from each lamp lit a circle round itself but was not strong enough to lighten the whole roof darkness. Anyone bending over a lamp was suddenly illuminated and Bea, bending to shift the oil round a wick, was lit, her shoulders, her neck, the line of her face, and her hair; she was gilded, and as she moved the oil she looked up at Valerie and laughed at what Valerie was saying. Harriet had noticed that Captain John had stood there, lost, and the oil in the lamp he held ran over the edge on to the floor and Valerie scolded him. 'Yes, he looks at Bea,' said Harriet mournfully.

She wished her big toe could reach the water. The river current gurgled against the poles of the jetty; its traffic floated down and Harriet watched it lazily, while her mind left that part of Captain John's idea and thought of the other. *'You are born with each new big thing that happens.'* 'I don't quite understand that,'

38

thought Harriet.

A boat floated down laden with bright red pots: then a boat laden with nothing at all; then a launch from up-river; Harriet noted its black funnel, blue-banded, and its white and red hull: 'From Brentford's,' she thought, 'the "Sprite".' On its deck sat a large lady dressed in white. 'Mrs Milligan,' Harriet identified her without a flicker of interest. 'How few, how very, very few people are important,' she thought, and lazily she began to think over the people who were important for her. 'Father-Mother-Bea-Bogey-Victoria.' That was automatic, and she did not realize that, as she said their names, she did not think of them at all. 'Nan?' Her thought made her think of Nan. 'No, not Nan,' thought Harriet as she watched a police motor boat, with the police flag almost touching the wash at its stern as it went by; the rolling wave behind it presently came in broken rifts to hit the jetty where she was sitting. 'Anyone else?' thought Harriet. Of course, children were not expected to have many people, but however she circumscribed herself, her thoughts came back to the question she wanted to ask. 'Captain John?' asked Harriet at last, and she answered as she had to answer because it was the truth, 'How can he be important for me? It is Bea he likes. At first we thought it was Victoria, but it is Bea he is interested in.'

A porpoise came down, turning slowly over

and over in midstream with a beautiful easy armchair rhythmical motion that lulled Harriet. She rubbed her back against the post and picked at her finger lump in her hand. 'Oh well,' thought Harriet comfortably, 'I shall meet heaps of people when I am older, when I am famous. Heaps of things are going to happen to me.'

A whirr and a splash made her jump so that she almost fell off the jetty. A kingfisher had struck from a branch above her. Now it sat on a post with the fish still bending and jerking in its beak. The poor fish had been placidly, happily, swimming and feeding somewhere under the jetty, and then, out of its element, from another, it had been seized and carried off. 'And swallowed,' thought Harriet regretfully, watching it disappear.

'I wonder what the other fishes think?' thought Harriet, but then, that was the same with any dying; one person was seized and taken away. 'But what does it feel like if that comes right plumb in the middle of your family?' She could not think of it, it seemed impossible and yet she had just seen it happen. 'Things do happen,' she told herself, but she was lulled again with the sound of the river running in her ears. 'Those were fishes,' Harriet told herself comfortably. 'Only fishes.'

There was no sign of the splash. The river ran steadily where it had been. 'There you see... Anything can happen, anything, and whatever happens the other fishes just go on wriggling and swimming and feeding because they have to,' said Harriet. 'It, the river, has to go on.' Whatever happened, a fish's death, a wreck, storm, sun, the river assimilated it all. The far bank showed as a line across the river, a line of fields, a clump of trees by the temple, and, further away, the walls and roofs and chimney and jetty of Valerie's father's works. 'I wonder what he thinks about dying; Captain John, not Valerie's father,' thought Harriet idly. 'I wonder if he thinks the same as he thinks about being born, if he really thinks you could die over and over again. Goodness,' thought Harriet, 'I nearly died just now when I nearly fell off the jetty. I would die if I saw that cobra!' But what Captain John meant was deeper than that. Harriet suspected that, but her mind was now too lazy, too happy, to explore.

★    ★    ★

Sometimes, in the night, Harriet thought about death. She thought about Father and Mother dying, or Nan, who was really very old; then she would hastily wake Bea to comfort her.

When Ram Prasad's wife died, she was carried on a string bed to the river and put on a pyre and burned. Afterwards her ashes were thrown on the water. Bogey and Harriet went to look, though they knew without being told that

Mother would not have allowed them.

'Did you mind it?' Harriet asked Bogey afterwards.

'Mind what?'

'The burning.'

'It looked just like burning to me.'

It had. The pyre was well alight when they arrived, hiding themselves behind a brick kiln on the edge of the burning ghat so that even Ram Prasad should not see them.

'I didn't like the smell,' said Harriet. 'Did you see them throw her ashes in the river?'

'I wasn't looking,' said Bogey, 'there was a frog...' His mind went off on the thought of the frog, but after a while he said, 'No, I didn't mind.'

'Nor did I,' said Harriet. She had not seen the body only those ashes, and they did not seem to be anything to do with a person who had lived and walked and talked and eaten food and played with her baby and laughed. No, it had been, up to now, birds like the kingfisher, and animals like the livestock of the nursery, guinea-pigs and rabbits and kittens, that had given Harriet her glimpses of birth and death.

Nan said if you were good you died and went to heaven. 'To Paradise.' Mother, not so certainly, half-heartedly, lent some support to that. Nan was quite certain.

'To eternal rest,' said Nan, looking at the swellings her bunions made in her shoes. 'To

42

have wings like the angels,' said Nan, as she toiled upstairs with the washing.

Harriet had seen heaven on the films, but it was Hindu heaven in an Indian film, Krishna playing his flute in a garden of roses and dancing girls. The Mohammedan heaven? She was not sure about that. She asked Father what Buddhists did when they died; he took down a book and read to her about a drop sliding into the crystal sea and being lost. She asked Mother, and Mother pointed out that Harriet knew already that Jesus rose from the dead; some people, she added, believed that you came back over and over again, to live another life each time. 'A better life,' said Mother.

'Goodness, how good you must be in the end,' said Harriet.

That was the idea, Mother thought, and if you were not good, she went on to say, you came back as something lower.

'Like?'

'An animal. An insect. A flea,' said Mother, smiling.

'I should rather like to be a flea,' thought Harriet, thinking of herself as a gay acrobatic jumping flea, but Bogey, who did not like to be labelled good or bad, was bored with the idea. 'I should rather have done with it,' said Bogey.

All these thoughts seemed like cracks in the wholeness of Harriet's unconsciousness. It had cracked before, of course, but now she was

43

growing rapaciously.

The winter drew on. Day succeeded day, and ended and went out of sight and was gone. 'There are such lots of days,' thought Harriet, 'but not more than there are drops of water in the river.'

She was on the jetty again. Very often now she went to watch the river. It flowed down in negroid peace, in sun, in green strong water. Harriet, now she was growing from a little girl into a big one, was beginning to sense its peace. 'It comes from a source,' said Harriet, who learnt geography. 'From very far away, from a trickle from a spring, no one knows where exactly, or perhaps they do know; it doesn't matter. It is going to something far bigger than itself, though it, itself, looks big enough. It is going to the sea,' said Harriet, 'and nothing will stop it. Nothing stops days, or rivers,' said Harriet with certainty.

Then the guinea-pig, Bathsheba, died.

The children had several scores of guinea-pigs, and they used to play shepherds with them, driving guinea-pig flocks over the lawn. One of the original stock was Bathsheba, an old white guinea-pig, who belonged to Harriet. One day, Harriet found her, lying limp, as if she were alseep, in a corner of the cage. When Harriet picked her up, she did not feel limp, but curiously stiff and resilient and her fur felt hard. 'She is dead, I think,' said Harriet, but she was

44

still not quite sure what dead was. She did not take Bathsheba in to Nan or Mother or anyone in the house; she carried her down the garden and out of the gate and into the Red House to find Captain John, but all the assistants were out except one, Mr Corsie, lying ill in bed with dysentery.

'May I come in, Mr Corsie?' asked Harriet.

'Wh't is it ye want?' asked Mr Corsie without enthusiasm. He was feeling ill.

'Please—is this dead?' asked Harriet, offering Bathsheba for inspection.

'Ugh! Take it away, oot o' heer,' cried Mr Corsie.

'*Is* it—ugh?' asked Harriet, doubtfully.

'Dae ye no heer me?' asked Mr Corsie. 'Take it oot. Or I'll tell yeer Pa.'

'But—is it dead?' asked Harriet.

'Daid as a doornail. Take it away. Good Lorrd! It is stinkin'.'

Harriet immediately dropped Bathsheba on the floor.

That night she was worried.

'Bea.'

'Sssh.'

'Bea.'

'What *is* it, Harriet? I am asleep.'

'Bea, when we are dead, do we go ... like Bathsheba?'

'How did she go?' asked Bea, yawning.

'Stiff. Hard. Stinking,' said Harriet tearfully.

45

'Yes, I suppose we do,' said Bea, who was sleepy. 'That is called a corpse.'

Harriet shivered, all over her skin, under the bedclothes.

'Bea.'

Silence.

'Bea.'

No answer.

'Bea. *Bea. BEA!*'

'Oh, Harriet! I am asleep. What is it?'

'Bea. I don't want to.'

'Don't want to *what?*'

'Be a corpse.'

'But you are not,' said Bea, practically.

'But I shall be,' said Harriet, and she began to cry.

'Don't you think you could wait till you are?' said Bea. 'I *am* so sleepy, Harriet.' Then as the fact of Harriet's sobs was borne in upon her, she said, more gently, 'Couldn't you wait till the morning, Harry?'

'No. No. I can't,' sobbed Harriet. 'I am frightened, Bea. I can't get the feeling of Bathsheba off my hands. I am frightened, Bea.'

'Don't cry,' said Bea, kindly. She sat up in bed, and by the verandah light Harriet could see her shoulders in her white yoked nightgown, and the fall of her dark hair. 'Don't cry, Harry. It isn't anything to cry about. I am sure it is not.'

The sound of her normal little voice was

comforting to Harriet, until she thought that Bea too must die, dark hair, voice and all. 'Then I shall never hear her voice again,' cried Harriet silently, 'and Mother must die, and Nan, and Nan is old and must die quite soon.'

'Why isn't it something to cry about?' cried Harriet bitterly, aloud.

'Oh, Harry. You ask too many questions.'

'Yes, but ... Don't *you* ever think about dying, Bea?'

'Well, yes I do,' said Bea.

'Then what do you think?' she asked.

'It is hard to know what I think,' said Bea's small voice out of the darkness. 'But I know a few things.'

'Wh-what do you know?' quavered Harriet, and she said suspiciously, 'Nan and Mother and Ram Prasad tell us things about heaven and Jesus and Brahma, but they don't really know.'

'I think they are all wrong,' said Bea severely. 'Mine are not things like that. They are more simple things.' And she added, as if this had only just occurred to her, 'More sensible things.'

'Wh-what sort of th-things?'

'This,' said Bea. 'When anything, anybody is dead, like Bathsheba, it is dead. The life, the breath, the ... the *warm* in it, is gone.'

'Nan calls it the spirit.'

'The spirit then,' said Bea. 'I call it the "warm", but the spirit or the warm is gone.'

47

'Yes,' said Harriet. 'Yes. It was gone out of Bathsheba.'

'The body is left behind,' said Bea, 'and what happens to it? It goes bad.'

'Don't!' said Harriet, and shuddered.

'You can't keep a body ...'

'Except mummies and those Rajahs who are pickled in honey,' said Harriet.

'Then I think,' said Bea, and she contradicted herself. 'Then I *know* that it isn't meant to go on. It is useless. The body isn't any use any more.'

'Yes?' said Harriet.

'But the other, the warm has gone. It doesn't stay and go bad. So I think,' said Bea, 'that it is of some use. That it has gone to something, somewhere.'

'But where?' asked Harriet. 'Where?'

'You ask too many questions, Harry,' said Bea.

'I wonder what Captain John thinks,' said Harriet in despair.

'Captain *John*?'

'Yes. He would think something,' said Harriet, and her curiosity got the better of her sense, and she said, 'What do you feel like with Captain John, Bea?'

Bea immediately lay down again. Harriet knew she would not tell.

But, as silence settled. Harriet felt obscurely comforted. Why? Bea had not said much, but

48

Harriet felt strengthened. She kept her head under the bedclothes for a little while and then found she was perfectly well able to come out, and she lay calmly, looking through her mosquito net at the starlight that fell dimly between the columns of the verandah, and listening to the puff-wait-puff of steam from the works and the ever-flowing gurgling of the river. 'I will learn more about it as I grow,' she thought comfortably. 'Living and dying and being born, like Captain John said,' she yawned. She naturally supposed that that growing was still a great way off.

She tried to remember the names of the stars as she lay, and she thought how much longer stars and things like trees and rocks went on than people: 'Mountains and islands and sands,' she thought, 'and man-made things as well; songs and pictures and rare vases and poems.' 'Things are the thing,' said Harriet sleepily, and then a thought came like a spear from one of those stars, but real, truthful. It had occurred to her that she, Harriet, might possibly, one day, if she were good enough, have some small part in that. 'One of my poems might still be alive in...' thought Harriet, '... say, A.D. 4000. It might. I don't say it will, but it might. I should be like the Chinese poets,' she thought dizzily. 'Or like Keats or Shakespeare,' she thought, and she was filled with a sense of her own responsibility. That was a new sensation for

Harriet. She was not given to responsibility and it gave her a feeling, more serious, more humble, than she had ever known. 'I must work,' said Harriet earnestly. 'I must work and work and work.' Like Queen Victoria she thought. 'I will be good. I will be good.'

*Saw roses wide that comforted her heart.*

*And saw their cr-im-son* ... but it was somehow not interesting. She gave a huge yawn, the poem grew fuddled, and she was asleep.

★    ★    ★

Next morning, when she went out before breakfast and stood on the jetty, she wondered what all the fuss had been about. Now she felt she had no need to stand there staring at the river, watching it flow, when it was such a glorious morning in the garden. 'What was I fussing about last night?' she asked. She was filled with such buoyancy of living, of happiness, that she could not stay still any longer; she had to move away, walking up and down the paths, beside the creeper screens, under the turrets of roses, touching the flowers, knocking the dew off them, letting the boughs touch her and spring back, until she came to the cork tree.

It was early. The garden shone. The cold weather light lay on the paths and unfolded across the green of the lawns and through the trees. There was brighter green in the wings of the flycatchers and in the flight of parakeets that flew in front of her and across the river.

Victoria came down the steps. She did not see Harriet. She had some straw under her arm and she was dragging a rug after her. Harriet knew what she was going to do; she was going to make a house. At the moment Victoria was like a snail, she always had a house attached to her somewhere. Now, dragging the rug over the dew and the gravel, she went away round the corner towards the swing.

Harriet had reached the cork tree. By standing very quietly under it, she could hear the woodpeckers tap-tapping on it far above her head. She put her head back and looked through the break in the branches and their canopy to the sky, and as she looked, the clouds, and the grey line with a stone daisy that was the parapet of the house, and the tall tree itself, seemed to tilt gently backwards. 'That is the world turning,' thought Harriet. It gave her a large feeling to see the tilt of the world. Clouds, house, tree, lawns, river, Harriet, were borne slowly backwards as the world turned, but the tree remained upright, steady, rising into the sky, spreading its branches that were coming into bud. Under Harriet's feet, where she stood among the red lilies, its roots went deep into the earth, down down into the pit of the earth. 'I believe,' said Harriet, 'I believe that this is the middle of the world. That I am standing in the middle of the middle of the world, and this tree is that tree, the axis tree, like the one in the story. It goes right through the earth. It goes up and up.'

She put her hand on the tree and she thought she was drawn up into its height as if she were soaring out of the earth. Her ears seemed to sing. She had the feeling of soaring, then she came back to stand at the foot of the tree, her hand on the bark, and she began to write a new poem in her head.

It took her a long time, walking on the lawn, pacing the paths, coming back to the tree, to finish it. She finished it in her head, then she felt for her book that was in the waistband of her dress, and her pencil that she kept in her stocking, and wrote the poem down.

When she looked at it, it did not look like any of her poems. She read it aloud. It did not sound like any of her poems. 'It is not like any poem I ever read,' she said doubtfully. 'It can't be good,' and immediately she had the feeling that it was good. It felt alive, as she did. She felt alive and curiously powerful, and full of what seemed to her a glory.

She glanced round. She could see Victoria's head rising and dipping by the swing, but it was no good reading poems to Victoria. Bea was out riding, she did not know where Bogey was, and every adult was always busy before breakfast.

Then, as she stood puzzled under the cork tree, Captain John came limping up the jetty and across the lawn towards her.

'Hullo,' said Captain John.

'Hullo,' said Harriet, considering him.

'I have been across the river.'

'Bea has gone riding,' said Harriet. She looked up at him. 'Captain John,' she said, and stopped.

'Yes?'

'I—' said Harriet slowly, and then easily it tumbled out. 'I have written a poem. It is— either very bad—I expect it is bad, or else it is good. It is so new, I don't know.'

'Show me,' said Captain John, and put out his hand. Harriet gave him the poem and he began to read it.

She had not expected he would read it aloud, quite naturally and unselfconsciously as he was doing, and prickings of acute shyness ran over her until she found that she was soothed, allayed, delighted by the sound of her own words:

'*This tree, my tree, is the pole of the world....*'

When he had finished it he looked at Harriet. Then he looked at the poem.

'Did *you* write this?' he asked. 'By yourself?'

Harriet nodded. She could not speak.

'Nobody helped you?'

'Of course not,' said Harriet indignantly.

'But it is good!'

Waves of bright-eyed satisfaction chased through Harriet's every vein. He looked at her as if he had not properly seen her before.

'It—felt good ... for me,' said Harriet huskily.

'I didn't know you wrote poems.'

'I—I do,' said Harriet. She had to bend her head down. She moved the toe of her shoe along the edge of a root. The silence went on and on. She could hear the woodpeckers again, tap, tap, tap.

'Har-ree!'

That was Bogey.

'Har-ree!' She raised her head.

'He-ah!'

Bogey came chasing round the corner of the house, past Victoria, past the swing.

'Here, Boge. I am here.'

'We are going to make bricks,' announced Bogey. ''n bake them in a n'oven, 'n build a tank for fishes. I have found some lovely mud. It is a little bit smelly, but you needn't mind. Come on, Harry.'

The gate opened and Bea came trotting up the drive on the white pony, Pearl. Bogey ran off and Harriet sped after him.

But when she reached the corner of the house she stopped and turned so fast that the short skirt of her dress whirled round her. She stood in the shadow of the poinsettias and looked back at Bea and Captain John. She saw how Captain

54

John went up and put his hand on the pony's neck and then how Bea let him help her off as if she were a grown-up, not a child. Harriet stood, frowning a little by the poinsettias, then slowly she walked away to look at Bogey's mud.

★    ★    ★

Now Harriet began to think a great deal about Captain John.

What was wrong with him? Something was wrong. There was that emptiness in his eyes. Though he was loosed, among people again, he was not like other people, and he knew it. 'But he was strong enough not to die,' argued Harriet. He was strong enough to bear the unbearable pain, and the prison camp, and to escape, and to live in the hospital through all those operations when no one expected him to live, and to go on working every day with his troublesome wound and the weight of his leg. He could joke about it; he could be kind to Victoria, and in the same way to Nan; he could understand her, Harriet: he had this ... 'this reverent,' said Harriet, wrinkling her brow to get the exact word, 'this reverent feeling for Bea'; and even someone as young as Harriet could sense he was no common thinker. There was no one she could talk to like Captain John. 'And he *ought* to talk to me,' said Harriet. 'When he talks to me he looks quite strong and

55

rested. He doesn't when he talks to Bea.'

'You can't talk to her, can you?' she asked him.

'No,' he said irritably. 'She is too confoundedly polite.' That was the first time Harriet had ever heard a word against politeness, but she saw immediately that it was true.

But it was not Bea who was wrong with Captain John. It was something in him, himself. 'Or not in him,' she said slowly.

'Leave him alone,' said Nan.

'But I want to *do* something for him.'

'You can pray for him.'

'Oh, *Nan!*'

'You can,' said Nan certainly, and then she added, as a warning, 'and Harriet, you are not to do anything else.'

But Harriet, being Harriet did, and was snubbed.

She went away with his snub stinging in her, into the Secret Hole, where she sat down on her box, in the darkest shade. She sat holding her knees in her arms, her face turned down on them, and the stinging passed into a peculiar hurt. 'I—I hate him,' said Harriet, with clenched teeth.

Ayah came presently and found her. 'What is it, Harry Baba? What is it, Harriet Rajah?'

'I have a pain,' said Harriet, she did not know what else to call it.

56

Ayah began to rub her legs, though the pain, of course, was not in her legs. Harriet had had pains in her legs and arms recently that Nan called 'growing pains'. Now she felt as if she were being stretched to hold this one. This was not exactly a pain, though it hurt. It ached, but it was not like the ache she had had with dysentery, it was not sore, and it was not like toothache, that awful toothache she had when her tooth fell out. Analysing her pain, it began to go away, and she immediately forgot what it had been like.

Every family has its milestones; the first teeth come and the first teeth go; there is the first short hair-cut, the first braces, the first number one shoes, the first birthday in double figures. Events happen, too, which change families and family relations, and sometimes, often, one member is struck at more than another. Now, this feeling of pain, of hurt, had come to Harriet. This winter strange things seemed to be happening to her, eventful things. She felt herself growing and growing as she sat there in the gloom of the Secret Hole.

But soon she had regained her halcyon insouciance.

'Har-ee!'

'He-ah.'

'Get the scissors, quick. Ram Prasad says the goldfish should have a worm and here is a worm, Harry. Cut him into bits, quick.'

57

'Harriet,' said Bogey, as they fed the fish. 'What do you think, Harry? The cobra comes out into our side of the garden now.'

'*Bogey!*' said Harriet appalled. 'Have you seen it?'

Bogey nodded. His face was illumined.

'Wha—what is it like?'

'It is lovely. It slithers.'

'Ugh!' said Harriet, and she asked. 'How did you make it come?'

'I did what they did. I put down saucers of milk.'

'Ugh!' said Harriet. 'Oh, Bogey!' and a quiver of sense, an antenna, lifted and pointed. 'Now I ought to tell Father. It is *in* the garden now.'

'But it is hardly ever in it,' said Bogey, earnestly. 'You can't say it is, Harriet. It lives the other side of the tree. That is where its hole is. It hardly ever comes out. Sometimes I watch for ages n'ages and it doesn't come.'

'Does Ram Prasad know?'

'No,' said Bogey absently. 'I don't *touch* it, Harry.' He added gently to himself so that even Harriet did not hear, his eyes bright and dreaming, 'I only poke it with a little bit of stick.'

Harriet was really too interested in herself to think about the cobra. She was hurt again. She was often hurt now. Things hurt her that would not have hurt her before, that she would have skimmed over without noticing. She was different. She was altogether puzzled, and on the afternoon of the second day she went to talk to Bea.

Bea was reading.

'Bea.'

Bea looked up. Her book was one of those books of Valerie's, 'The Girl's Own Annual' or 'The Rose Book for Girls', books that Harriet was not addicted to. Harriet liked 'The Orange Fairy Book' and 'Arabian Nights'. Or did she? Did she like anything? 'Bea,' she said, and Bea looked up but kept her finger on her place to let Harriet know that the interruption was to be only temporary, and Harriet, with Bea in that mood, could not talk about the nebulous things she had come to talk of. She had to think of something else, something important, if only to rivet Bea's attention.

She said, 'I have lumps.'

'Lumps?' asked Bea.

'Yes. On my chest. You know, my two chests, like swellings, and they hurt.'

'Those are your two little new breasts,' said Bea, and went on reading.

'Mine? But ... I am too young.' Harriet shrank back into her frock. 'I am far too young,' she said, shocked.

'You can't be or they wouldn't come,' said Bea reasonably. 'They don't come until you are ready.'

That was interesting. Harriet looked down,

59

inside her frock, at her chest. Her frock was of blue cotton and the light on her skin was therefore blue as well; her chest no longer had a plain bow; its topography had altered to two soft warm swellings, and in between them the skin was wonderfully tender, fine and silken. 'It is pretty,' said Harriet, looking down inside her frock. 'And my veins *are* blue. It isn't only the light.' That skin, those veins were older than Harriet. They were the sign of a woman. She was visibly growing. 'Were these signs something only for girls?' she wondered, and she tried to think of something male which was a counter-part, a visible growth, like this, and she could only think of stags, of the antlers of a stag. 'I hurt rather like a stag,' she said. 'Like a stag's new antlers hurt. Have you got them, Bea?'

'What? Antlers?'

'Breasts.'

'Yes,' said Bea shortly.

'I never noticed them.'

'You never notice anything that isn't yourself,' said Bea, which was largely true, though lately Harriet was noticing in this new acute way.

'Bea.'

'Do go away, Harry. I want to read.'

'But I want to talk . . . about you, Bea.'

'I hate talking about me.'

'How odd,' thought Harriet, who loved above all things to talk about herself.

It was true. Bea had slipped off from Harriet and a space was widening between them. They were still officially 'the big ones,' while Bogey and Victoria were 'the little ones,' but like most labels, these were not true. Harriet, if she played at all, played with Bogey nowadays, and the truth was, that the completeness went out of their play if Bea played too. 'Not in the doing games,' said Harriet to herself. 'She can still play those: rounders, and flying kites and "animal-mineral-vegetable".' They played rounders on the lawn with the young men from the Red House after a Sunday tea that had plum cake and chocolate tarts; for Harriet it always meant running when she was too full to run. Bogey had a curious inability to grasp what he was doing, Victoria was allowed to play by courtesy, but Bea really played, gracefully and competently. She was good at the game of flying kites too; that was, flying paper kites off the roof with strings glassed with ground glass, when you challenged other unknown kites, crossed strings with them and tried to cut them adrift; your kite wore a bob on its tail for every kite it cut. 'Animal-mineral-vegetable' was agony to Harriet, because she inevitably forgot in the middle and let her mind go off cantering free in questions of its own: 'What-would-I-feel-like - if - I - were - vegetable - scarlet - flower - flesh - or - if - I - were - silver - or - tin - with - tin - fingers - and - tin - toes - and - little - tin - ears-

61

and-tin-hair?' She saw her hair flashing with curls of shining tinfoil and, of course, she lost her place and Father called her a dunce. Bea was never a dunce at this, but she could not play 'being' games any more; being Rowena or a Cavalier, or Arabs or highwaymen or pirates, or even Minnehaha. Bea was still not bad as Minnehaha, not bad, but not really Minnehaha; it seemed she could not be anything but Bea just at present; and now... 'Am I going to be like this too?' asked Harriet.

As Bea grew into being only Bea, she grew mysteriously better-looking. She grew beautiful.

'What a beautiful child,' people said when they saw her.

Harriet and Bogey went behind a bush to discuss whether or not they would tell this to Bea.

'We don't want to make her conceited,' said Harriet and she did not know herself why she said that.

'Oh, tell her. Tell her. Tell her,' begged Bogey.

When they told Bea she did not become conceited. She seemed simply to take it as her due and to be unmoved by it, in a way that made Harriet feel breathless.

Now, as Bea was reading, Harriet took a long firm view of her. Over the edge of the bright blue-bound book, Harriet was impressed again by the withdrawn look on Bea's face, by its shape, oval and clear, with the clear modellings of the cheekbones under their soft skin, her straight small nose, and the fine lines of her eyebrows; as she read, looking down, her lashes were spread, fine and curled, along her lids, and her dark hair fell on to her shoulders. Round her neck, on a black ribbon, she was wearing a carved ivory rose, tinted pink; her skin was tinted in exactly the same way, pink on ivory.

Harriet went away and looked at herself in the glass.

'What are you doing, Harriet?' said Mother.

'I am wondering if I am as beautiful as Bea,' said Harriet.

'You have a little face full of character,' said Mother kindly, 'and you have nice eyes and hair.'

'That means I am not,' thought Harriet. She could see for herself that her face looked pink and commonplace after Bea's; it was speckled with freckles, it had a large nose, green-brown speckly eyes under tawny eyebrows, and something tawny and rampant in her hair. 'It is more like Bogey's face,' thought Harriet. 'But no, it is not even as nice as Bogey's. Bogey has such dear little bones. He is more like Bea, really. No, mine is nothing, nothing at all, like hers.'

'Why do I want to be pretty suddenly?' asked Harriet, and she did not know. Certainly she had never bothered about it before, but then she had never bothered about anything very much. 'What is the matter with me?' thought Harriet. 'Why do I keep on having these ... cracks? Why is everything suddenly so funny?'

She was unhappy again in rifts, in, as she called them, cracks: for ten minutes, or for a minute only, or for a whole half hour. 'It isn't fair,' said Harriet in a temper, 'for a family not to be the same. To be half ugly and half pretty, to grow up at different times,' complained Harriet. With all she felt, and truly felt, another part of her was watching and found it interesting. She watched herself when she went to brood in the Secret Hole, when she went to sit on the jetty or under the cork tree. 'I give up,' said Harriet crossly, but the other part of her was far too interested to give up.

Meanwhile she was separating from Bea. Bea had passed into a kind of upper society with Valerie or Captain John. Harriet used to overhear them talking; she listened, not to Valerie of course, but to Captain John.

'What is the name of those flowers?' He was always asking Bea the names of flowers. He did not appear to be able to remember any for himself, or to know the commonest flower names. He went on asking them. 'I believe he likes doing it,' thought Harriet, and she marvelled that Bea never lost patience or let him know she knew he was pretending.

'What is the name of those flowers?'

'Petunias,' said Bea.

He bent down to smell one. 'They remind me of you,' he said to Bea. 'No, you remind me of them, one of those purple ones,' he said, 'or a white one.'

Bea took it with the same calmness, almost with primness, but Harriet was dizzy. 'They are both behaving like grown-up people,' she thought indignantly, 'or they are both behaving like children. Why?' And then Captain John turned and said, 'Why don't you go away and play, Harriet? Don't tag on to me all the time.'

Harriet became scarlet to the tips of her ears. 'I don't ... tag,' she said in a muffled voice. 'I was only here, that is all,' and she rushed away, up the side stairs to the Secret Hole, and cast herself down on the floor. 'I hate him. I hate him,' said Harriet again, crying into the floor.

Her tears fell into the dust and it mingled with the tears on her face. When she came out Nan said she was not fit to be seen, and made her have her tea in the nursery.

'I warned you,' said Nan.

Harriet hunched her shoulders.

'If I were you,' said Nan, 'I should keep to playing with Bogey.'

'I am too big to play with Bogey,' said Harriet angrily.

'You are too small for Captain John,' said Nan.

*     *     *

More and more Harriet was thrust with
Bogey, and this meant, usually, being alone.
Whatever she started to do with Bogey, he
eventually and cheerfully left her alone. After a
few minutes, she would look up, and there
would be no Bogey.

They were beginning to find that out in
lessons. Bogey had just started lessons. 'He
really must learn to read,' said Mother. 'It is
disgraceful, at his age, not to be able to read.'

Why had no one taught him to read before?
Because he defied them completely. Yet he was
not naughty. He was perfectly docile.

'M.A.T. Bogey?'

'Mat.'

'F.A.T. Bogey?'

'Fat.'

'C.A.T. Bogey?'

'Cat.'

'R.A.T. Bogey?'

'Sailor' and Bogey was entirely absent. Nor
could they get him back.

'Why did the Ancient Britons find it so hard
to make their boats, Bogey?'

'Because they had to make the inside bigger
than the outside,' said Bogey gravely, his eyes
on the sky.

He was not capable of being made to feel

66

guilty, like Harriet, who knew she dreamed. He simply removed himself, and they were tired of the chase long before he was caught.

'One day you will have to learn to read,' said Harriet. 'Imagine a man who couldn't go to office, nor sign letters, nor read newspapers.'

'I am not going to be any of those men,' said Bogey. 'I am not ready to learn to read.'

'You can't always do what you like, you know,' said Harriet, who was still feeling sore and angry.

'I can,' said Bogey. 'I always do.' That was true. He always did, and if he found trouble he kept it to himself. Once he fell down the back stairs and broke his front teeth. He never told anyone till Nan saw his swollen lips. Once he set his sock alight when he was cooking on a secret fire. He put out the sock and tied a rag on the burn. He never told. It was of no use. Bogey was no companion. Harriet still needed Bea. She could not, in any ultimate move, do without Bea. Bea still had to be her mentor, her help and her confidante, her guide and her public opinion. She tried to bid for her attention; or now, better than Bea, Captain John.

She painted a picture; it was of a lotus on blue water, and when it was done, looking at it critically, she could see that it was nothing like a lotus, it was more like a pig in bluish mud. She did not show that to Bea. 'I am not a painting person,' said Harriet. 'I am a writer,' and she tried for a little while to recapture the status of the poem she had written under the cork tree; she wrote a book, at least the beginnings of a book, and it kept her happy for some days. Then she showed it to Bea, who had not any great desire to look at it.

'*And they had four children,*' read the reluctant Bea, '*called Olive, Bice, Emerald and Spinach, all green as grass and slimy.*'

'Queer children!' commented Bea.

'This is a book about frogs,' said Harriet huffily.

'Well, you should say so.'

'You are supposed to understand that from reading the book.'

'Well, *I* don't,' said Bea.

It was no good. This was a thoroughly tiresome time, and Harriet could not do anything with it.

\*     \*     \*

It was nearly Christmas. 'It must be a quiet Christmas,' said Mother as she had said about the winter. 'A quiet Christmas, and you must be content with little presents.'

'The war again,' thought Harriet angrily. She wanted Christmas to have its full panoply, she wanted the right to be happy and excited without this horrible onus of caring about other people, the hungry children, the wounded

68

soldiers, the women left without husbands and fathers. 'And even if there isn't a war, it is just the same,' she said. 'There are always hurt people and starved people, and beaten people and misery.'

'And there are always the people who don't care,' said Bea.

'Well, I care really, I have to,' said Harriet.

'Of course you care,' said Captain John, and he smiled kindly at her. Now Harriet came to think of it, he did not often smile, and when he did . . . 'Why, he most often smiles at me,' thought Harriet dazzled. 'Not at Bea, nor Victoria; at me, at something I say or do. It is as if he couldn't help smiling then. Yes, I am the one who makes him smile.'

'Do you ever feel you want to fight again, Captain John?' asked Valerie.

'No,' said Captain John curtly.

'When I am grown up,' said Harriet, 'I am not going to fight in wars. I am going to fight the people who make wars.'

'Is that any better?' asked Bea. 'Everyone seems to be always fighting and fighting, and it doesn't do any good. If I were a man, I should be one of those people who say they won't fight.'

'I wonder if you would,' said Captain John.

'Why didn't you?' asked Bea. It was seldom she asked a point-blank question, especially of Captain John, and he answered it with the seriousness it deserved.

'I wanted to . . . but I couldn't trust myself.'

'How—not?' asked Harriet, puzzled, 'if you wanted to.'

'At the last pinch,' said Captain John, 'at the last pinch I think I should have been angry and fought to save myself—and it is no use unless you can go through that last pinch.'

They did not understand.

'But what good does it do?' asked Bea. 'Fighting?'

'Well, that is not the only point,' said Captain John slowly.

'Why not? What other point could there be?'

'It is something,' he said, 'to believe enough to die for that belief. Perhaps it is more than something, perhaps it is everything—to—aspire—to try.

'Yes,' breathed Harriet. 'Like martyrs.'

'I think the martyrs were stupid,' said Bea. 'I think soldiers are too. Fighting is stupid.'

'Perhaps it is,' said Captain John. 'But perhaps that is neither here nor there. Perhaps the the thing is, to believe.'

'And get killed for it?'

'If necessary.'

'I think so,' said Harriet. 'If I were brave enough . . . only I wouldn't be,' she said. 'But I believe in things.'

'Oh, you!' said Valerie. 'You will believe in anything.'

'That is better than believing in nothing,' said

Captain John.

'Is it?' said Bea.

'Yes.'

'I don't think so,' said Bea.

'I do,' said Captain John.

Harriet stared at them. They were quarrelling.

They had been having tea in the garden, in fact Victoria, who ate inordinately, had still not finished and Nan was pouring out more milk for her. Harriet had left the table early and come to stand under the cork tree, listening to the woodpeckers, while she decided what she would do with the rest of the afternoon. Bea came after her, Captain John came after Bea and Valerie had brought a chair for Captain John. Valerie's fussing and homage annoyed him. It was true it took him ages to lower himself on to the grass, 'but it is better to let him take ages than to notice him,' thought Harriet, and now, he held on to the chair and deliberately let himself down to sit with them on the grass.

Harriet began to build a fence of twigs. Somewhere, in the distance, she could hear Bogey hallooing. Bea sat with her legs curled under her, sitting sideways into her white skirts that were patterned with a pattern of old rose stencillings. Harriet's dress was the same, except that it was patterned with China blue; that difference changed its whole character, it looked merely crisp and fresh, while Bea's ...

71

'looks like ... poetry,' said Harriet. Why are some colours filled with poetry and others not? 'Why can't *I* choose my clothes?' she had said to Mother. 'Why can't I wear what I like?' 'Now, Harriet,' began Mother, 'you are very nicely and suitably dressed. . . .' Harriet sighed.

The quarrel was continuing.

'Your ideas are so ... unsteady,' said Bea to Captain John. Once more they were like two children, or two grown-ups, 'and that isn't Bea's word,' thought Harriet. 'She learnt that from Father.' 'So ... unsteady,' said Bea.

'Are they?' said Captain John. 'Once they were burningly steady.'

That silenced Bea and moved Harriet. She stopped her play with the twigs and put her hand on his knee. It was the knee of his artificial leg, but he seemed to feel it. 'Won't they ever be again?' asked Harriet.

'No. I don't think they will,' he said, looking down at her hand. It was a little dusty from the twigs, but he did not tell her to take it away.

'I think they will,' said Harriet.

'Valerie,' said Bea getting up, 'come and practise,' and she and Valerie walked away, arm-in-arm, linked together. Presently the not-quite-synchronized sounds of their new duet came down to the garden from upstairs. Harriet looked down at the grass because she knew that Captain John cared. The silence, broken only by the duet, grew too long.

'You shouldn't care,' said Harriet severely, speaking into the grass. 'You are a man and she is a little girl.'

'If I were ninety and she were nine, or the other way round, it would be all the same,' said Captain John. She could hear him breathing.

'Do you—love her?' asked Harriet, digging with her finger in the grass.

'Yes and no,' said Captain John. 'Never mind, Harriet,' and he added, 'There are some things you understand better than Bea,' and he said, speaking lightly, 'We can't change her.'

That was true. Bea would not change. Under her charm and softness she was adamant, and people never guessed how adamant she was because she was resilient. 'I expect you find Harriet the difficult one,' they said to Nan, and Nan shook her head and pursed her lips. With the deadly knowledge that old servants have, Nan could have told a thing or two of Bea, though she never did. 'Bea is by far, far, the most difficult,' was all that Nan would say.

'She knitted more Red Cross scarves than any of us,' said Harriet now, and then she added truthfully, 'But it was because she wanted to be the best at knitting,' but she did not say that aloud because after all Bea was as good a sister as could be expected.

She tilted her head and looked up through the branches of the cork tree to see the clouds moving and the house and tree tilting back

73

against the clouds.

'Funny,' said Harriet to himself. 'The world goes on turning, and it has all these troubles in it.' She looked down the garden to the tea-table, where Victoria still sat. 'Horrible-wounds-and - milk - and - bread - and - butter - and - loving - and-quarrelling-and-wars.' What was a quarrel but a little war? And there were wars all over the world. 'They have even come in here,' thought Harriet, looking at the big stone house that was her home. 'But,' thought Harriet, 'this *is* the world.'

The sound of playing had stopped and there was no sign of Valerie and Bea. That probably meant they had gone up on the roof; the roof was a favourite place for walking or pacing; its flatness and its four parapets like walls were restful; there you could not see anything but the sky and the hawks circling and a few bright dots of paper kites. If you climbed up on the parapet, of course, you saw the whole wide vista of the land: 'town - river - boats - trees - works - Ram - Prasad's - little - house - by - the - gate - the - faraway - temple - another - temple - across - the -river,' thought Harriet. Climbing up on the parapet was forbidden, but she and Bogey climbed.

Every family has something, when it has left home, that is for it a symbol of home, that, for it, for ever afterwards, brings home back. It may be a glimpse of the dappled flank of a rocking-horse, a certain pattern of curtain, of firelight shining on a brass fender, of light on the rim of a plate; it may be a saying, sweet or sharp, like: *'It will only end in tears.' 'Do you think I am made of money?' 'It is six of one and half a dozen of the other'*; it may be a song or a sound; the sound of a lawnmower, or the swish of water, or of birds singing at dawn; it may be a custom (every family has different customs), or a taste: of a special pudding or burnt treacle tart or dripping toast; or it may be scent or a smell: of flowers, or furniture polish or cooking, toffee or sausages, or saffron bread or onions or boiling jam. These symbols are all that are left of that lost world in our new one. There was no knowing what would remain afterwards of hers for Harriet.

Being European in India, the flavour of Harriet's home was naturally different from most; it was not entirely European, it was not entirely Indian; it was a mixture of both. The house was a large oblong of grey stucco, flat-roofed, its parapet ornamented with those improbable daisies. The river ran past its garden and the tree rose high in front of its serpentine drive.

It was a double-floored house, with long verandahs. The rooms were all high, cavernous, stone-floored and white-washed; shaded by the verandahs, they were always dim, though the end rooms had green-shuttered windows. For nine months of the year electric fans moved the upper air. They did not at first appear the kind of rooms that made a home, but Harriet's home was a peculiarly pleasant place.

On the ground floor was the dining-room, red-floored, pillared, with large pictures in large frames, reproductions of Gainsboroughs, Reynolds and Romneys. The dining-table was oval and capable of taking extra leaves; at night it had an embroidered cloth and pink-shaded candelabra above its bowl of roses or pink sandwich creeper; those candles always woke excitement in Harriet. There was also a barrel, hooped with brass, that had once held salt meat on a sailing ship; now it was used for drinks and the children could just manage to raise the lid and all of them, often, had small secret swigs. There was the high chair that even Victoria had outgrown, and there were Father's silver cups, won by his charger Maxim when he was a younger man in the Bengal Volunteer Horse; there, too, were all the children's christening mugs.

On one side of the dining-room was Father's room; it had his desk, papers, cupboards, his two guns, the telephone and Sally's, his fox-terrier's, basket. At the other end of the house on the ground floor was the double nursery with its battered furniture, the children's own personal bookshelves and small wicker armchairs and the Millais pictures that had been in Mother's nursery. Nan's bed, Bogey's and Victoria's cot were at the back of the room in a row and there was an ironing-board where the iron seemed perpetually heated. Nan's red lamp burnt in front of the holy picture over her chest of drawers; she always kept a sprig of jasmine in her vase. The guinea-pig's cage, the rocking-horse and the scooters that no one ever touched, were out on the verandah.

Upstairs was Mother's bedroom where she and Father slept and where anything private and serious in the family was discussed: 'talks', and what Mother called 'reasoning' and whippings; temperatures were taken there, the doctor examined throats and chests and ears and stomachs. Harriet, Bogey and Victoria had all been born in that bedroom.

Next door was Harriet's and Bea's room and their two white beds from which they talked at night; next door to that again was the drawing-room.

The drawing-room was always confused for Harriet; there were so many things in it, both objects and happenings, that she could never remember it exactly. It was a large room and one end of it was left almost bare, with its green floor holding only the piano and the music rack and a tiger skin with a snarling head on the wall. The other end of the drawing-room was furnished very thoroughly with chairs and couches, bookcases and a cabinet, a fireseat and, in the centre, a low brass tea-table on carved wooden legs. The tea caddy was tortoiseshell and very old; it stood on the mantelpiece with the Worcester cups and a tiny Dresden china cup that belonged to Bogey. Harriet never knew why it should belong to Bogey. Mother's writing-table held a pile of account books, and notes, and catalogues. There was a sweet-pea chintz on the chairs and real sweet peas in bowls, or else sweet sultanas and gypsophila, or else, when it was getting hot, vases of tuberoses. There were small rubbed leather books that were sets of the classics, Scott and Thackeray and Dickens, and there was a scrapbook made for Harriet's grandmother when she was a child. The cabinet held a compendium of games.

The house had three staircases, a main one of dark wood, a side one painted white under which was the Secret Hole, and a back one for the servants which the children were not allowed to use, though Bogey and Harriet used it. Double flights of stone steps led from the downstairs verandah into the garden at the front of the house. The kitchen and the servants' quarters were outside, and there were stables, a washerman's yard, an electric-light-machine shed, a garage, and the porter's, Ram Prasad's, house beside the gate.

'It is more comfortable than anywhere on earth,' Harriet would have said of her home. It had fitted her like her own skin, but just lately she had come to see it more critically and more clearly. 'Is it that I am getting old?' wondered Harriet. 'I am getting old, look at my little breasts. Or is it Valerie and Captain John?' And she added honestly, 'It is something to do with knowing Valerie and Captain John.'

Certainly, since she had known them, everything in the house had been thrown into sharper focus, but then they, particularly Captain John, had coincided in a curious way with her growing up. Had she grown up because of them. She could not tell, but she knew now, for instance, that her parents had not as much money as Valerie's. Her eyes had been opened to contrasts: Valerie's clothes and their own home-made handed-down dresses; Nan and Valerie's travelling governess; Harriet's family had no car, they had only one child's pony. 'When the cradles fill,' said Harriet's father, 'the stables empty.' 'Of course we do have a lot of children,' thought Harriet, 'but we have no Persian rugs, no wine at dinner, no ice cream, and when we go for picnics we don't have a basket with plates and cups and everything to match.' 'Yes. I suppose we are poor,' said Harriet. 'Compared to Valerie . . . we haven't been anywhere, and we don't know anything at all.'

She felt crushed. Captain John raised his head.

'What is the matter, Harry?'

'I was thinking—of us—our family.'

'And what did you think of it?'

'Not very much,' answered Harriet.

'Then I will tell you what I think,' he said. 'I think you are the very best family I have ever known.'

'D-do you?'

'Yes, I do. And don't you forget it,' said Captain John.

Something fell with a small soft plop on Harriet's head. It was a cork-tree flower just breaking into cream petals from its bud.

'Look,' cried Harriet in an excess of happiness. 'Look. That means that it is nearly Christmas. The tree is always in flower for Christmas.' Her face clouded. 'But it can't be as good a Christmas this year,' she said.

'It may be the best you have ever had,' said Captain John.

★    ★    ★

Of the families who keep Christmas, some keep it rather more, some rather less. Harriet's family kept it implicitly.

Besides the cork tree, the chrysanthemums were always out for Christmas; their scent was a part of it, like the smell of the withering fir tree and of hot candle wax and raisins and tangerines. Any of those scents, for ever afterwards, filled Harriet with the brand of quivering excitement she had known as a child at Christmas.

Their Bengali Christmas had its own brand too; it was always perfect weather, the weather of a cool fresh summer day. The day began the night before, as Bogey said, with carols and hanging up stockings; that led to the opening of stockings the next morning and early church in the Masonic Lodge (the town had no church) where the gardeners gave each person, even children, a bunch of violets wired with ferns. Then the merchants and clerks of the works and the district came to call on Father with baskets of fruit and flowers and vegetables and nuts and whisky and Christmas cakes decorated with white icing, tinsel and pink-paper roses. The servants' children came to see the tree and be given crackers, oranges and four-anna pieces. The young men from the Red House came to lunch and in the evening there was a Christmas tree.

All this happened every year, but there was, besides this, a thread of holiness, a quiet and pomp that seemed to Harriet to have in it the significance of the Wise King's gold. It linked Christmas with something larger than itself, sometimes as large as...? Harriet thought it was a largeness that had something to do with the river, that began as a trickle and ended in the sea. Afterwards she wondered if this feeling in Christmas came from Nan. This year, as the time drew on and there was much less of

81

everything, less buying and hiding and writing and planning, it was there again and it was more pronounced.

Bogey did not want anything for Christmas.

'But you must,' said Harriet. 'You must have something. Mother didn't mean you to have nothing.'

'But I want nothing,' said Bogey obstinately.

'You can't want nothing. You must want something.'

'But I don't. I have what I want.'

'You must want new things,' argued Harriet.

'I don't like new things. I like what I have.'

'What have you?' Bogey did not know. 'You haven't anything. You buried all your soldiers.'

'If I get any more I shall bury those,' said Bogey darkly.

'Pooh! You only like insects and horrid snakes.'

'Harry,' said Bogey, his face changing. 'I have been thinking. You know how the snake-charmers play on their pipe things? Well, I am going to play on my whistle. You know my whistle that Captain John gave me? I am going to play like a charmer on that. My snake might like it.'

This was the season for snake-charmers. This was the time they came walking through the East Bengal towns and villages, black-skinned men with beards, dressed in dark orange clothes. They carried a pole on their shoulders, and from each end of the pole hung down a loop of cloth in which were round shallow baskets that would just hold the coils of a snake. Baskets were piled on baskets, but many of the snakes were great worms, harmless and thick and stupid, not like a cobra with its strong strike and beauty and interesting wickedness. Very often the snake-man would have a mongoose, tied around the neck with a cord, its little red eyes gleaming. The mongoose would be put to stage a fight with a snake. 'I wish we had a mongoose here,' thought Harriet, 'and he would kill that cobra.' 'I don't think you ought to play with it, Bogey,' said Harriet aloud.

'It—doesn't come now. I think it has gone,' said Bogey quickly, but he lied.

The snake-man's pipe was a pipe on a gourd that made a sound like a bagpipe, sinuous and mournful. Bogey's whistle sounded merely hopeful after it.

'Why do you want to whistle if it has gone?' said Harriet sternly.

His eyes flickered. 'Oh . . . just 'cos.'

'If a snake-charmer hears about your snake,' said Harriet, 'he will come and take it away. They are always looking for cobras. You had better take care.'

'I should like to be a snake-charmer,' said Bogey dreamily.

Harriet was tired and cross with her own preparations, which were always elaborate and always caused her family a good deal of tribulation before they were given.

'And what are *you* giving, Victoria?' she asked.

'I?' said Victoria, surprised. 'Nothing.'

'But *Victoria*, you must give people things.'

'Must I?'

'Yes. You can't take things and not give them.'

'But I like taking, not giving,' said Victoria contentedly.

Bea had made a handkerchief for Captain John and hemmed it with even small stitches and competently embroidered his initials in the corner. 'But—I haven't anything nice to give him.' wailed Harriet.

'Why should you give him anything?' said Mother calmly. 'He is more Bea's friend than yours.'

Harriet knew that, but for some reason, to hear Mother say it, filled her with a storm of torment and rage. 'I—I—hate Bea!' she cried, but fortunately Mother had gone out of earshot and Harriet was left to swallow it alone.

All her auguries were for a miserable Christmas, but still that holy quiet persisted, even in her, and besides she had a secret, a secret iron in the fire. She tried to be gloomy about that too, but she could not: the warmth of her secret persisted in the quiet.

Every year Nan made a crib with a set of old

German figures of the Nativity. They were of painted wood, older than Nan knew. Harriet could never see them without a great fascination, and now, when they were brought out of their boxes, ten days before Christmas, to stand in their cave of moss and sawdust lit by candles, Harriet's imagination was touched again. In her restlessness and unhappiness they touched her so deeply that a familiar urge rose up in her. 'I am going to write about them,' said Harriet suddenly. 'What shall I write about them? A Carol? A hymn? An Opera,' thought Harriet modestly. 'Or an "Ode to the Three Wise Men"?' But there were so many odes.

There was a blue angel kneeling with a lap full of roses. Her legs and her face were salmon pink, she had a gilt halo with blue in its diadem and she was always the one Harriet remembered best, for the expression of pain and smugness on her face. She looked as if she had a remarkable headache. 'What is the matter with her?' thought Harriet now as she had thought every Christmas. 'Is she too good?' she wondered. 'Why does she pull that face?' And an idea came to her and filled her mind, so that she went straight away into the Secret Hole and wrote down her idea in her book. It took most of the day, but when it was finished and she read it over, she was not surprised as she had been when she read her poem; she was tickled and delighted, as she had thought she would be.

'Good,' said Harriet, biting her pencil. (She bit her pencils so badly that Nan said her inside must be like the floor of a carpenter's shop.) Now, as she remembered to take her pencil out of her mouth, a second idea, an idea of what to do with her idea, came to her, and this was of such dimensions that she was dazzled. 'But— could I?' asked Harriet. 'How could I?' and she looked doubtfully at the pencil-writing in her round handwriting in the book. Could I?' and then her face and her voice hardened. 'I could,' said Harriet. 'I shall.'

Captain John was staying with them for Christmas. She went to find Captain John.

'Come into Father's office,' said Harriet to him. 'I want to speak to you.'

He obligingly came, but like Bea, he kept his finger in his book. 'Put your book down,' said Harriet. 'I need you.'

'But—' he said. 'But—' he said again when she had explained.

'It is no use saying "but",' said Harriet firmly, and she began to uncover Father's typewriter that she was forbidden to touch. 'You can type,' she said. 'You said you could. This must catch to-morrow's steamer. And you must write a letter for me too.'

'But—the "Speaker" is a grown-ups' paper,' objected Captain John.

'This is a grown-ups' story,' said Harriet. 'And they do put things like this in at

86

Christmas-time.'

'Yes. But ... you are far too late. They choose articles for their Christmas number weeks before.'

'They may have kept a little space,' argued Harriet. 'And mine may be so much better than the things they have, that they may put it in after all.'

'That isn't very likely,' said Captain John.

'No, but it is possible,' said Harriet.

He put out his hand for her story as he had for her poem once before. Harriet gave him the book and waited, quiveringly expectant.

'"*The Halo that was too Tight*"' read Captain John. He glanced up at Harriet with a twinkle in his eyes and down again. '"*An angel complained that her halo was too tight.*"' He read on and his lips twitched, and once he laughed.

When he had finished it he did not say anything, except, 'Very well, I will type it for you,' but he gave her shoulder a small squeeze.

'I expect I am a nuisance,' said Harriet humbly.

'Yes. You are,' he said, sitting down to the typewriter.

'I expect you will have to alter the spelling a bit, if you don't mind,' said Harriet happily.

'I expect I will,' said Captain John.

On occasions, very occasionally, things happen as you feel they will, as you feel in your bones they will. Once or twice more in her life,

Harriet was to know that calm certainty, that power of will, and have it answered. She was quite right to be certain. There was a surety of touch in that small story; it was small to change, to crystallize and confirm, as it did, Harriet's whole life, but she had known it could not go wrong, and on Christmas morning, when the mail bag was brought in to Father as they were having breakfast, he stopped as he looked over the letters and said, 'Why, Harriet. There is one for you.' Then he looked at it more closely. 'It can't be for her,' he said. 'It is from the "Speaker." There must be a mistake,' and he was raising his knife to slit it open when Harriet called out in agony, 'But it is for me. Don't open it, Father. It is for me. I . . . I am expecting it.'

Everyone turned to look at her.

Father, still doubtful, handed it to her, and now she learned what facing an inquisition meant; no one spoke; they waited for her to open it. The envelope was buff-coloured, addressed in typescript; in its corner the printed, *Speaker Ltd., Speaker House, Calcutta.* The blood began to drum oddly in Harriet's ears. 'I - expect - I - am - sure - it - is - only - to - say - it - is - no - good - to - send - it - back,' she thought rapidly to herself. She wanted to hide the envelope quickly in her hand and rush away with it and open it by herself.

'Go on. Open it, Harriet,' said Father. 'We are dying of curiosity.'

Harriet gave one appealing glance at Mother and opened it. A typed letter and pink cheque form fluttered out.

'*Harriet!* What have you been up to?' said Mother sternly.

'I haven't been up to anything,' said Harriet. 'I—I don't understand what it says.' And she burst into tears.

It was quite true. Father read the letter aloud, and then Captain John came limping in with a paper in his hand. Harriet's story had been there all the time in the folded Christmas edition of the 'Speaker' by Father's plate. 'Well. I am absolutely damned!' said Father.

The rest of the day passed in bliss. 'I never want it to end,' said Harriet, and when it had run its full gamut it stayed, still perfect, in her mind. 'It will stay with me for ever,' she said. 'It is my new beginning. Today I have been born again,' said Harriet, 'as Captain John said.'

Father had cut the story out and pasted it into his scrap-book. He showed Harriet when he had written. '*Harriet's first published work*,' and the date. 'First!' With the feeling of elation there came to Harriet a feeling of responsibility. She had avowed herself. She had signed herself away. It was public now. She was different. With all the glory, she wished she could have kept herself a secret.

That night she could not sleep. She was too excited to sleep. She lay listening to the pulse of the steam escape and to the river; she looked out through the doors, where Mother had left the curtains looped, where the light was clear moon blue. 'There must be a moon,' thought Harriet. 'I can see branches, but I can't see the top of the tree. I wonder...' What she wondered she did not say. From Bea's bed there came the sound of a sob. She listened. There came another.

'Bea!'

Instant silence.

'Bea. Are you crying?'

Silence.

'Bea. You are crying.'

No answer.

Harriet left her bed and went across in her nightgown to Bea's. It was cold and Bea made no move to let her in, but she remained sitting on the edge of Bea's bed. It was shaken slightly up and down every second. Bea was crying.

'Are you—feeling sick?'

No answer.

'Is it—because—is it anything to do with to-day?'

No answer.

'Did anyone get angry with you?'

Only a shake in the bed.

'Is it Valerie?' asked Harriet angrily.

'No.'

'Is it ... Bea, is it because I wrote the story and you didn't?'

'Of *course* not!'

'Is it—is it anything to do with Captain John?' said Harriet delicately.

Silence and complete stillness.

'What is it about him, Bea?'

'It is—it is—'

'You made up your quarrel, didn't you?'

'It—wasn't a—real—quarrel.'

'Shall I call Mother?' asked Harriet out of her depth.

'N-no. W-we mustn't d-disturb her. You kn-know that.'

'But you can't go on crying,' said Harriet.

Bea made an effort to be quiet. She sat up, but the sobs began again.

'Tell, Bea.'

'He ... he is ... going away,' said Bea, in a rush, without any breath.

'Is he?' said Harriet stunned. 'Going away,' and she went on repeating 'Going away. Going away,' till the words felt like two hammers hitting a sore place. 'Ouch!' said Harriet, wincing.

'Yes. He is going away. We sh-shan't see him any more.'

'No,' agreed Harriet. 'Then we shan't.' She sat on the bed feeling more sore, more than ever cold and separated. 'But not yet, Bea,' she said, 'not yet. Not now.'

'No, not yet,' said Bea, but she cried as hard as ever.

'Bea, don't cry so hard. Don't, Bea. He isn't

91

going yet.'

'I am not crying because he is going,' said Bea. 'I am crying because . . .'

'Because?'

'Because *it* is going,' said Bea in another rush.

'It? What "it", Bea?'

'It is all going so quickly,' said Bea. 'Too quickly. It is going far too fast.'

'Mmm,' said Harriet, beginning to understand.

'Much too quickly and too fast,' cried Bea. 'It is all changing, and I don't w-want it to change.'

'But it hasn't changed,' said Harriet. As she said that she knew that it was false. How much had changed even since this morning? Everything had changed.

'I like it to stay as it is,' said Bea. 'I don't want this to end, ever. I want it to stay like this always, but it won't.'

'No, it won't.' Harriet had to agree again sadly. There was nothing else for her to do.

'We can't keep it, and to-day was so l-lovely— happy.' Bea's head went down in her pillow again. 'I want to be like this for ever and ever,' she cried.

So did Harriet. She sat hurt and cold and silent on Bea's bed until Bea put out a hand to her. 'Don't you stay, Harry,' she said. 'There isn't anything we can do, you're c-cold. Your hand feels like a frog.'

Harriet crept, cold and helpless, back to bed,

but long after Bea was quiet, she lay awake. She thought Bea was awake too, and this was the first time they had ever lain awake without talking. The day was gone. However they might lie awake and cry or ache, they could not claim it back again. Who was it who had said you could not stop days or rivers? Harriet could hear the river running in the dark, that was not really dark but moonlight. She shivered. 'In six or seven weeks perhaps he will go away.' She tried to make herself believe that, but it did not seem, nor feel, true. 'What will Bea feel then?' wondered Harriet. 'Will she feel worse than I shall? In books people are happy for ever and for ever. But those books are nonsense. Nothing is for ever and for ever,' thought Harriet. 'It all goes away. But does it?' Again she was struck by a doubt. Does it all go, be lost and ended—or in some way do you have it still? Could that be true? 'Is everything a bit true?' she had said to Captain John. Then she lost that hope. 'No. It is gone,' thought Harriet. 'I didn't notice it before, but now I see. I see it—horribly. Why didn't I see it before? Because I was little?' And aloud she said, 'Bea. Are you asleep?'

'No,' said Bea.

'Bea, does it show you are getting old?'

'Does what? I do wish, Harry, you wouldn't think in between the things you say. As Valerie says, how do you expect us to understand?'

Bea was cross, but Harriet persisted.

'What are the signs of getting old—like us?' asked Harriet.

'Lots of things, I expect,' answered Bea wearily. 'Do you want to know now?'

'Yes.'

'Growing up, of course—'

'Growing pains?' asked Harriet.

'I suppose so. Learning more. Being more with Mother and less with Nan; not liking playing so much, nor pretending; understanding things more and feeling them longer; wearing liberty bodices; and oh, yes,' said Bea, 'I remember when we came down from Darjeeling this year, finding everything had grown far more little than I expected. When I went away it all seemed so big. When I came back, it was little; and I suppose,' said Bea slowly, 'being friends with Captain John has made me old.'

'I am not so far behind all that,' thought Harriet to herself.

*       *       *

Soon after that conversation with Bea, that talking of growing, Mother sent for them.

'Harriet and Bea. Mother wants to speak to you—in her room.'

'What about?' said Bea instantly and suspicious.

'She didn't tell me,' said Nan smoothly.

94

'But Nan knows,' said Harriet to Bea. Bea shrugged her shoulders.

It was January. The Christmas holidays were over and life had entered on the second lap of the cold weather. Lessons had begun. The bignonia venusta creeper in the garden and along the front of the house was out in orange-keyed flowers. The cork tree had its full spread of blossom. There was, all day long, a smell of honey in the garden and of honey in the fields where the mustard was in flower. It was still cool; there were still cold morning mists that blew over the garden at dawn and gathered on the river. The excitement was all over. Life had settled to its tenor. Harriet's story, with other happenings, had lost its point of interest and been fined down by the passing of the days until now the family took it for granted.

'I want to talk to you,' said Mother. 'I think you are old enough to have this talk with me.'

Harriet, as a matter of fact, was not at all old that morning. She looked down, as she sat, at her brown scratched knees with their sprinkling of golden hairs, and at the shortness of her green -and-white checked gingham dress. The dress bore all the stains and marks of that morning's experiences: papaya - juice - from - breakfast Prussian - blue - from - painting - the - Sea - of - Azov - a - little - torn - hole - from - climbing - trees - a - long - mark - from - falling - down - while-chasing-Bogey-on-the-dewy-lawn.

Mother was looking at the dress too. 'What have you been doing, Harriet?'

Harriet hung her head. 'Playing.'

'A big girl like you! Perhaps you had better not stay,' said Mother. 'Perhaps you are not old enough. I will talk to Bea.'

Bea sat with a stony face her shoulders hunched. She said nothing.

'Oh, Mother, please let me stay. I am old enough, really I am. It is only sometimes, when I play with Bogey. Mother, let me stay.'

Mother looked at Bea and Bea looked resentfully at the floor. Mother sighed. 'Well,' she said with another glance at Bea, 'perhaps you had better stay.'

Then there was complete silence, with only the regular steam puff from the Works and the steady sound of the river.

'You are getting to be big girls now,' said Mother.

Another silence. Bea sat stiff, withdrawn as far as she could be. Harriet began to be agog.

'Every day you grow a little more,' said Mother.

'Willy-nilly,' said Harriet suddenly.

Bea shot an angry glance at her from under her eyebrows, but Mother smiled. 'Yes, exactly,' she said. 'Willy-nilly. Soon, sooner than we guess perhaps, you will become women.'

'Yes, I suppose we will,' said Harriet.

96

'I don't know,' said Mother, 'I have never asked you how much you both know about—life.'

'Life?' asked Harriet puzzled.

'Babies being born,' said Bea shortly, breathing through her nose.

'Everything,' said Harriet with certainty.

'A little,' said Bea reluctantly.

'Well—' said Mother. She sighed again. 'We had better begin from the beginning. . . . You know it is the women who bear the babies, carry them in their bodies—as I am doing.'

'Yes, Mother,' said Harriet, and she and Bea both averted their eyes from Mother.

'We—women have to make our bodies fit for that,' said Mother. 'Like a temple.'

'A *temple*?' asked Harriet surprised.

'Yes,' said Mother. But still it did not seem quite certain, the idea did not quite fit.

'Because you see, Harriet, the bearing of children, for the man you love, and who loves you, is very precious and sanctified work.'

'Do you love Father?' asked Harriet immediately.

'Yes,' said Mother, 'I am glad to say I do.'

At that small statement, typical of her mother, the conversation became suddenly and intimately true. Harriet felt a surge of love for her. She put her hand on Mother's knee and Mother pressed her hand, but Bea still sat aloof, still as if she were angry.

Harriet was unable to prevent herself from talking, from forcing this on.

'But—having babies, doesn't it hurt—horribly?'

'Yes, it does,' said Mother. 'But nowadays they have so much to help you that you hardly feel the pain, at least, not very much. You needn't be frightened. The doctors are clever.'

'But—suppose there isn't a doctor. Suppose you were caught out in—the jungle—or a desert—or there was a *flood!*' said Harriet.

'Oh, *Har-ri-et! Do* let Mother go on,' said Bea.

'To get ready this temple . . .' said Mother, and her voice sounded uncertain again as if she again had been thinking over how to put what she had to say, and was not sure of the result.

'To make it ready, changes happen in your body, when you are beginning to be big girls.'

'I know,' said Harriet, nodding. 'They have happened to me.'

Mother looked surprised and Bea impatient.

'You needn't snort at me. They have,' said Harriet.

'Yes, I expect they have. You are growing, but wait, Harriet,' said Mother. 'Listen.'

'Mother,' broke in Bea, '*must* we talk about this now? Can't we wait till this does happen? And *must* we have Harriet here?' She glared at Harriet as if she hated her.

And Harriet herself suddenly felt that she

would prefer to postpone it, though she did not know why.

A sound came from the river, an approaching churning with a regular pulsing of engines. It was the twelve o'clock mail steamer. The noise grew louder as it passed the house, upstream, and then grew fainter; presently there came the sound of waves, its wash slapping against the garden bank. Mother, who had seemed to waver, gathered herself again.

'You can be patient for a few minutes longer,' said Mother. 'I shan't keep you long. It is always better for things to be talked of plainly.'

Bea looked as though she did not agree. 'And,' added Mother dryly as she watched Bea's face, 'it won't do you any harm to hear this from your mother, even if you have been told it by someone else already.'

'She means Valerie,' thought Harriet. 'Valerie has told her. Good for you, Mother,' thought Harriet, refreshed to find how little of a fool her mother was.

Mother's eyes were resting on Bea's head as she began to talk again. Bea bent her head so that neither of them could see her face and her fingers picked, picked at the wicker stool she sat on. Why was Bea so funny, so resentful? And now Harriet found herself wishing that Mother would not keep them there, keep Bea, at any rate, there, to be talked at against her will.

But Mother talked on calmly and firmly, and

99

soon Harriet forgot to look at Bea. She was listening with all her ears.

Mother's voice went steadily on. Then there was a third silence.

'Well!' said Harriet. 'Well!'

She looked down at herself, and it was true that she was exactly as before, the same knees, the same hairiness, the dress with the same stains and marks. 'But—I didn't know what I was, what I am, what I am going to be,' said Harriet. For all she knew, had known up to now, she might have been the same as Bogey. Gone, and she thought regretfully of them for a moment, gone were some pleasing vistas she had seen for herself and Bogey; running away to sea and becoming cabin boys; turning into Red Indians, 'I should have to be a squaw, and I don't like squaws,' thought Harriet; being an explorer, 'No, I suppose women are not really suitable for explorers,' thought Harriet, 'they would be too inconvenient. And every month . . . like the moon and the tides . . . the moon brings tides to the world and the world has to have them . . . it can't help its tides, and no more can I.' All at once it seemed exceedingly merciless to the small Harriet, sitting on just such another wicker stool as Bea's in Mother's room.

'I wish I were Bogey,' said Harriet.

'I know,' said Mother. 'I often wanted to be a boy.'

100

'You?' asked Harriet in surprise. 'You did?'

'Yes, I,' said Mother, 'but it is no good, Harry. You are a girl.'

'But ... I don't think it *can* happen to me,' thought Harriet, and aloud she said, 'Mother, I don't think it will ...'

'Will what, Harriet?'

Bea made an impatient movement. 'That is what she always does, thinks, and then expects you to know what she is thinking.' It seemed to help Bea if she attacked Harriet. 'She is a perfect little silly. Can I go, Mother?'

'Bea ...' Mother began, but Harriet had to interrupt.

'To me? In *my* body? Are you sure, Mother?'

'I hate bodies,' burst out Bea, 'I want to go.'

'Very well then, go, Bea,' said Mother.

After Bea had gone, Mother sat still, and once again Harriet heard her sigh, but she herself was too engrossed with herself, with being Harriet, to feel this. 'I don't think,' she said, 'that I can be—quite an ordinary woman, Mother.'

'You will be the same as every woman when your turn comes,' said Mother, 'and so will Bea ... just as you said, willy-nilly. And now,' she said, 'perhaps you had better go back to your playing.'

'Play!' said Harriet. 'Play! I shall never play again.' But she did. The same day she was chasing Bogey on the lawn again.

* ★ ★ ★

In the early afternoon, everyone rested. Father snatched an hour before he went back to the office, Mother rested monumental on her bed from two till four; Harriet and Bea read, Bogey was banished to a camp cot in Father's room, while Victoria slept and Nan sat in her chair in the darkened nursery and sewed under the window and sometimes dozed off. It was the servants' siesta time; even the birds were silent; even the lizards lay asleep in the sun.

If, however, Harriet had any pressing business she did not postpone it; she left her book and slipped off to her bed and no one was any the wiser. 'I am going to rest in the Secret Hole,' she said to Bea. She was not, but Bea nodded quietly. Then Harriet went downstairs and almost always, as she passed Father's room, Bogey's camp cot was likewise empty.

This was Bogey's supreme time for his adventures, when there was no one to see him or hinder him or even be aware of him. It was the time, too, when the garden was least disturbed, when his insects and his reptile friends were most accessible. Harriet never remembered yet getting up and finding him in bed.

One afternoon, in later February, Harriet needed Bogey. She went downstairs to find him, but of course he was not there. She could not see him in the garden either as she stood on the verandah.

'Bother,' said Harriet, 'I shall have to go out,' and she went on tiptoe to the nursery to fetch her hat.

Nan was asleep. On her lap lay a pair of Victoria's knickers into which she was putting new buttonholes as Victoria grew too fat for the old; she still held her needle and her lips, as she slept, blew gently in and out. Harriet fetched her hat and went out.

She could not see Bogey anywhere. 'He is playing Going-round-the-garden-without-being-seen,' said Harriet annoyed, and she began to follow him over the customary tracks that only she and Bogey knew. The garden was empty, brilliant with sun. Its colour blazed at Harriet. Here, as she went between the plinth of the house and the poinsettias, their flowers, as big as plates, long-fingered, scarlet, looked into her face as she passed; she half expected to see Bogey's face amongst them, Bogey's face screwed up in the sun, under his shock of hair. She crept between the poinsettias and the house just as he crept, but there was no Bogey there. He was not by the morning glory screen trumpeting its blue and purple flowers into the sun, nor under the swinging orange creeper at the house corner. He was not in the bougainvillæa clumps nor anywhere near the rose turrets, nor under the jacaranda trees, nor by the tank. Harriet went into the vegetable garden between the rows of peas and white-flowering beans, and pushed through the tomato bed, malodorous with its yellow flowers, but he was not here. He was not in the stable where Pearl stood looking stupidly out of her stall, half asleep herself. Harriet stopped to pat her, to smell her warmth, but Pearl did not alter her expression at all. She only twitched her ear at a fly.

Bogey was not behind the little midden of manure, not in the servants' quarters where Harriet could see forms, stretched out asleep on the string beds, under the trees and the eaves of each hut.

She went behind the hibiscus standards, their flowers hanging pink and scarlet and yellow and cream in lantern shapes with tasselled stamens; she swung them as she passed, but nothing else stirred or shook them. She went where Bogey went, along the drain by the wall behind the bamboos whose pipe stems stood, green and bronze and canary yellow with only the sunlight filtering between them. She went stealthily along expecting Bogey to spring out on her with a cat-call any moment, but the garden was as still and blank as ever. She went into the fern-house and round the goldfish pond. Bogey was not there either.

Out on the open lawn, the sun beat down on the grass that had a haze of its own heat, and sent off a warm dry smell. All the scents of garden mixed with it, but still the scent of the yellow Maréchal-Niel roses and of the petunias and of the cork-tree flowers was distinguishable. The lawn, too, was quite empty. The whole garden was empty, and Harriet flung herself down on the grass and looked back up at the house and the tree still making their journey against the sky. Far up the hawks still went round and round in their rings. They made her dizzy. 'I rather wish I had stayed in and had my rest,' said Harriet, yawning. 'I don't know where Bogey is. He plays 'Going-round-the-garden' far too well. Probably he is here, quite close to me and laughing,' said Harriet crossly; but no, she had no feeling of Bogey being near and laughing. She had only a feeling of blankness, a complete blank. 'Blank,' thought Harriet aridly, and yawned again. 'Blank.'

All at once she sat up. 'I believe,' she thought. 'I believe he is waiting for that snake. I believe he is by the peepul tree.'

She did not want to go near the peepul tree; even the thought of the cobra made her spine go cold. 'Ugh!' said Harriet. 'Ugh! I wish he wouldn't. I don't know how he can. I must tell Father. I am going to tell Father,' said Harriet, and she jumped up and dusted the dust of the grass off her hands and knees and elbows.

She went to the gate where the bridal creeper, over now, hung in a tangle of dried green. The gate was open a crack. That meant Ram Prasad was out. His house was empty. Harriet looked in as she passed, and saw his 'lota', his washing-pot, and his lantern and his green tin trunk painted with roses standing neatly under his bed; his coat hung from a peg, his cut-out pictures were pasted on the wall and in the corner, near his earth cooking-oven, were his brass platters, his spoon and his brass drinking cup and his hookah. They were all utterly familiar to Harriet; she had seen them all hundreds of times.

Now she had come to the space round the peepul tree. Here, where the earth was bare because of the peepul roots, there was an empty space like a courtyard edged and screened with bamboos. There was nobody there, not even the cobra; her eyes had looked at once quickly among the roots, under the bamboos, to see a dark heap, a sliding coil. There was nobody, nothing, and then the blankness ran up into the sky, her feet were clamped to the earth; she had seen something else. It was not Bogey; not the snake, but an earthenware saucer of milk lying upset and broken on the ground near a small bamboo stick and, further off, towards the bamboos, on the ground too, Bogey's sun hat was lying by itself. 'He has been bitten,' said Harriet's mind distinctly as she stood there.

'It—it came out for the milk and he touched it with a stick and it struck. It struck,' and again the blankness ran into the sky into a long pause.

Then close to her feet, lying on the ground, she saw Bogey's whistle.

With trembling legs she bent to pick it up, and as she bent, she saw him.

He was lying in the bamboos, only a few yards away, spread starfishwise as if he had flung, or tried to fling, his arms and legs away from him; he was lying on his face, his body drawn up from his arms and legs in a small heap. 'I see,' said that dreadful clearness in Harriet's mind, 'he would do that. Try and hide in the bamboos. He would go off to hide it, not tell—and then when it hurt,' and she knew snake bite was a terrible pain, 'why, then, I suppose he couldn't tell. No one would hear him. There was no one near enough to hear.'

She went towards him on shaking legs. 'Bogey,' she said in a voice that was a croak, 'Bogey. Bogey.'

She went nearer, her eyes looking in and out of the bamboos, on the ground, near him, away from him. There was nothing there. Only Bogey on his face.

She looked down on him, at the seat of his shorts, old grey-blue linen, and at his rucked-up shirt that showed his naked back and his spine. His hands were clutched and filled with earth and bamboo bits, and his hair was dirty with them too. 'He must have rolled about in them,' thought Harriet. Her throat grew drier, her breath hurt, her neck was cold. 'Bogey,' she croaked. 'Bogey—'

There was a rustle in the bamboos behind her, and she jumped so that her skin tingled. It was a bird, a jay. It made a harsh whirring and clapped its wings and flew. 'Don't they do that when a snake is near?' thought Harriet, and now, where she had been cold, she was wet. She bent and took hold of Bogey's foot in its sock and brown shoe and gave it a little pull. 'Bogey,' she tried to say. 'Boge. Bogey. Boge.'

She had not expected Bogey to answer, and he did not answer. He did not move, and she had not expected him to move. 'The—the warm is gone,' thought Harriet. The side of his face she could see was scratched and the skin was blue.

'Blue?' asked Harriet numbly, staring down at him. 'Blue? Why should he be blue?' She went on saying that as she looked and looked and looked. She said it until she heard the gate creak on its hinge. Ram Prasad had come back.

Then she broke the quiet. She screamed louder than the jay. 'Look. Look. Look,' she screamed. 'Ram Prasad! Ram Prasad! *Sarpe. Sarpe.* Snake, Snake, Snake.'

★  ★  ★

In India, when anyone dies, it is necessary that they are buried at once, and by sunset of that same day Bogey was lying in the small

108

cemetery where the trees, that had honey-balls like mimosa, dropped their pollen on the old graves and the new graves, on the short earth mound that was Bogey's, on the stone of the other boy, John Fox, piper, who was fourteen when he died, two hundred years ago.

With the resource that a small far-away town often shows, a coffin was found and made to fit Bogey by the carpenters in the Works. The Works were stopped; the coolies went home, but the clerks gathered in a silent and respectful throng just inside the gate. The firm's small launch, the 'Cormorant', left her moorings and came up to the jetty; from other jetties, up and down the river, other launches put out, and on them were people from the other Works, and flowers from the other gardens. The gardeners knew what ought to be done; without being told they cut all the white flowers, white petunias and roses and candytuft and dianthus and gypsophila. In Harriet's garden they sat in the shade making wreaths though no one told them, and they made a cross, too, of yellow roses.

'Why can't I go out? Why can't I go *out*?' whined Victoria.

'Be quiet,' said Harriet.

'Hush,' said Bea.

People, ladies and gentlemen, gathered under the cork tree. Abdullah and Goffura, who also knew what should be done, carried out chairs and trays of tea, but no one of the family came down to speak to anyone; everyone sat or stood talking in low voices while the cork blossom, that was falling, dropped on their heads or into their cups of tea.

'We haven't had any tea,' said Victoria. 'I want some tea.'

'Hush,' said Harriet.

'Be quiet,' said Bea.

'Why did all the people come?' wondered Harriet. They came as if they had a right to come, as if it were their duty. Now Mr Marshall, who was wearing a grey suit, not whites as he usually did, came and stood talking with a set grave face. They had come for Bogey? Why? 'Why do—they—all come?' Harriet asked Bea.

'It is the custom,' said Bea. 'Bogey has to be buried.'

'Buried?' said Harriet startled.

'Yes. You know that,' said Bea.

Harriet knew. She had always known, but it had not come to her before. When you died, you did not belong to yourself, nor to your family; you belonged to custom, and places and countries and religions; even a small boy like Bogey. Harriet remembered Father telling her about the Registration of Births and Deaths, the birth and death of a citizen. 'Then Bogey was a citizen,' she said aloud.

They huddled under Bea's bookshelf, straining to listen, trying to see and not see.

110

'I want to go out,' said Victoria. 'Why *can't* I *go out?*'

Then Nan came in.

'Why are you not dressed?' said Nan.

'Dressed?' They stared.

'Yes. You always get dressed for the afternoon?'

'Yes—but—but—'

'You would think no one had ever taught you how to behave,' said Nan. 'Take off that dirty frock, Harriet, and go and wash your face. You too, Bea. Victoria, come here and let me unbutton you.'

'But are we—is—Bogey—'

'Bogey is dressed,' said Nan with dignity. 'The house is full of ladies and gentlemen. We must show them that we—we care for him. You will get dressed and then come with me.'

'Shall we—see him?'

'I don't want to see him,' said Victoria. 'Ayah says he is all black.'

Nan's face folded in on itself suddenly, the lines by her mouth and her eyes folded in, and she shut her lids. Then she picked up the brush and without answering began to brush Victoria's hair. When they were dressed she walked them out on the verandah, between more people who parted and made way for them, and into Father's room. It was very dim, but Nan had lit two candles on the writing-table. There was only Bogey's coffin there heaped up with

111

flowers.

'I don't know what Mother would wish,' said Nan, 'and I cannot ask her, but I think you should *not* see Bogey. You must say good-bye to him here.'

They stood close in the candlelight, in the smell of flowers where again the roses were the strongest. 'Why again?' wondered Harriet. 'When—in what age had she thought that before?' Then Nan took then out into the garden, away from the people, by the river.

The river ran with no noise of steam from the Works. It sounded queer.

Father and Mr Marshall came from the house carrying Bogey in his coffin. They carried him down to the jetty and put him on the deck of the 'Cormorant' and the people followed with flowers, till there was a hill of flowers on the deck. Some of the flowerheads fell off into the river, and were floated down and away. Then the 'Cormorant' cast off from the jetty and backed and turned in a half circle to go upstream, and the other launches, with their people, cast off too, and followed behind. Each launch left a pointed wake in the water.

'The river can't close over this,' thought Harriet; then she seemed to see again in the water the handful of ashes that had been Ram Prasad's wife, and she remembered how they had been washed, round and round, gently, on the water, before the current took them away.

Now the launches had passed out of sight.
The colours in the garden were deepening in late
afternoon sunlight; it was nearly evening.

★    ★    ★

Pieces of the next two days broke through to
Harriet.

They found and killed the snake, not one but
two, two cobras. Harriet saw Ram Prasad
stretch them out on the ground when they were
dead, one five feet, the other more than four.
Bogey had been bitten in the neck, the right side
below his cheek, Nan said. 'He was quickly
dead,' said Nan.

After the cobras were killed, Harriet began to
be sick. She was sick on and off, all those two
days. In spite of that there was no respite. There
were still things to do. Nan told her to go and
find all Bogey's toys. She was packing his things
away, out of Mother's sight.

Harriet could not find any toys except an old
arrow, thrown down and rusty; she knew where
Bogey had buried his soldiers, but she let them
stay buried; she found a mud garden under a
tree, but you could not pack a mud garden. She
wandered round the garden that was the same
garden, not changed, not different, but she
walked in it not thinking, not touching, merely
walking.

There was no clergyman in the town. Mr

113

Marshall had read the service for Bogey. In the evenings, Mr Marshall and Dr Paget came to be with Mother and Father. One evening Mr Marshall stopped to speak to Harriet who sat on the steps looking at the darkness, not thinking, only looking.

'I expect you to miss your brother,' said Mr Marshall kindly.

The jackals howled far out on the lawn.

'Well, it is a good thing it wasn't Victoria,' said Harriet.

Mr Marshall seemed slightly taken aback. 'Why?' he asked.

'Victoria is afraid of jackals,' Harriet explained. 'Bogey isn't.'

Nan forgot to pack Bogey's toothbrush. When Harriet was having her bath she saw it still there: Bea, pink; Harriet, green; Bogey, red; Victoria, blue. Harriet stood up in the hot water and took Bogey's down.

'What are you hiding in your hand, Harriet?'

When Harriet showed, Nan turned her back and tidied the towels on the rack.

'You can't keep that, Harriet,' she said.

'No,' Harriet agreed forlornly.

She put her head down on the zinc edge of the bath. Nan stayed by the towels, smoothing them down.

'We don't need to keep things, Harriet.'

'No,' said Harriet, not arguing; then, as she relinquished the toothbrush, it was true. The less she had of Bogey, the more clearly she saw him.

There began to be shoots of life. Whether they were wanted or not, there were shoots of life.

Father went back to the Works. Mother came downstairs. Harriet heard her ordering the meals again. 'Soup. Celery soup with cream,' said Mother, 'mutton, mint-sauce, peas, the garden peas.''

'Roast potatoes,' said the cook, entering it in Hindi in his notebook. He was an educated cook.

'Then orange baskets,' said Mother, and Harriet found herself chiming in, 'Yes. Can't we have orange baskets too, Mother? For our supper?'

Victoria made herself a new kind of house on the verandah table. She said it was a 'think house'. It was nothing but Victoria herself sitting on the table. 'Where are the walls? The roof? The front door?' demanded Harriet.

'It is a think house,' said Victoria.

'You mean you think it is a house, and it is?'

Victoria nodded.

'But what can you *do* with it?' asked Harriet.

'You can think in it,' said Victoria, with dignity.

Lessons began again. Lessons with Mother, with Father. Eating - sleeping - getting - up - going - to - bed - resting - washing - brushing -

115

and - combing - and - doing - your - teeth - reading - swinging - riding - Pearl - knitting. All the outward things went on. Surprisingly, the inward things began to go on too. Nothing had changed. 'But everything,' Harriet thought, 'has shrunk. Everyone has shrunk somewhere inside themselves, as if they are hiding and you are afraid to find them because you are afraid of what you may find.' Occasionally, you would discover. Mother cutting roses, stooped and picked up a lead highlander off the path. It was one of Bogey's soldiers that Sally had dug up. Mother went indoors, dropping her scissors and the roses she had picked on the verandah table.

Harriet came into the nursery and there was Nan just as before, making buttonholes for Victoria. Harriet stopped, and her sickness came back again.

'What is it, Harriet?'

'It is so—horrid—so cruel,' Harriet burst out.

Nan went on with her sewing.

'Going on and on. We go on as if nothing had happened,' wept Harriet.

'No, we don't,' said Nan. 'All we do is to go on. What else are we to do, Harriet?'

'It is as if we had wiped Bogey away. Look at you, making *button*-holes!' wept Harriet.

'What do you think I should do?' asked Nan quietly.

'That is just it,' Harriet could not hold her tears. 'It happens, and then things come round again, begin again, and you can't stop them. They go on happening, whatever happens.'

'Yes, they go on happening,' said Nan, 'over and over again, for everyone, sometime, Harriet.'

Harriet sat down on the floor, and wiped her eyes on the back of her hand. She felt hollowed with her unhappiness, and then, as she sat there, leaning against Nan's chair, another astonishing shoot came up in her mind. 'No,' said Harriet, horrified at herself. 'No. No, I can't. I mustn't. *Write* about this? No. No. I can't,' but it was already forming inside her head, as Nan stitched buttonholes again, and again she heard the sound of her life, the steam puff-wait-puff and the river. It was true; on the surface, even deeper, it was all exactly and evenly the same.

*The world goes round.*

'No,' thought Harriet, trying not to listen to herself; it carried her on.

*The river runs, the round world spins.*

'*Dawn and lamplight*,' thought Harriet. '*Midnight Moon.*' She shut her eyes and said it over to hear, in the old familiar way, if the words ran. It seemed to her that they ran properly and she went on:

> *The river runs, the round world spins.*
> *Dawn and lamplight. Midnight. Noon.*
> *Sun follows day. Night, stars and moon.*

**117**

The customary happiness and suspense and power filled her. She felt lifted again, as if she were rising up. She was ashamed, she tried to crush the words down, but they could not keep down. They insisted on rising.

*Sun follows day. Night, stars and moon*
*. . . . the end begins.*

'Nan,' said Harriet, shocked.

'Yes, dear?'

'Nan, how can I be happy? How *can* I?'

If surprising things came out of Harriet, no surprises ever came out of Nan.

'It isn't for us to dictate, Harriet.'

'Oh, Nan!'

'That is so,' said Nan, snipping her thread. 'If you are happy, you are. You can't make yourself unhappy. We are something, part of something, larger than ourselves, Harriet.'

Harriet was silent, remembering Christmas, and how little she had felt below the stars, remembering Bea and what Bea had said about growing smaller as you grew older, only perhaps Bea meant that this otherness grew larger; she thought suddenly of the fish that the kingfisher had taken out of the river and of the splash it had made and of how the splash had gone and the river, with its other fish, it porpoises, its ships, had gone on running on.

'Then what is the good of my writing my poem,' thought Harriet, 'if it is all so big and I am so small? It wouldn't make a mark as big as a—a fly's leg against the whole world. I shan't write anything.'

*The river runs*—it immediately began again.

'I have to go to the Secret Hole, Nan,' said Harriet, jumping up from the floor. 'I have a poem that I have to write down.'

But when she reached the Secret Hole, her box was empty. Her book was not there.

She came downstairs, hurtling down, and there was Valerie reading her book on the lawn.

'What are you doing with my book?' Harriet was scarlet.

'Reading it,' said Valerie, absolutely cool. Bea was standing by as if she did not quite know what Valerie was doing; she made no attempt to stop her reading Harriet's book, and worst of all, Captain John was reading his own book near lying on the grass.

'Give it to me.'

'No, I shan't,' said Valerie, turning over a page. 'I think it is very funny. Listen, Bea: *When I have thoughts they hum. I might have I think a little top in the top of my head—*'

'Bea. Make her give it to me.'

'Valerie. It is Harriet's private book.'

'Yes. I should think so,' said Valerie giggling. 'How could you, Harriet? There are all kinds of things in it. Captain John, here's one about you.

119

There are a great many about you,' and she read out, '*I think that Captain John's face is like one of those plants you touch . . .*'

'You are not to read it. You are not to,' screamed Harriet, flying at Valerie, but Valerie dodged away, nearer to Captain John, who had lifted his head to listen and look at them.

'*Captain John's face is like one of those plants that if you touch roughly they shrink and close up. I think it is true. Father calls him "a sensitive plant."* Oh, Captain John!' laughed Valerie, and Bea had to laugh too.

'You beast!' screamed Harriet. 'You beastly girl.'

'*I think he is like Antinous whose face you never do forget,*' read Valerie, dodging Harriet. '*Today I am so alive I am glad I am me and am born—*' Valerie ended in a shriek as Harriet tore the book away and pulled her hair.

'Harriet. You mustn't hurt her.'

'She has hurt me,' shouted Harriet, 'the mean sneaking hateful beastly pig. How dare she!'

'I don't want to read your silly diary,' said Valerie, rubbing her shoulder where Harriet had wrenched her. She put back her hair and fastened her tortoiseshell slide that had come undone. Harriet hated her fuzzy brown hair and she hated her face, which looked considerably heated and a little uncomfortable. 'Why be so angry?' said Valerie lightly.

'It was her private book,' said Bea.

120

public not private, so that they were not by themselves any more. 'I wish I had died with Bogey,' whispered Harriet.

There was a knock on the shutters behind the curtain.

'Harriet, can I come in?'

'Captain John!' cried Harriet, shrinking in her bed.

'Yes. Can I come in?'

'No. Please no.'

'I am coming in,' said Captain John.

He came in. Made dim by the shadows of the room, he looked large, his movements very jerky. Harriet could not see his face.

'I have brought your book,' he said, and laid it at the foot of her bed.

'Than-k you.'

She did not move. She did not want him to see her face.

'Don't you want it?'

Harriet shook her head. 'I won't be doing any writing any more,' she said.

He did not answer that. Instead he said, 'I have come to take you for a walk.'

'Me?' said Harriet.

'Yes. Along by the river. It is beautiful there in the evening. Nan says you can come. Come along, Harriet.'

'But—' Harriet sat up and put her legs down over the edge of the bed, 'don't you want to be with Bea?'

124

'She is quite right to be angry,' said Captian John, who with difficulty had risen from the grass and come to them. 'You had no right to take it, Valerie.' He looked almost as angry as Harriet, and Valerie saw that everyone was against her. She looked hotter than ever and her eyes grew bright with spite.

'I don't see why *Harriet* should be so haughty,' said Valerie, 'when everyone knows it was her fault Bogey died.'

It was said.

There was complete silence in front of the steps, except again, in this pause, the steam puff and the river. Then Harriet turned and ran upstairs.

\*       \*       \*

No one had spoken very much to Harriet about the cobra. She knew and they knew, and they knew that she knew. Father had questioned her. Her face and her voice had shown him how guilty and wretched she was, and he did not punish her. 'What,' said his whole attitude as he turned away, 'is the use of punishing now?' and that had twisted Harriet's heart more than any words.

Mother had said nothing either till Harriet had come and stood in front of her. 'Mother— I — I knew about — the — the — cobra — Mother.'

121

'Yes, Harriet. I know you did,' said Mother.

'Mother—I—'

'It is no use talking about it now,' said Mother.

There had been shocks. Ram Prasad was sent away. 'But why?' demanded Harriet. 'Why? He only knew it was there. *He* didn't know that Bogey—'

'There is no excuse for Ram Prasad. No excuse at all,' said Nan hardly.

Ram Prasad was, later, forgiven and reinstated, but that had given Harriet a glimpse of how people felt. Did they, then, think as hardly of her? She had only, so far, thought hardly of herself. Now Valerie's words burnt into her. *'Everyone knows.' 'Everyone knows.'*

Harriet lay on her bed, her face turned to the wall.

Nan came in.

'Harriet,' said Nan.

'Please go away.'

'Harriet,' said Nan, 'I think you should get up.'

'I—can't.' Harriet's voice was muffled.

'You will have to get up some time,' said Nan reasonably, 'so I should get up now.'

'I can't, Nan. How can I?'

'With a girl like Valerie,' said Nan, 'a spiteful girl, you have to very proud. You should not let her see she can hurt you.'

'It isn't only Valerie,' cried Harriet in despair.

122

'You didn't hear what she said. Oh, Nan, do[es] everyone know? Does everyone say—*that*?'

'I expect they do,' said Nan calmly. 'You hav[e] to expect that because it is partly true, Harriet.'

'Yes, but—*who* could have thought—'

'You could have thought,' said Nan. 'You didn't use your sense. You know you didn't, and for that a cruel lesson has been given.' Her voice trembled and she looked with indescribable pity at Harriet, but she went on. 'Very cruel, but perfectly just,' said Nan. 'You can't complain about it. You must not.'

'What am I to do? What can I do?' cried Harriet.

'It is a thing that will have to pass away from you, Harriet.'

'It never will, Nan. Never! Never!'

'Yes, Harriet, it will,' said Nan. 'You have plenty of courage and you are strong. I have faith that it will,' and she pressed Harriet gently on the thigh and said, 'Get up now and face that Valerie.'

She rustled gently out, but Harriet did not get up. She lay on her bed engulfed with misery. All the sounds of the late afternoon came up to her and she could identify each one, but she lay cut off from them all. 'I feel as if I had thorns in my heart,' said Harriet. 'How hard Nan is. Ho[w] hard,' she said. Now she could not be unhapp[y] for Bogey by himself any more. Mixed wit[h] him, irretrievably, was the guilt and indictmen[t]

123

'No,' said Captain John, 'I want to be with you.'

They went downstairs together and out along the drive and past the jetty and along the footpath, that lay beside the river.

The up steamer and the down steamer, the mail steamers, had passed for the day and the river flowed calm and untroubled between its banks. Now under the bank it showed shallows of light, yellow, where the late sun struck down into it; further out the water was deeply green, and beyond, in midstream, it showed only a surface with flat pale colours. On the further bank, a mile across stream, there was a line of unbroken brilliant yellow above a line of white, the mustard fields in flower above the river's edge of sand. The temple showed its roof among the trees and country boats, their sails set square, moved gently down before the current and the wind. Other boats passed, towed upstream by boatmen leaning on long towing lines. A peasant was washing the flanks of his cows in the river above the garden, and on the sand and in the mud lay the halves of empty shells, bleached white, that had baked all day in the hot sun.

'How beautiful it is,' said Harriet. Its beauty penetrated ino the heat and the ache of the hollowness inside her. It had a quiet unhurriedness, a time beat that was infinitely soothing to Harriet. 'You can't stop days or rivers,' not stop them, and not hurry them. Her cheeks grew cool and the ferment in her heart grew quieter too, more slow.

She was silent trying to think of it: then, 'I feel better already,' she said sadly.

'Don't you want to feel better?'

'No, I don't' and she said with the same forlornness, 'I need some time to be unhappy.'

He did not answer, but he bent and took her hand, and holding his hand, she went on walking beside the river, her steps made a little jerky by his. His hand was very comforting to her.

'Soon—you will be going away though—won't you?' said Harriet.

'Yes,' said Captain John.

'What will you do? Do you know?'

'I don't know yet, but something.'

When the sun had gone, they turned and came back. Now the colours had drawn in to tints of themselves in the water and in the sky, but the mustard still showed its brilliant clashing yellow; the last clouds of the sunset hung over the temple. 'They are like cherub's wings,' said Harriet. 'We always call them cherub's wings.'

He made no answer to that.

They heard all the Indian evening sounds, sounds that were alien to him, utterly homely and familiar to Harriet: the gongs beating far off in the temple in the bazaar, the creak and knock

126

of the ferryman's paddle as the ferry came near the bank; the sound of cooking-pots being scoured with mud and of a calf bellowing while its mother was milked. There was an evening smell of cooking too, pungent, too raw for their noses with its ghee and garlic and mustard oil; there was the smell of dung fuel burning, and, as they came near the house again, they smelled the cork-tree flowers on the air.

'Those flowers are falling off the tree,' said Captain John.

'It is nearly the end of the cold weather, of the winter then,' said Harriet.

'I must go,' said Captain John, but he did not go. 'Harriet, will you come for another walk with me?' he said.

'Of course. Can we go for a walk when it is dark, and look at the fireflies? I have always wanted to do that,' said Harriet.

'Yes.' He still lingered. Then he said, 'Harry. Put your book back in its place. Promise.'

Harriet nodded.

'I like to think of it back in its place. And I am glad I am in it,' said Captain John.

\*       \*       \*

As Harriet came into the nursery, where the lights were already on, Nan and Bea were kneeling on sheets of newspaper spread round Victoria's old basket cot. They were painting it

127

with fresh white paint.

Harriet stood rooted to the threshold, staring. 'Goodness!' she said. 'My goodness!' And she asked startled, 'Is the baby coming then?'

They laughed at her startled face. 'Didn't you think it would?' asked Bea.

Harriet came slowly into the room, stilll staring.

'There,' said Nan, standing up and cleaning her brush in the jar of turpentine. 'That will be dry tomorrow. It is such excellent enamel,' she said with satisfaction. 'Look, it is nearly dry already.'

Harriet looked at Nan sharply. There was no sign in Nan's face of anything but satisfaction over the excellence of the enamel. 'Nan is like a clock,' said Harriet to herself. 'Every minute she ticks just that minute. Nothing else.' She said it irritably, but she sensed that all the other minutes were in Nan was well, a tremendous aggregate of minutes. She said slowly, 'Nan, have you seen hundreds of babies born?'

'Not hundreds,' said Nan, 'but many. Very many.'

'And have you seen a great many people die?'

'Don't, Harriet,' said Bea sharply.

'But have you, Nan?'

'A great many, Harriet.'

'I don't understand,' said Harriet more slowly. 'I don't understand how you keep yourself so clear.'

128

'Don't you?' said Nan, but she did not tell them. 'I must go and see about your suppers,' she said.

After she had gone Harriet was left alone with Bea. Bea was still painting a leg of the cot, working the paint very carefully into the basketwork.

'Captain John has been so nice to me,' said Harriet.

'Has he?' said Bea.

'He took me for a walk.'

'Did he?' said Bea.

'He is—different, Bea.'

'Is he?'

Bea did not seem interested. She painted with small firm even strokes. Harriet could not see her face for her fall of hair.

'Bea,' said Harriet, 'are you unhappy?'

'Well, we all are,' said Bea, without looking up.

Harriet did not think it wise to continue, but she did. She could not go away.

'Does Captain John make you more unhappy, Bea?'

'No,' said Bea shortly.

'What do you do when you are unhappy?' asked Harriet.

'Oh, what a lot of questions you ask, Harriet. What is there to do? I am unhappy, that is all.'

She finished the leg and stood up and began to put her brush away with Nan's.

'I can't believe in this baby,' said Harriet, looking at the cot.

'It will be born all the same.'

'What happens, Bea?'

'Don't you remember when Victoria was born?'

All Harriet could remember was a story she had heard. When Victoria was born the head clerk of the Works, Sett Babu, came to Father and said, 'Sir, I hear you have another little calamity.' That was because Victoria was a girl and a girl to Sett Babu meant a dowry to be given when she was married. 'Do we have to have them?' she asked aloud.

'Have what? Babies?'

'Dowries,' said Harriet, but Bea did not answer.

'I don't see how we can,' said Harriet. 'How can we?'

'What? Have dowries?' asked Bea irritably.

'How can we be expected to have another baby and to like it? That is asking too much,' said Harriet. 'How *can* Mother?'

'If she is, she can. That is the answer,' said Bea. 'Harry, we ought to go and wash for supper.'

Harriet was silent, thinking, and then she said, 'It is too hard to be a person. You don't only have to go on and on. You have to be—' she looked for the word she needed and could not find it. Then, 'You have to be tall as well,' said

Harriet.

★  ★  ★

In spite of the sadness and the quiet in the house there began to be a thread of expectation; then a stir.

The nurse came, Sister Silver, and Bea and Harriet were moved out of their room. Harriet went to sleep with Nan and Victoria; Bea went to stay with Valerie.

'Then—will Captain John go there—to see her?' thought Harriet. 'Won't he come here any more?' said Harriet.

An overwhelming loneliness filled her and the old misunderstood pain. She went again to the Secret Hole and again sat there by her soap-box, with her knees under her chin, brooding. 'Am I always going to be lonely?' thought Harriet, and the right answer seemed to be, 'Yes, I expect I am.'

She had kept her promise and put her book back and now she picked it up, but all the writing in it seemed broken and flat. 'How silly I was when I wrote it,' thought Harriet. Valerie was right. It was all babyish and silly or else crude; the funny bits were not funny; the beautiful bits were too beautiful. 'I hate my writing,' said Harriet.

*The day ends, the end begins.*

She had not finished the poem. She looked at

131

it. 'Nothing leaves off,' said Harriet crossly. 'But I shall leave off,' and she threw the book back in the box.

★     ★     ★

In the night she did not sleep well. She did not often sleep well now. Her dreams were too intimately concerned with Bogey, with the cobra. That night she woke in her customary cold sweat, and slowly, as she forced open her eyes, she saw that she had not woken to the frightening darkness when everything had long lithe shapes and might, or might not, be sliding, coming, moving towards her. The light was on, and what had woken her was not a dream, but the sound of heavy treads. They came along the verandah and up the stairs past the nursery, and she heard a commonplace loud and cheerful voice, Dr Paget's voice. She lay and listened to it sleepily; then in a moment she sat up.

'Nan,' she said, 'is it the baby? Is the baby born?'

'Shsh,' said Nan's voice. 'You will wake Victoria.'

'Nan. What is—'

Harriet's voice stopped when she saw what Nan was doing. In front of a hot low brazier, Nan was airing the small clothes Harriet had often seen put away in Mother's trunk; Harriet looked dumbfounded. Washed, ironed and

ready, a vest, a flannel nightgown, a coat, a
white shawl, were airing there. 'It *is* the baby,'
said Harriet in awe. 'The baby is going to come.'

Outside, in the night, a gong struck once.
Harriet listened. 'One.' No more. It was the
Works' gong, beaten at the hours. 'It is one
o'clock in the middle of the night,' said Harriet.
'Is the baby born?'

'Not yet. Come,' said Nan. 'Get up. As you
are awake. You shall help me make some tea.'

'Tea? Now? In the middle of the night?'

In the dining-room the tea things were laid
out, sandwiches were cut. Harriet was
astounded and Nan laughed at her face as she
put on the kettle. 'Whom do you think I first
put the kettle on for, here, in the middle of the
night?' asked Nan.

'Who?'

'For you, Harriet.'

'For me?'

'Yes. You were born just after I came here.'

'And then—Bogey?'

'Then Bogey.' Nan said his name as if it were
the same as anyone's else's.

'Nan, you have seen so many babies,' said
Harriet. 'Do they always seem new and exciting,
like this, to you?'

'Always new,' said Nan, 'and exciting.'

'Every time?'

'Every time.'

Harriet pondered. 'But we don't want another

133

boy, do we?' she said jealously.

'That isn't left to us,' said Nan. 'It won't be another anything. It will be itself.'

Sister Silver came down.

'Is the baby born?' asked Harriet.

'Why isn't that child in bed?' said Sister. 'Nurse, I think we shall want those clothes soon.'

'I am ready,' said Nan. She had poured out a cup of tea before she took up the tray. 'Now, Harriet, here is a cup of tea for you. Can I trust you not to wake Victoria?'

Harriet took her tea and went to sit by the brazier that shed a dim warm circle of light in the nursery. Even the tea had a different flavour in the middle of the night, dark and strong and hot. It was too hot. She put the cup down and went to look out of the window.

The house was so warm and sheltered, so full of light and hush and life, that it did not know the night. At the window, Harriet met the chill of the early hours. There was no freshness in it yet, the dew had not fallen; the night was still strong. Far away, over and over again, she could hear the jackals howling and the two sounds, always present, always reminding her: puff-wait-puff, and the running of the river.

The strong night scent came to her again from the Lady of the Night; it was heavy, more than ever drenching, in the dark. She did not like it. She shivered.

134

Usually now all of them in the family would have been asleep, like any sleeping family. She thought of all the families safely and unadventurously asleep and then of how her own was scattered. Only Victoria was in her place. Mother's room was out of bounds, she could not know what was happening to Mother; Father was awake, walking between the verandah and the drawing-room, she had heard him while Nan poured out tea. Bea was across the river, and she herself was standing here tied with excitement so that she felt as if she had a knot in her stomach with the coldness of the night blowing on her forehead and the cold howling of the jackals in her ears. And Bogey ... where was Bogey? The warm of him was gone. 'It didn't stay—it wasn't made blue by the cobra ... then where ... where?' Harriet knew that it would be better, much better, not to think of Bogey now, in the middle of the night.

'If you are cold,' she told herself reasonably, 'why not drink your tea?' She went back to the heater and sat warming herself, her hands cold on the cup, her lips shivering as she drank. She could hear footsteps going backwards and forwards over her head in Mother's room.

Then she decided she would go out on the verandah and wait there. It was nearer. She could hear more clearly there.

The verandah showed her the night and now she saw the stars behind the cork tree, but the

135

tree did not appear to be moving at all. 'But it is,' argued Harriet. 'It is, because it always does.' The scent of the night bush was softened here by the circle of cork-tree flowers, by the thin dew scent of Mother's petunias in the pots.

'She is very quiet,' thought Harriet. 'I thought people screamed and shrieked and cried when they had babies.' She strained to hear and went to the foot of the stairs. No sound at all. Nothing. She began to walk upstairs.

It was dark on the centre landing, but the upper flight was lit and the lights were on outside Mother's room as well. Harriet kept in the shadow of the banisters. She could hear Father's steps, and cautiously she raised her head to look up. At that moment Sister Silver came out of Mother's room. Sh had her sleeves rolled, her face looked busy. As Harriet saw her, she saw Harriet.

'What are you doing up here?'

'Is it born?' asked Harriet.

'You go downstairs directly, Miss,' said Sister sharply, and Harriet retreated.

She did not retreat far, about nine steps. There she waited, and presently, when she judged it was safe, she came up again.

Then down the stairs a smell filtered to Harriet. She sniffed it. She knew it, and she had known what it was going to be. It was chloroform. She knew it from her operation for tonsils. There was no mistaking it. She came a little further up the stairs.

Nan was standing there outside Mother's door, but her back was turned to Harriet.

'Is it born?' That was on Harriet's tongue again when Nan's attitude arrested her.

Nan was standing and waiting for the moment to come. The light showed her thin shoulder blades under the straps of her apron crossed on her back; it showed the combs holding her thin bun of hair, and her old black jacket that she wore under her apron, her print skirts, and slippers. As she stood there, she looked small and quiet and humble to Harriet, who felt she herself had been making something of a clamour. She felt ashamed, but not so ashamed that she went away. 'I couldn't, I couldn't go down now,' argued Harriet. 'Nobody could. Not now.' She stood, trying to emulate Nan in stillness, on the stairs.

Then Nan started, her hands unclasped, and a sound ran through Harriet from her scalp to her feet and from her feet up again.

It was a new sound. First it was a sound like birds chirping; like sparrows in twigs; a twig sound; then it grew; it was broken into hiccoughs: coughs; it was like a little engine starting; it grew again, and it was the baby crying. It was the actual baby crying.

★      ★      ★

137

There had never been any days as peaceful as those late winter days after the baby was born.

There was no ripple of disturbance in them. Mother lay in bed, and Harriet only saw her to say good morning and good night; Father was away, up-river, on a jute conference; Sister Silver lived apart with the baby and Mother; Bea was still with Valerie; Nan and Victoria were the only two with Harriet, and Nan was never a disturbance, and Victoria never, in any case, made ripples.

Now the days were tinged with heat at midday, cool again at mornings and evening. It was almost spring. In the fields the early sowing was finished and the young jute and rice made dark-green and light-green patches over the land. The yellowness of the mustard had dimmed and the first great red pods of the simul, the wild cotton trees, had opened their colour. In the sky, the clouds were soft and puffed as cotton-wool. The sky itself had altered. This was the time of its deepest blue; later the heat took its colour, and later still the monsoon broke and turned it heavy and grey, with intervals that were pale, washed out. Now Harriet, by looking at the sky, knew it was nearly spring.

The sky so attracted her that she opened her moneybox and took out two annas and asked Ram Prasad to fetch her two new kites from the bazaar. He bought an excellent one, striped red and white with emerald corners, and a second one of plain pink paper. He helped Harriet to pierce the first, and fix it to her glassed string that was wound on a light polished roller made of bamboo with two long handles. Then they went up together on to the roof.

'You launch it,' said Ram Prasad, 'and I will get it up for you.'

'No. I want to get it up myself,' said Harriet.

'You never will. You never can.'

'I can. I shall,' said Harriet. 'Stand out of my way.'

She took the roller on the palms of her hands and allowed plenty of space behind her in which to run back. Ram Prasad took the kite between his fingers and walked with it to the other end of the roof.

Above them the sky waited for the kite. Nothing showed between the grey stone parapet walls, not a tree, not a roof, not a mast, except only the top of the cork tree flowering in its green and, far up, the specks of the hawks making their circles on the edge of the wind current. 'I am going to send it as high as that,' said Harriet.

'Ready?' called Ram Prasad, holding it up.

'Ready.'

Ram Prasad sent it up in a strong flight. The string pulled taut, Harriet jerked it higher twice, the kite found the wind, rose and jerked away of itself in a short cornerwise dance.

139

Harriet pulled backwards, it rose again, and then suddenly made an arc in the air and fell, dashing itself against the parapet.

'I told you so,' said Ram Prasad.

'Is it broken?'

She stood there while he looked at the torn kite. She kept her lips stiff. She meant to fly that kite. It was important to her that she should, because she had, in true Harriet fashion, made it into an omen. 'If it flies, I shall fly,' is what Harriet had decided.

'It can be mended,' grunted Ram Prasad. As always when they sailed kites, he had brought the second kite up on the roof and with it a pot of flour-and-water paste, a stick with a rag round it and some strips of coloured paper. Squatting on their heels, he and Harriet began to mend the kite; they first patched the torn place, then they weighted the opposite tip with the same amount of paper and paste; they added a blob to the tail to steady it and laid the kite in the sun to dry.

Nowadays Ram Prasad and Harriet were neither of them conversational. While the kite dried Harriet went to lean over the parapet by herself, looking down on the garden as if it were a map in another focus. She saw a small launch tied to the jetty and a pigmy Captain John walking up the drive. She felt herself pause; she looked down on him, held in her thoughts. Then Ram Prasad called her. He held the roller.

140

'Pick up the kite,' he said, 'and I will get it up for you.'

'No,' said Harriet, 'I shall get it up for myself.'

'You will never do it.'

'Then it shall not be done,' said Harriet.

'If you have husband, poor Godforsaken man,' said Ram Prasad, 'he will need a padlock and a stick.'

'Put it up,' said Harriet, standing ready. She hoped she would get it well up before Captain John found out where they were.

Ram Prasad put it up, clumsily. Harriet stepped back, pulled and the kite came down flat on the roof in front of her, flat on its back with its string doubled up.

'See how clever you are,' said Ram Prasad.

Harriet did not contradict him. 'Is it broken?' she said.

'No. No thanks to you, thanks to God.'

'Then put it up and more carefully this time.'

Her lips were in a firm straight line as Ram Prasad sent the kite into the sky. Captain John appeared in the stairway.

Harriet jerked her roller, the kite rode up; out of the corner of her eye she saw his eyes follow it. It rode up well, and she brought it up again strongly. The she let it go a little and it danced away down the current of the wind.

'Bring it up,' said Ram Prasad.

'Leave me alone,' said Harriet.

141

She brought it up herself, riding straight again, then to the left, to the right, another cornerwise dance off, and a bold fresh flight taking the string. Now it was safe, right up riding the wind, taking the string out, further and further away, higher and higher.

'You do it well,' said Captain John.

'At the third try,' said Ram Prasad. 'Bogey Baba could get it up first time, every time.'

The kite string sang in the wind; it pulled and tugged at Harriet's hands... 'This is me—me—me,' she was singing triumphantly to herself. The string seemed to go up until the kite was among the hawks' rising in the sky.

'Feel it,' she said, and put the roller into Captain John's hands.

It was handing him something that was alive. His arms jerked and his hands had to close quickly to hold it and he had to use his strength on it. She saw his cheeks flush and his eyes grow darker with the excitement of the kite. Soon she saw that he was nearly as moved and as exhilarated as she.

They flew the kite while the afternoon grew later and richer in the world beyond the parapet, until the small clouds took the sunset as they had on the walk by the river. The same sounds, the same smells, came up to them.

'Now I have been up here long enough,' thought Harriet. 'I am tired.' She began to wind the kite in.

142

'Are you bringing it down?' he asked regretfully.

'Yes.' She added, 'I always like them to be in before the first star comes.'

'Why?'

'Because it would be fatal for them to be out then,' she said seriously. 'The star would turn them back into paper.'

He did not laugh as she had been half afraid he would. He gravely helped her to wind the string in and the kite came back to them, fluttering, pulling away, getting larger in the dusk until it was over their heads, and Ram Prasad put up his hands and caught it level with his turban, as the last wind sank out of its sides. 'That was not so bad,' said Ram Prasad, 'but not as well done as Bogey Baba could have done it.'

Captain John took Harriet downstairs to ask permission from Nan to go out. 'It is very late,' said Nan, looking at them over her spectacles. 'It is dark.'

'Yes, but we wanted it to be dark. I want to show Captain John the fireflies,' pleaded Harriet.

Nan appeared to be thinking it over. Harriet checked her own arguments, of which she had a torrent ready, and waited too.

'Very well,' said Nan at last. She wisely did not say anything about time, nor bed.

'Shall we say good night to the baby?' asked Harriet.

143

'Very well,' said Captain John.

The cot was on the verandah, and all they could see in the folds of shawl was the baby's head and face asleep, and her fist doubled up. As they looked, the shawl moved up and down with her breathing.

'Feel how warm she is,' said Harriet.

Captain John held his finger near.

'She is very ugly, isn't she?' said Harriet.

'Look again,' said Captain John.

Harriet looked, at the line of cheek and the forehead where the veins spread, at the tiny mottled lids, like seals or sleeping shells, that showed a line of hairs that were lashes. She saw the nose and the mouth whose corners folded as it slept, and the chin. 'There is a dimple in her chin, like Father's,' she whispered, and Captain John nodded. The lobe of the one ear Harriet could see was laid flat to the head with a glimpse of tender skin behind it, going into the line of the back of the head turned into the shawl. The head was covered with fluff, a down, that was gold too. Harriet looked at the doubled fist, and at the hand and the fingers and the nails. 'I like her nails,' said Harriet. 'And Mother made her,' she thought, 'finished, complete outside and inside.' That was the wonder. This, this like to like. That was the wonder: foals, little horses, to horses; rabbits to rabbits; people to people; all made without a mistake. 'And without a pattern,' thought Harriet, touching the baby's

144

hand. It was always a fresh shock to find it warm, soft and firm, the feel of a real hand . . . 'Where did Mother—what did Mother—' she thought. 'Queer, what people can make: the flight of a kite—and poems—and babies. What a funny power—and I too, one day!' thought Harriet, 'see, how I have grown already.'

All at once she said to Captain John, 'Could I go just one minute? There is something I very badly want to write down.'

The minute was half an hour, but when Harriet came out of the Secret Hole, Captain John was waiting quietly for her.

It was nearly dark. They did not walk along the river. 'The villages are interesting at night,' said Harriet, 'and the fireflies are in the village tanks.' They walked away from the Works and the bazaar along the road, where it began to run through the fields and villages. Soon they came to a village. There was a stucco house on the edge of the huts, and, as they passed, a man whose white clothes shone in the darkness stepped through its gateway with a floating oil lamp in his hand. By this house there was an orange tree; it was in blossom like the cork tree, and its flowers glimmered as they passed it, and its scent followed them up the road.

'This is a very smelly time of year, isn't it?' said Harriet.

'You mean scented,' corrected Captain John.

'Yes. All the flowers smell,' said Harriet.

145

Here was a village tank, a sheet of water with a black shine, with the fireflies they had come to see along its bank and under its trees. Now they came to the huts built of earth, mud-walled with reed and bamboo roofs; every doorway, as they passed, was lit and showed a still life of figures or of things, lit and quiet. Here, on the earth floor, was a block of wood with a hollow in it, and a handful of spices and a pestle. 'That is where they grind spices for curry,' Harriet interpreted. By the block on the floor were chilis, bright red in the lamplight, and behind them on the wall hung a wicker scoop. 'That is for separating the husks from their rice,' said Harriet. Here a woman in a cotton cloth crouched down on her ankles, while she turned the stone handmill for grinding grain to flour; with her other hand she threw in the grain, and on her turning arm her silver bangle caught and lost the light. Two old men, next door, sat by the bamboo pole that held the roof up and shared a waterpipe, passing it from one to another politely. Here a mother sat and oiled another baby, her own baby, in her lap; the baby had a girdle of silver bells round its waist. There were sounds too of a tap, a goat bleating, of bullock-cart wheels in the road, of a passing bicycle's bell.

They went further, to another village and another, and then turned to come back. When they came to the first village again, some of the doorways were already dark, and the mother was singing to her baby, a song that was ineffably sleepy and low with only half cadences of notes.

'That is like Nan sings to our baby,' said Harriet. 'Nan sings like that.' The other woman was still grinding, the old men were still smoking and no one put the spices away.

From the stucco house, as they passed it, came music, a flute, cymbals, the interpitched grasshopper-playing of a sitar, and a drum. As they came nearer, a man's voice began to sing.

'What is he singing?' asked Captain John.

Harriet listened, but she could not make out the words. 'It will be about Radha and Krishna, I expect, and their love. They are always singing about that. Or else about Ajunta and his wars. It is always love and war,' she said.

Now they had come back to the house again, and they went in at the gate and up the drive, where the cork tree stood in its complete wheel of fallen flowers. Its branches were quite bare.

'So the winter is over,' said Harriet, as they stood under it.

The drum gave two throbs, a beat, and was still. 'It has done, for to-night,' said Harriet. 'Do you remember Diwali, Captain John? There were drums there too.'

'Diwali?'

'The Feast of Lights.' He nodded. 'Funny,' said Harriet. 'We talked about living, and being born and dying, and we didn't know then about... Bogey... nor the baby really ... nor anything...' And she said under her breath, *'Bellum ... Belli... Bello... Bello... Amamus... Amatis... Amant.* I was doing those then.' 'How young I was,' thought Harriet. 'Now how I have grown,' and she said aloud to Captain John, 'Are you any different?'

'I think I am,' said Captain John.

'Because you have decided to go?' asked Harriet.

'Partly, perhaps.'

Harriet nodded. 'That is what Nan used to say. "Leave him. He will go on when he is ready." I used to wonder what was wrong with you,' she said candidly. 'You hadn't died ... but...'

'I wasn't alive?' he suggested.

'You hadn't come alive,' said Harriet, and she said, 'You were like the baby ... you had to be born. ... You were quite right when you said that,' said Harriet. 'I died a bit ... with Bogey. I died much more when Valerie said that to me ... for a long time I didn't come alive ... not the whole afternoon!' she said.

'You are alive now, Harriet.'

'Yes, and so are you...'

She had a sudden excess of happiness as she had had that other morning, long ago.

'Look at my tree,' she said. 'Do you see it turning... Up in the stars? Sometimes,' she

148

said, remembering that morning, 'I write poems that are taller than I am.'

Captain John brought his eyes down and looked at her. 'I thought you were not going to write any more.'

'That was—' but Harriet did not say what it was.

'You can't help it, can you?' said Captain John. 'And what is this one? A story? A poem?'

'It is a poem.'

'And I have to read it, don't I, Harriet?'

'It is too dark to read,' said Harriet.

'Well, say it to me then,' said Captain John.

'It is good enough to say,' said Harriet. 'Really it is. This one is good. You will enjoy it. You will really. I wrote it after my other poem. It is much older.'

'I see,' said Captain John.

'This is it,' said Harriet, and she said it aloud:
*The day ends. The end begins . . .*

'Hm!' said Captain John when she had finished. 'You will be a real writer one day, Harriet.'

'Oh, yes,' said Harriet. 'I shall be very great and very very famous.'

He did not say anything to that and she ran her hand up and down the tree's smooth bark. The woodpeckers, of course, had gone to bed. 'Does everyone have one?' she asked.

'Have what? A poem?'

'No, a tree.'

149

'Not everyone finds theirs so soon,' said Captain John. 'You are lucky, Harriet. That is where I am going,' he said more firmly. 'I am going to look for mine.'

A launch, as it passed on the river, gave a mournful little hoot that sounded like an owl. A real owl hooted a minute after.

'I must go,' said Captain John.

'It is so dark you can hear the river,' said Harriet. She meant 'quiet' but dark was better. 'Time to go? Oh, no!' but that tag of remembrance came in her mind. When had she said it? 'You can't stop days or rivers?'

Captain John smoothed his hair with his hand, smiled once more at Harriet, and went.

'But ... you haven't said good-bye to me,' she called, caught unawares, in dismay, but he did not answer and limped steadily away until his footsteps died in the distance, and she knew he had reached the Red House.

Slowly she turned the edge of the thick carpeted wheel of flowers over in the grass with her foot; over and over and over.

'To-morrow we shall have to sweep these up,' said Harriet. 'They don't smell nice when they wither.'

She remembered something she had forgotten all these days and weeks and months. She stepped over the old lily shoots up to the tree and put her hand down into the hollow she had found, all that time before. Cold, sticky from dew and tree-mould, her charm was still there.

'My world,' thought Harriet. She was pleased to have it again, but she thought regretfully, 'I have it still, but I never found out what it meant.'

Holding it in her hand she went slowly across the drive and up the steps and into the house.

'Puff-wait-Puff' sounded the escape steam from the Works, and the water ran calmly in the river.

# AN INDEPENDENT
# WOMAN

# AN INDEPENDENT WOMAN

BY

BETTY NEELS

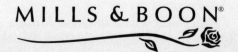

MILLS & BOON®

*First published in Great Britain 2001
Large Print edition 2001
Harlequin Mills & Boon Limited,
Eton House, 18-24 Paradise Road,
Richmond, Surrey TW9 1SR*

© Betty Neels 2001

ISBN 0 263 17235 X

*Set in Times Roman 16½ on 18½ pt.
16-0901-47756*

*Printed and bound in Great Britain
by Antony Rowe Ltd, Chippenham, Wiltshire*

# CHAPTER ONE

THE street, like hundreds of other streets in that part of London, was shabby but genteelly so, for the occupants of the small turn-of-the-century houses which lined it had done their best; there were clean net curtains at the windows and the paintwork was pristine, even if badly in need of a fresh coat. Even so, the street was dull under a leaden sky and slippery with the cold sleet.

The girl, Ruth, looking out of the window of one of the houses, frowned at the dreary view and said over her shoulder, 'I don't think I can bear to go on living here much longer...'

'Well, you won't have to—Thomas will get the Senior Registrar's post and you'll marry and be happy ever after.'

The speaker who answered, Julia, was kneeling on the shabby carpet, pinning a paper pattern to a length of material. She was a pretty

5

girl, with a quantity of russet hair tied back carelessly with a bootlace, a tip-tilted nose and a wide mouth. Her eyes under thick brows were grey, and as she got to her feet it was apparent that she was a big girl with a splendid figure.

She wandered over to the window to join her sister. 'A good thing that Dr Goodman hasn't got a surgery this morning; you've no need to go out.'

'The evening surgery will be packed to the doors...'

They both turned their heads as a door opened and another girl, Monica, came in. A very beautiful girl, almost as beautiful as her elder sister. For while Julia, she of the russet hair, was pretty, the other two were both lovely, with fair hair and blue eyes. Ruth was taller than Monica, and equally slender, but they shared identical good looks.

'I'm off. Though heaven knows how many children will turn up in this weather.' Monica smiled. 'But George was going to look in...'

George was the parish curate, young and enthusiastic, nice-looking in a rather crumpled way and very much in love with Monica.

They chorused goodbyes as she went away again.

'I'm going to wash my hair,' said Ruth, and Julia got down onto her knees again and picked up the scissors.

The front doorbell rang as she did so, and Ruth said from the door, 'That will be the milkman; I forgot to pay him…I'll go.'

Professor Gerard van der Maes stood on the doorstep and looked around him. He had, in an unguarded moment, offered to deliver a package from his registrar Thomas, to that young man's fiancée—something which, it seemed, it was vital she received as quickly as possible. Since the registrar was on duty, and unlikely to be free for some time, and the Professor was driving himself to a Birmingham hospital and would need to thread his way through the northern parts of London, a slight deviation from his route was of little consequence.

Now, glancing around him, he rather regretted his offer. It had taken him longer than he had expected to find the house and he found the dreary street not at all to his taste. From time to time he had listened to Thomas's diffident but glowing remarks about his fiancée, but no one had told him that she lived in such a run-down part of the city.

The girl who answered the door more than made up for the surroundings. If this was Ruth, then Thomas must indeed be a happy man.

He held out a hand. 'Van der Maes, a colleague of Thomas. He wanted you to have a parcel and I happened to be going this way.'

'Professor van der Maes.' Ruth beamed up at him. 'How kind of you.' She added, not quite truthfully, 'I was just going to make coffee…'

He followed her into the narrow hall and into the living room and Ruth said, 'Julia…'

'If it's money you want there's some in my purse…' Julia didn't look up. 'Don't stop me or I'll cut too much off.'

'It's Professor van der Maes.'

'Not the old man from across the street?' Julia snipped carefully. 'I knew he'd break a leg one day, going outside in his slippers.'

Ruth gave the Professor an apologetic glance. 'We have a visitor, Julia.'

Julia turned round then, and looked at the pair of them standing in the doorway. Ruth, as lovely as ever, looked put out and her companion looked amused. Julia got to her feet, looking at him. Not quite her idea of a professor: immensely tall and large in his person, dark hair going grey, heavy brows above cold eyes and a nose high-bridged and patrician above a thin mouth. Better a friend than an enemy, thought Julia. Not that he looked very friendly...

She held out a hand and had it gently crushed.

'I'll make the coffee,' said Ruth, and shut the door behind her.

'Do sit down,' said Julia, being sociable.

Instead he crossed the room to stand beside her and look down at the stuff spread out on the carpet.

'It looks like a curtain,' he observed.

'It is a curtain,' said Julia snappishly. It was on the tip of her tongue to tell him that by the time she had finished with it it would be a dress suitable to wear to an annual dance which the firm she worked for gave to its employees. A not very exciting occasion, but it was to be held at one of London's well-known hotels and that, combined with the fact that it was mid-February and life was a bit dull, meant that the occasion merited an effort on her part to make the best of herself.

She remembered her manners. 'Do you know Thomas? I suppose you're from the hospital. He's Ruth's fiancé. He's not ill or anything?'

'I know Thomas and I am at the same hospital. He is in splendid health.'

'Oh, good. But horribly overworked, I suppose?'

'Yes, indeed.' His eye fell on the curtain once more. 'You are a skilled needlewoman?'

'Only when I am desperate. What do you do at the hospital? Teach, I suppose, if you are a professor?'

'I do my best...'

'Of what? Professor of what?'

'Surgery.'

'So you're handy with a needle too!' said Julia, and before he could answer that Ruth came in with the coffee.

'Getting to know each other?' she asked cheerfully. 'Thank you for bringing the parcel, Professor. I'm sorry you won't see Monica— she runs the nursery school here. Luckily I've got the morning off from the surgery, and Julia is always here, of course. She works at home—writes verses for greetings cards.'

Ruth handed round the coffee, oblivious of Julia's heavy frown.

'How very interesting,' observed the Professor, and she gave him a quick look, suspecting that he was amused. Which he was, although nothing of it showed on his face.

Ruth asked diffidently. 'I suppose Thomas hasn't heard if he's got that senior registrar's job? I know he'd phone me, but if he's busy...'

'I think I can set your mind at rest. He should hear some time today. He's a good man and I shall be glad to have him in my team in a senior capacity.' He smiled at Ruth. 'Does that mean that you will marry?'

She beamed at him. 'Yes, just as soon as we can find somewhere to live.' She went on chattily, 'An aunt left us this house, and we came here to live when Mother and Father died, but I think we shall all be glad when we marry and can leave it.'

'Your other sister—Monica?' encouraged the Professor gently.

'Oh, she's engaged to the local curate; he's just waiting to get a parish. And Julia's got an admirer—a junior partner in the firm she works for. So you see, we are all nicely settled.'

He glanced at Julia. She didn't look at all settled, for she was indignantly pink and looked as though she wanted to throw something. She said coldly, 'I'm sure the Professor isn't in the least interested in us, Ruth.' She picked up the coffee pot. 'More coffee, Professor?'

Her tone dared him to say yes and delay his departure.

He had a second cup, and she hated him. And she thought he would never go.

When he did, he shook hands, with the observation that the dress would be a success.

Ruth went with him to the door. When she came back she said, 'He's got a Rolls; you ought to see it.' She glanced at Julia's kneeling form. 'You were a bit rude, dear. And he's such a nice man.'

Julia snipped savagely at a length of curtain. 'I hope I never meet him again.'

'Well, I don't suppose you will. He's a bit grand for us…'

'There's nothing wrong with a rising young surgeon and a member of the clergy.' She'd almost added *and a junior partner in a greetings card firm,*' but she didn't, for Oscar, accepted as her admirer by everyone but herself, didn't quite fit. Curiosity got the better of her.

'Why do you say he's grand?'

'He's at the very top of the tree in the medical world and he's got a Dutch title—comes from an ancient family with lots of money. Never talks about himself. Thomas says he's a very private man.'

'Huh,' said Julia. 'Probably no one's good enough for him.'

Ruth commented mildly, 'You do dislike him, don't you?'

Julia began to wield her scissors again. 'Dislike him? I don't even know him. Shall we have Welsh rarebit for lunch? I'll make some scones for tea. Monica will be ravenous when she gets home; she never has time to eat her sandwiches. And if you're going to the shops you could bring some steak and kidney and I'll make a pudding.' She added, 'Filling and cheap.'

She spoke without rancour; the three Gracey sisters, living together for the sake of economy in the poky little house a long-dead aunt had bequeathed to them, had learned to live frugally. The house might be theirs, but there were rates and taxes, gas and electricity, clothes and food to be paid for. None of them had been trained to do anything in the business world, having been left suddenly with nothing but memories of their mother and father, killed in a car accident, and a carefree life in a pleasant old house in the country with never a thought of money worries.

It had been Julia who'd got them organised, refusing to be daunted by unexpected debts, selling their home to pay off the mortgage, arguing with bank managers, solicitors, and salvaging the remnants of her father's ill-advised investments. Once in their new home, it had been she who had urged the rather shy Ruth to take the part-time job as a receptionist to the local doctor while she looked for work for herself and Monica joined the staff of the local nursery school. But Julia had had no luck until, searching through the ads in the local paper, she'd seen one from the greetings card company.

Nothing ventured, nothing gained, she had decided, and had sat down to compose a batch of verses and send them off. Much to her surprise, the firm had taken her on. It was badly paid, but it meant that she could work at home and do the housekeeping and the cooking. And they managed very well.

Ruth had met Thomas when she had gone to the hospital to collect some urgent path. lab. Results for Dr Goodman, and soon they would marry. Monica, although she liked children, had never been quite sure that she wanted to stay at home, especially in such alien surroundings, but then George had come one day to tell the children Bible stories and all ideas of going out into the glamorous world to find a job more to her liking had faded away. They would have to wait to marry, of course, until George had a parish. In the meantime she was happy.

Which left Julia, twenty-four years old, bursting with life and energy. Because she had a happy nature she didn't allow herself to dwell on what might have been, but wrote her sentimental little verses, kept the house clean and tidy and, being clever with her needle, dressed herself in a style which, while not being the height of fashion, was a passable imitation.

It was fortunate, she supposed, that Oscar, her admirer—for he was only that at the moment, although he promised to be rather more when it was convenient for him to be so—had absolutely no taste in clothes. That horrible professor might sneer in a well-mannered way at the curtain, but Oscar wouldn't suspect. Indeed, even if he did, he would probably approve, for he was of a frugal nature when it came to spending money. He was persistent too. She had tried, over and over again, to shake him off, to suggest that she would make him a most unsuitable wife, but he refused to be shaken and, despite the countless excuses she had given, she was committed to attend the annual dance given by the greetings card firm.

Rightly, Ruth and Monica had urged her to go and enjoy herself. But neither of them had met Oscar, and she had given way because she knew that they both felt unhappy at the idea of her being left alone when they married. When she allowed herself to think about it she felt unhappy about that too.

She put away her sewing and started on the household chores, and found herself thinking about the Professor. He seemed a tiresome man, and she suspected that it would be hard to get the better of him. Probably he was horrid to his patients.

Professor van der Maes, contrary to Julia's idea, was treating the endless stream of patients attending his clinic with kindness and patience, his quiet voice reassuring, his smile encouraging. He was a tired man, for he worked too hard, but no patient had ever found him uncaring. But that was a side which he seldom showed to anyone else. The nursing staff who worked for him quickly learnt that he would stand no nonsense, that only their best efforts would suit him, and as for his students—he represented the goal they hoped to obtain one day. A good word from him was worth a dozen from anyone else, just as a quiet reprimand sent them into instant dejection. They called him the old man behind his back, and fiercely defended any criticism anyone was foolish enough to utter.

The Professor remained unmoved by other people's opinion of him, good or bad. He was an excellent surgeon and he loved his work, and he had friends who would be his for life, but he had no use for casual acquaintances. He had a social life when his work permitted, and was much sought after as a dinner party guest. Since he was unmarried, he could have taken his pick of any of the women he met. But, although he was a pleasant companion, he showed no interest in any of them. Somewhere in the world, he supposed, there was the woman he would fall in love with and want for his wife, but he was no longer young and he would probably end his days as a crusty old bachelor.

It wasn't until he was driving back to London a few days later that he thought about the three Gracey sisters. Ruth would make Thomas a good wife: a beautiful girl with her shy smile and gentle voice. He thought only fleetingly of Julia. Pretty, he supposed, but sharp-tongued, and she made no effort to be pleasant. She was the last person he imagined would spend her days writing sentimental verses for greetings cards, and what woman in her senses wore dresses made from curtains? He laughed, and forgot her.

The dance was ten days later, and, since the firm had had a good year, it was to be held at one of the more prestigious hotels. There was to be a buffet supper before everyone went to the hotel ballroom, and Ruth and Monica, anxious that Julia should enjoy herself, lent slippers and an old but still magnificent shawl which had belonged to their mother. They sent her there in a taxi—an unnecessary expense, Julia protested; the journey there would have been a lengthy one by bus but far cheaper. However, they insisted, privately of the opinion that Oscar could have come and fetched her instead of meeting her there...

The dress, despite its origin, was a success, simply made, but it fitted where it should, and unless anyone had actually seen the curtain, hanging in the spare bedroom, one would never have known...

Julia walked out of the taxi feeling quite pleased with herself, straight into the Professor's person.

He set her tidily on her feet. 'Well, well, Miss Julia Gracey. Unexpected and delightful.' He looked around him. 'You are alone?'

She bade him good evening in a choked voice. 'I am meeting someone in the hotel.'

She glanced around, looking without much hope for Oscar. There was no sign of him, of course. He had said that he would be at the hotel entrance, waiting for her. She supposed that she would have to go inside and look for him. She was not easily daunted, but the hotel's imposing entrance and the equally imposing appearance of the doorman daunted her now, and how and by what misfortune had the Professor got here? Surely he hadn't anything to do with greetings cards?

It seemed not. He said easily, 'I'm meeting friends here. We may as well go in together.'

He paid the cabby and took her arm. 'Your friend will be looking for you inside?'

He was being kind, with a casual kindness it was impossible to resent. She sought frantically for something to say as the doorman opened the doors with a flourish and they joined the people in the foyer.

There was no sign of Oscar. She had been a fool to accept his invitation; she didn't even like him much.

'Let me have your shawl,' said the Professor. 'I'll let the girl have it.' And he had taken it from her and left her for a moment, returning with a ticket which he tucked into the little handbag hanging from her wrist.

She found her tongue then, 'Thank you. I'll—I'll wait here. Oscar will find me…'

'Oscar?' She mistrusted his casual voice. 'Ah, yes, of course. And if I'm not mistaken this must be he…'

She should have been glad to see him, and she might well have been if he had expressed regret at not meeting her promptly. But all he did was thump her on the shoulder and say heartily, 'Sorry old lady. I got held up; so many people wanted to have a chat.'

He looked her up and down. 'Got yourself a new dress for the occasion? Not bad, not bad at all…'

His glance fell upon the Professor, who had made no attempt to go away.

'Do I know you?'

Julia, aware of the Professor's eyes fixed on the curtain, said tartly, 'No, Oscar, you don't. This is Professor van der Maes. He knows Ruth's fiancé.'

Oscar looked uneasy under the Professor's cool gaze. 'Nice to meet you. Come along, Julia, I'll find you somewhere to sit; I've one or two important clients to talk to, but we'll be able to dance presently.'

He nodded in a condescending manner at the Professor, who took no notice but said pleasantly to Julia, 'I do hope you have a happy evening,' and, as Oscar turned away rudely to speak to a passing couple, 'but I doubt it.' He looked amused. 'I can't say that

I agree with Oscar about your dress, but then I know it's a curtain, don't I?'

He was sorry the moment he had said it; for a moment she had the look of a small girl who had been slapped for no reason at all. But only for a moment. Julia stared up into his handsome face. 'Go away, Professor. I don't like you and I hope I never see you again.'

She had spoken quietly but she looked daggers at him. She turned her back then, surprised at how upset she felt. After all, she hadn't liked him the first time, and she couldn't care less if he jeered at the dress or liked it. If Oscar liked it, that was all that mattered, she told herself, not believing a word of it. But presently, when Oscar had finished his conversation, she went with him to the hotel ballroom, to be sat on one of the little gilt chairs and told to wait awhile until he had the leisure to dance with her.

A not very promising prospect—but quickly lightened by a number of men who, seeing a pretty girl sitting by herself, danced her off in rapid succession. Which served Oscar right by the time he found himself ready to partner her.

'Some of these modern dances are not dignified,' he told her severely, propelling her round the ballroom with correct stiffness. 'You would have done better to have sat quietly until I was free to come to you.'

'But I like to dance, Oscar.'

'Dancing in moderation is splendid exercise,' said Oscar, at his stuffiest.

They came to a dignified halt as the music stopped. Julia spoke her thoughts out loud. 'Do you want to marry me, Oscar?' she asked.

He looked at her with astonishment and displeasure.

'My dear Julia, what a very—very…' he sought for the right word '…unwomanly remark to make. I must only hope it was a slight aberration of the tongue.'

'It wasn't anything to do with my tongue; it was a thought in my head.' She looked at him. 'You haven't answered me, Oscar?'

'I have no intention of doing so. I am shocked, Julia. Perhaps you should retire to the ladies' room and compose yourself.'

'You sound like someone in a Victorian novel,' she told him. 'But, yes, I think that would be best.'

The ballroom was at the back of the hotel; it took her a few moments to find the cloak-room where the Professor had left her wrap. She would have to take a bus, she hadn't enough money for a taxi, but it wasn't late and there were plenty of people about. She wrapped the vast mohair shawl she and her sisters shared for evening occasions round her and crossed the foyer, comfortably full of people. And halfway to the door the Professor, apparently appearing from thin air, put a hand on her arm.

'Not leaving already?' he wanted to know. 'It's barely an hour since you arrived.'

She had to stop, his hand, resting so lightly on her arm, nevertheless reminding her of a ball and chain. She said politely, 'Yes, I'm leaving, Professor.' She looked at his hand. 'Goodbye.'

He took no notice; neither did he remove his hand.

'You're upset; you have the look of some-one about to explode. I'll take you home.'

'No, thank you. I'm quite capable of getting myself home.'

For answer he tucked her hand under his elbow. 'Your Oscar will come looking for you,' he said mildly.

'He's not my Oscar...'

'Ah, I can't say that I'm surprised. Now, come along. This is indeed a splendid excuse for me to leave with you—a pompous dinner with endless speeches to which I have been bidden.'

He had propelled her gently past the door-man, out into the chilly night and, after towing her along gently, popped her into his car, parked nearby.

Getting in beside her, he asked, 'Are you going to cry?'

'Certainly not. And I have no wish to be here in your car. You are being high-handed, Professor.' She sniffed. 'I'm not a child.'

He looked at her, smiling a little. 'No, I had realised that. Are you hungry?'

She was taken by surprise. 'Yes…'

'Splendid. And, since you are not going to cry and I'm hungry too, we will go and eat somewhere.'

'No,' said Julia.

'My dear girl, be sensible. It's the logical thing to do.' He started the car. 'Let us bury the hatchet for an hour or so. You are free to dislike me the moment I see you to your front door.'

She was hungry, so the prospect of a meal was tempting. She said, 'Well, all right, but not anywhere grand—the curtain…'

He said quietly, 'I'm sorry I said that. You look very nice and it was unforgivable of me. We will go somewhere you won't need to be uneasy.'

He sounded kind and her spirits lifted. Perhaps he wasn't so bad… He spoilt it by adding, 'Is your entire wardrobe made up of curtains?' He glanced at her. 'You must be a very talented young lady.'

She was on the point of making a fiery answer when the thought of a meal crossed her mind. She had no idea why he had asked her out and she didn't care; she would choose all the most expensive things on the menu...

He took her to Wilton's, spoke quietly to the *maître d'*, and followed her to one of the booths, so that any fears concerning her dress were instantly put at rest.

'Now, what shall we have?' asked the Professor, well aware of her relief that the booth sheltered her nicely from the other diners. 'I can recommend the cheese soufflé, and the sole Meunière is excellent.' When she agreed he ordered from the waitress and turned his attention to the *sommelier* and the wine list. Which gave Julia a chance to study the menu. She need not have bothered to choose the most expensive food; everything was expensive.

When it came it was delicious, and cooked by a master hand. She thought fleetingly of Oscar, and applied herself to her dinner, and, being nicely brought up, made polite conversation the while. The Professor replied suitably, amused at that and wondering what had possessed him to take her to dinner. He went out seldom, and when he did his companion would be one of his numerous acquaintances: elegant young women, dressed impeccably, bone-thin and fussing delicately about what they could and couldn't eat.

Julia, on the other hand, ate everything she was offered with an unselfconscious pleasure, and capped the sole with sherry trifle and drank the wine he had ordered. And that loosed her tongue, for presently, over coffee, she asked, 'If you are Dutch, why do you live in England?'

'I only do so for part of the time. My home is in Holland and I work there as well. I shall be going back there in a few weeks' time for a month or so.'

'How very unsettling,' observed Julia. 'But I suppose you are able to pick and choose if you are a Professor?'

'I suppose I can,' he agreed mildly. 'What are you going to do about Oscar?'

'I dare say he won't find me a suitable wife for a junior partner...'

'And will that break your heart?'

'No. He sort of grew on me, if you see what I mean.'

He said smoothly, 'Ah—you have a more romantic outlook, perhaps?'

She took a sip of coffee. 'It's almost midnight. Would you take me home, please?'

Not one of the women he had taken out to dinner had ever suggested that it was getting late and they wished to go home. On the contrary. The Professor stifled a laugh, assured her that they would go at once, and signed the bill. On the journey through London's streets he discussed the weather, the pleasures of the English countryside and the prospect of a fine summer.

The street was quiet and only barely lit. He got out and opened the car door for her, before taking the door key from her. He opened the door and gave her back the key.

Julia cast around in her mind for something gracious to say. 'Thank you for my dinner,' she said finally, and, since that didn't sound in the least gracious, added, 'I enjoyed the dinner very much and the restaurant was—was very elegant. It was a very pleasant evening…'

She didn't like his smile in the dimly lit hallway. 'Don't try too hard, Julia,' he told her. 'Goodnight.'

He pushed her gently into the hall and closed the door soundlessly behind her.

'I hate him,' said Julia, and took off her shoes, flung the shawl onto the floor and crept upstairs to her bed. She had intended to lie awake and consider how much she disliked him, but she went to sleep at once.

The Professor took himself off home, to his elegant Chelsea house, locked the Rolls in the mews garage behind it, and let himself into his home. There was a wall-light casting a gentle light on the side table in the hall and he picked up the handful of letters on it as he went to his study.

This was a small, comfortably furnished room, with rows of bookshelves, a massive desk, a chair behind it and two smaller ones each side of the small fireplace. Under the window was a table with a computer and a pile of papers and books. He ignored it and put the letters on his desk before going out of the room again and along the hall, through the baize door at the end and down the steps to the kitchen, where he poured himself coffee from the pot on the Aga and acknowledged the sleepy greetings from two small dogs.

They got out of the basket they shared and sat beside him while he drank his coffee: two small creatures with heavily whiskered faces, short legs and long, thin rat-like tails. The professor had found them, abandoned, terrified and starving, some six months earlier. It was apparent that they weren't going to grow any larger or handsomer, but they had become members of his household and his devoted companions. He saw them back into their basket, with the promise of a walk in the morning, and went back to his study. There were some notes he needed to write up before he went to bed.

He sat down and pulled the papers towards him and then sat back in his chair, thinking about the evening. What had possessed him to take Julia out to dinner? he wondered. A nice enough girl, no doubt, but with a sharp tongue and making no attempt to hide the fact that she didn't like him. The unknown Oscar was possibly to be pitied. He smiled suddenly. She had enjoyed her dinner, and he doubted whether Oscar rose much above soup of the day and a baked potato. He acknowledged that this was an unfair thought; Oscar might even now be searching fruitlessly for Julia.

When Julia went down to breakfast in the morning, Ruth and Monica were already at the kitchen table, and without wasting time they began to fire questions at her.

'Did you dance? Was it a splendid hotel? What did you eat? Did Oscar propose? Did he bring you home?'

Julia lifted the teapot. 'I danced three and a half times, and the hotel was magnificent.'

She shook cornflakes into a bowl. She didn't like them, but, according to the TV ad, the girl who ate them had a wand-like figure—a state to which she hoped in time to subdue her own generous curves. She said, 'I didn't eat at the hotel.' She took a sip of tea. 'Oscar didn't propose. I don't think he ever will now. And he didn't bring me home.'

'Julia, you didn't come home alone?'

'No, Professor van der Maes drove me back.'

She finished the cornflakes and put bread in the toaster.

'Start at the beginning and don't leave anything out,' said Ruth. 'What on earth was the Professor doing there? He doesn't write verses, does he?'

'No. Though I'm sure he is very handy with a needle.'

Her sisters exchanged glances. 'Why did you dance half a dance?' asked Ruth.

Julia said through a mouthful of toast, 'Oscar was annoyed because I hadn't stayed on my chair to wait for him, so I asked him if he wanted to marry me.'

'Julia, how could you...?'

'He told me to go to the ladies' room and compose myself, so I found my shawl and left, and the Professor was at the entrance. He said he was hungry and asked me if I was, and when I said yes, he took me to Wilton's.'

'Wilton's?' chorused her sisters, and then added, 'The dress…?'

'It was all right. We sat in a booth. It was a nice dinner. And then, when I asked him to bring me home, he did.'

Two pairs of astonished blue eyes stared at her. 'What about Oscar?'

'He was shocked.'

'And the Professor? Whatever did he say?'

'He said he wasn't surprised that Oscar wasn't mine. You will both be late for work…'

'But why should the Professor take you out to dinner?' asked Ruth.

'He said he was hungry.'

'You can be very tiresome sometimes, Julia,' said Monica severely.

When they had gone Julia set about the household chores and then, those done, she made coffee and a cheese sandwich and sat down to write verses. Perhaps Oscar would be able to get her the sack, but on the other hand her verses sold well. The senior partners might not agree. For it wasn't the kind of work many people would want to do and it was badly paid. She polished off a dozen verses, fed Muffin, the family cat, and peeled the potatoes for supper. Oscar, she reflected, wouldn't bother her again.

# CHAPTER TWO

OSCAR came four days later. Julia was making pastry for a steak pie and she went impatiently to the front door when its knocker was thumped. Oscar was on the doorstep. 'I wish to talk to you, Julia.'

'Come in, then,' said Julia briskly. 'I'm making pastry and don't want it to spoil.'

She ushered him into the house, told him to leave his coat in the hall, and then went back into the kitchen and plunged her hands into the bowl.

'Do sit down,' she invited him, and, when he looked askance at Muffin the household cat, sitting in the old Windsor chair by the stove, added, 'Take a chair at the table. It's warm here. Anyway, I haven't lighted the fire in the sitting room yet.'

She bent over her pastry, and presently he said stuffily, 'You can at least leave that and listen to what I have to say, Julia.'

She put the dough on the floured board and held a rolling pin.

'I'm so sorry, Oscar, but I really can't leave it. I am listening, though.'

He settled himself into his chair. 'I have given a good deal of thought to your regrettable behaviour at the dance, Julia. I can but suppose that the excitement of the occasion and the opulence of your surroundings had caused you to become so—so unlike yourself. After due consideration I have decided that I shall overlook that...'

Julia laid her pastry neatly over the meat and tidied the edges with a knife. 'Don't do that,' she begged him. 'I wasn't in the least excited, only annoyed to be stuck on a chair in a corner—and left to find my own way in, too.'

'I have a position to uphold in the firm,' said Oscar. And when she didn't answer he asked, 'Who was that man you were talking to? Really, Julia, it is most unsuitable. I trust you found your way home? There is a good bus service?'

Julia was cutting pastry leaves to decorate her pie. She said, 'I had dinner at Wilton's and was driven home afterwards.'

Oscar sought for words and, finding none, got to his feet. 'There is nothing more to be said, Julia. I came here prepared to forgive you, but I see now that I have allowed my tolerance to be swept aside by your frivolity.'

Julia dusted her floury hands over the bowl and began to clear up the table. Listening to Oscar was like reading a book written a hundred years ago. He didn't belong in this century and, being a kind-hearted girl, she felt sorry for him.

'I'm not at all suitable for you, Oscar,' she told him gently.

He said nastily, 'Indeed you are not, Julia. You have misled me...'

She was cross again. 'I didn't know we had got to that stage. Anyway, what you need isn't a wife, it's a doormat. And do go, Oscar, before I hit you with this rolling pin.'

He got to his feet. 'I must remind you that your future with the firm is in jeopardy, Julia. I have some influence...'

Which was just what she could have expected from him, she supposed. They went into the hall and he got into his coat. She opened the door and ushered him out, wished him goodbye, and closed the door before he had a chance to say more.

She told her sisters when they came home, and Monica said. 'He might have made a good steady husband, but he sounds a bit out of date.'

'I don't think I want a steady husband,' said Julia, and for a moment she thought about the Professor. She had no idea why she should have done that; she didn't even like him…

So, during the next few days she waited expectantly for a letter from the greetings card firm, but when one did come it contained a cheque for her last batch of verses and a request for her to concentrate on wedding cards—June was the bridal month and they needed to get the cards to the printers in good time…

'Reprieved,' said Julia, before she cashed the cheque and paid the gas bill.

It was difficult to write about June roses and wedded bliss in blustery March. But she wrote her little verses and thought how nice it would be to marry on a bright summer's morning, wearing all the right clothes and with the right bridegroom.

A week later Thomas came one evening. He had got the job as senior registrar and, what was more, had now been offered one of the small houses the hospital rented out to their staff. There was no reason why he and Ruth shouldn't marry as soon as possible. The place was furnished, and it was a bit poky, but once he had some money saved they could find something better.

'And the best of it is I'm working for Professor van der Maes.' His nice face was alight with the prospect. 'You won't mind a quiet wedding?' he asked Ruth anxiously.

Ruth would have married him in a cellar wearing a sack. 'We'll get George to arrange everything. And it will be quiet anyway; there's only us. Your mother and father will come?'

Julia went to the kitchen to make coffee and sandwiches and took Monica with her. 'We'll give them half an hour. Monica, have you any money? Ruth must have some clothes…'

They sat together at the table, doing sums. 'There aren't any big bills due,' said Julia. 'If we're very careful and we use the emergency money we could just manage.'

Thomas was to take up his new job in three weeks' time: the best of reasons why he and Ruth should marry, move into their new home and have a few days together first. Which meant a special licence and no time at all to buy clothes and make preparations for a quiet wedding. Julia and Monica gave Ruth all the money they could lay hands on and then set about planning the wedding day. There would be only a handful of guests: Dr Goodman and his wife, George, and the vicar who would take the service, Thomas's parents and the best man.

They got out the best china and polished the teaspoons, and Julia went into the kitchen and leafed through her cookery books.

It was a scramble, but by the time the wedding day dawned Ruth had a dress and jacket in a pale blue, with a fetching hat, handbag, gloves and shoes, and the nucleus of a new wardrobe suitable for a senior registrar's wife. Julia had assembled an elegant buffet for after the ceremony, and Monica had gone to the market and bought daffodils, so that when they reached the church—a red-brick mid-Victorian building, sadly lacking in beauty—its rather bleak interior glowed with colour.

Monica had gone on ahead, leaving Julia to make the last finishing touches to the table, which took longer than she had expected. She had to hurry to the church just as Dr Goodman came for Ruth.

She arrived there a bit flushed, her russet hair glowing under her little green felt hat—Ruth's hat, really, but it went well with her green jacket and skirt, which had been altered and cleaned and altered again and clung to, since they were suitable for serious occasions.

Julia sniffed appreciatively at the fresh scent of the daffodils and started down the aisle to the back views of Thomas and his best man and the sprinkling of people in the pews. It was a long aisle, and she was halfway up when she saw the Professor sitting beside Mrs Goodman. They appeared to be on the best of terms and she shot past their pew without looking at them. His appearance was unexpected, but she supposed that Thomas, now a senior member of the team, merited his presence.

When Ruth came, Julia concentrated on the ceremony, but the Professor's image most annoyingly got between her and the beautiful words of the simple service. There was no need for him to be there. He and Thomas might be on the best of terms professionally, but they surely had different social lives? Did the medical profession enjoy a social life? she wondered, then brought her attention back sharply to Thomas and Ruth, exchanging their vows. They would be happy, she reflected, watching them walk back down the aisle. They were both so sure of their love. She wondered what it must feel like to be so certain.

After the first photos had been taken Julia slipped away, so as to get home before anyone else and make sure that everything was just so.

She was putting the tiny sausage rolls in the oven to warm when Ruth and Thomas arrived, closely followed by everyone else, and presently the best man came into the kitchen to get a corkscrew.

'Not that I think we'll need it,' he told her cheerfully. 'The Prof bought half a dozen bottles of champagne with him. Now that's what I call a wedding gift of the right sort. Can I help?'

'Get everyone drinking. I'll be along with these sausage rolls in a minute or two.'

She had them nicely arranged on a dish when the Professor came into the kitchen. He had a bottle and a glass in one hand.

He said, 'A most happy occasion. Your vicar has had two glasses already.'

He poured the champagne and handed her a glass. 'Thirsty work, heating up sausage rolls.'

She had to laugh. Such light-hearted talk didn't sound like him at all, and for a moment she liked him. She took her glass and said, 'We can't toast them yet, can we? But it is a happy day.' And, since she was thirsty and excited, she drank deeply.

The Professor had an unexpected feeling of tenderness towards her; she might have a sharp tongue and not like him, but her naïve treatment of a glass of Moet et Chandon Brut Imperial he found touching.

She emptied the glass and said, 'That was nice.'

He agreed gravely. 'A splendid drink for such an occasion,' and he refilled her glass, observing prudently, 'I'll take the tray in for you.'

The champagne was having an effect upon her empty insides. She gave him a wide smile. 'The best man—what's his name, Peter?—said he'd be back...'

'He will be refilling glasses.' The Professor picked up the tray, opened the door and ushered her out of the kitchen.

Julia swanned around, light-headed and light-hearted. It was marvellous what a couple of glasses of champagne did to one. She ate a sausage roll, drank another glass of champagne, handed round the sandwiches and would have had another glass of champagne if the Professor hadn't taken the glass from her.

'They're going to cut the cake,' he told her, 'and then we'll toast the happy couple.' Only then did he hand her back her glass.

After Ruth and Thomas had driven away, and everyone else was going home, she realised that the Professor had gone too, taking the best man with him.

'He asked me to say goodbye,' said Monica as the pair of them sat at the kitchen table, their shoes off, drinking strong tea. 'He took the best man with him, said he was rather pressed for time.'

Julia, still pleasantly muzzy from the champagne, wondered why it was that the best man had had the time to say goodbye to her. If he'd gone with the Professor, then surely the Professor could have found the time to do the same? She would think about that when her head was a little clearer.

\*     \*     \*

Life had to be reorganised now that Ruth had left home; they missed her share of the house-keeping, but by dint of economising they managed very well.

Until, a few weeks later, Monica came into the house like a whirlwind, calling to Julia to come quickly; she had news.

George had been offered a parish; a small rural town in the West country. 'Miles from anywhere,' said Monica, glowing with happiness, 'but thriving. Not more than a large village, I suppose, but very scattered. He's to go there this week and see if he likes it.'

'And if he does?'

'He'll go there in two weeks' time. I'll go with him, of course. We can get married by special licence first.' Then she danced round the room. 'Oh, Julia, isn't it all marvellous? I'm so happy...!'

It wasn't until later, after they had toasted the future in a bottle of wine from the supermarket, that Monica said worriedly, 'Julia, what about you? What will you do? You'll never be able to manage...'

Julia had had time to have an answer ready. She said cheerfully, 'I shall take in lodgers until we decide what to do about this house. You and Ruth will probably like to sell it, and I think that is a good thing.'

'But you?' persisted Monica.

'I shall go to dressmaking classes and then set up on my own. I shall like that.'

'You don't think Oscar will come back? If he really loved you…?'

'But he didn't, and I wouldn't go near him with a bargepole— whatever that means.'

'But you'll marry…?'

'Oh, I expect so. And think how pleased my husband will be to have a wife who makes her own clothes.'

Julia poured the last of the wine into their glasses. 'Now tell me your plans…'

She listened to her sister's excited voice, making suitable comments from time to time, making suggestions, and all the while refusing to give way to the feeling of panic. So silly, she told herself sternly; she had a roof over her head for the time being, and she was perfectly able to reorganise her life. She wouldn't be lonely; she would have lodgers and Muffin…

'You'll marry from here?' she asked.

'Yes, but very quietly. We'll go straight to the parish after the wedding. There'll be just us and Ruth—and Thomas, if he can get away. No wedding breakfast or anything.' Monica laughed. 'I always wanted a big wedding, you know—white chiffon and a veil and brides-maids—but none of that matters. It'll have to be early in the morning.'

Monica's lovely face glowed with happi-ness, and Julia said, 'Aren't you dying to hear what the vicarage is like? And the little town? You'll be a marvellous vicar's wife.'

'Yes, I think I shall,' said Monica compla-cently.

Presently she said uncertainly, 'Are you sure you'll be all right, Julia? There has always been the three of us…'

'Of course I'll be fine—and how super that I'll be able to visit you. Once I get started I can get a little car…'

Which was daydreaming with a vengeance, but served to pacify Monica.

After that events crowded upon each other at a great rate. George found his new appointment very much to his liking; moreover, he had been accepted by the church wardens and those of the parish whom he had met with every sign of satisfaction. The vicarage was large and old-fashioned, but there was a lovely garden... He was indeed to take up his appointment in two weeks' time, which gave them just that time to arrange their wedding—a very quiet one, quieter even than Ruth's and Thomas's, for they were to marry in the early morning and drive straight down to their new home.

Julia, helping Monica to pack, had little time to think about anything else, but was relieved that the girl who was to take over Monica's job had rented a room with her: a good omen for the future, she told her sisters cheerfully. Trudie seemed a nice girl, too, quiet and studious, and it would be nice to have someone else in the house, and nicer still to have the rent money...

She would have to find another lodger, thought Julia, waving goodbye to George's elderly car and the newly married pair. If she could let two rooms she would be able to manage if she added the rent to the small amounts she got from the greetings card firm. Later on, she quite understood, Ruth and Monica would want to sell the house, and with her own share she would start some kind of a career...

She went back into the empty house; Trudie would be moving in on the following morning and she must make sure that her room was as welcoming as possible. As soon as she had a second lodger and things were running smoothly, she would pay a visit to Ruth.

A week went by. It was disappointing that there had been no replies to her advertisement; she would have to try again in a week or so, and put cards in the windows of the row of rather seedy shops a few streets away. In the meantime she would double her output of verses.

Trudie had settled in nicely, coming and going quietly, letting herself in and out with the key Julia had given her. Another one like her would be ideal, reflected Julia, picking up the post from the doormat.

There was a letter from the greetings card firm and she opened it quickly; there would be a cheque inside. There was, but there was a letter too. The firm was changing its policy: in future they would deal only with cards of a humorous nature since that was what the market demanded. It was with regret that they would no longer be able to accept her work. If she had a batch ready to send then they would accept it, but nothing further.

Julia read the letter again, just to make sure, and then went into the kitchen, made a pot of tea and sat down to drink it. It was a blow; the money the firm paid her was very little but it had been a small, steady income. Its loss would be felt. She did some sums on the back of the envelope and felt the beginnings of a headache. It was possible that Oscar was behind it... She read the letter once again; they would accept one last batch. Good, she would send as many verses as she could think up. She got pencil and paper and set to work. Just let me say on this lovely day…she began, and by lunchtime had more than doubled her output.

She typed them all out on her old portable and took them to the post. It would have been satisfying to have torn up the letter and put it in an envelope and sent it back, but another cheque would be satisfying too.

The cheque came a few days later, but still no new lodger. Which, as it turned out, was a good thing…

Thomas phoned. Ruth was in bed with flu, could she possibly help out for a day or two? Not to stay, of course, but an hour or two each day until Ruth was on her feet. There was a bus, he added hopefully.

It meant two buses; she would have to change halfway. The hospital wasn't all that far away, but was awkward to get to.

Julia glanced at the clock. 'I'll be there about lunchtime. I must tell Trudie, my lodger. I'll stay until the evening if that's OK.'

'Bless you,' said Thomas. 'I should be free about five o'clock.'

Trudie, summoned from a horde of toddlers, was helpful. She would see to Muffin, go back at lunchtime and make sure that everything was all right, and she wasn't going out that evening anyway. Julia hurried to the main street and caught a bus.

The house was close to the hospital, one of a neat row in which the luckier of the medical staff lived. The door key, Thomas had warned her, was under the pot of flowers by the back door, and Julia let herself in, calling out as she did so.

It was a very small house. She put her bag down in the narrow hall and went up the stairs at its end, guided by the sound of Ruth's voice.

She was propped up in bed, her lovely face only slightly dimmed by a red nose and puffy eyes. She said thickly, 'Julia, you darling. You don't mind coming? I feel so awful, and Thomas has to be in Theatre all day. I'll be better tomorrow...'

'You'll stay there until Thomas says that you can get up,' said Julia, 'and of course I don't mind coming. In fact it makes a nice change. Now, how about a wash and a clean nightie, and then a morsel of something to eat?'

'I hope you don't catch the flu,' said Ruth later, drinking tea and looking better already, drowsy now in her freshly made bed, her golden hair, though rather lank, it must be admitted, neatly brushed. All the same, thought Julia, she looked far from well.

'Has the doctor been?' she asked.

'Yes, Dr Soames, one of the medical consultants. Someone is coming with some pills...'

Thomas brought them during his lunch hour. He couldn't stop, his lunch 'hour' being a figure of speech. A cup of coffee and a sandwich was the norm on this day, when Professor van der Maes was operating, but he lingered with Ruth as long as he could, thanked Julia profusely and assured her that he would be back by five o'clock. 'I'll be on call,' he told her, 'but only until midnight.'

'Would you like me to keep popping in for a few days, until Ruth is feeling better?'

'Would you? I hate leaving her.'

He went then, and Julia went down to the little kitchen, made another hot drink for Ruth and boiled herself an egg. Tomorrow she would bring some fruit and a new loaf. Bread and butter, cut very thin, was something most invalids would eat.

It was almost six o'clock when Thomas returned, bringing the Professor with him. The Professor spent a few minutes with Ruth, assured Thomas that she was looking better, and wandered into the kitchen, where Julia was laying a tray of suitable nourishment for Ruth.

'Get your coat,' he told her. 'I'll drive you home.'

Julia thumped a saucepan of milk onto the stove. 'Thank you, but I'll get a bus when I'm ready.'

Not so much as a hello or even a good evening, thought Julia pettishly.

His smile mocked her. 'Thomas is here now. Two's company, three's none.'

'Thomas will want his supper.'

Thomas breezed into the kitchen. 'I'm a first-rate cook. We're going to have a picnic upstairs. You go home, Julia. You've been a godsend, and we're so grateful. You will come tomorrow?'

'Yes,' said Julia, and without looking at either of the men went and got her coat, said goodnight to her sister and went downstairs again.

The two men were in the hall and Thomas backed into the open kitchen door to make room for her, but even then the professor took up almost all the space. He opened the door and she squeezed past him into the street. Thomas came too, beaming at them both, just as though he was seeing them off for an evening out.

The Professor had nothing to say. He sat relaxed behind the wheel, and if he felt impatience at the heavy traffic he didn't show it. Watching the crowded pavements and the packed buses edging their way along the streets, Julia suddenly felt ashamed at her ingratitude.

'This is very kind of you,' she began. 'It would have taken me ages to get home.'

He said coolly, 'I shan't be going out of my way. I'm going to the children's hospital not five minutes' drive away from your home.'

A remark which hardly encouraged her to carry on the conversation.

He had nothing more to say then, but when he stopped before her house he got out, opened the car door for her and stood waiting while she unlocked the house door, dismissing her thanks with a laconic, 'I have already said it was no trouble. Goodnight, Julia.'

She stood in the open door as he got into the car and drove off.

'And that's the last time I'll accept a lift from you,' she said to the empty street. 'I can't think why you bothered, but I suppose Thomas was there and you had no choice.' She slammed the door. 'Horrid man.'

But she was aware of a kind of sadness; she was sure that he wasn't a horrid man, only where she was concerned. For some reason she annoyed him...

She got her supper, fed Muffin, and went to warn Trudie that she would be going to Ruth for the next few days. 'No one phoned about a room, I suppose?' she asked.

'Not a soul. Probably in a day or two you'll have any number of callers.'

But there was no one.

For the next few days Julia went to and fro while Ruth slowly improved. Of the Professor there was no sign, although her sister told her that he had come frequently to see her. Dr Soames came too, and told her that she was much better. 'Though I look a hag,' said Ruth.

'A beautiful hag,' said Julia bracingly, 'and tomorrow you're going to crawl downstairs for a couple of hours.'

Ruth brightened. 'Tom can get the supper and we'll have it round the fire, and I dare say Gerard will come for an hour...'

'Gerard?'

'The Professor. I simply couldn't go on calling him Professor, even though he seems a bit staid and stand-offish, doesn't he? But he's not in the least, and he's only thirty-six. He ought to be married, he nearly was a year ago, but he's not interested in girls. Not to marry, anyway. He's got lots of friends, but they're just friends.'

'You surprise me...'

Ruth gave her a thoughtful look. 'You don't like him?'

'I don't know him well enough to know if I like or dislike him.'

Ruth gave her a sharp look. 'I'm feeling so much better; I'm sure I could manage. You've been an angel, coming each day, but you must be longing to be let off the hook.'

'There's nothing to keep me at home. Trudie looks after herself and keeps an eye on Muffin. And if you can put up with me for another few days I think it might be a good idea.'

'Oh, darling, would you really come? Just for a couple more days. I do feel so much better, but not quite me yet...'

'Of course I'll come. And we'll see how you are in two days' time.'

After those two days Julia had to admit that Ruth was quite able to cope without any help from her. It was all very well for her to spend the day there while Ruth was in bed, but now that she was up—still rather wan—Julia felt that Ruth and Tom would much rather be on their own.

The moment she arrived the next morning she told Ruth briskly, 'This is my last day; you don't need me any more...'

Ruth was sitting at the table in the tiny kitchen, chopping vegetables. She looked up, laughing. 'Oh, but I do. Sit down and I'll tell you.'

Julia took a bite of carrot. 'You want me to make curtains for the bathroom? I told you everyone could see in if they tried hard enough.'

'Curtains, pooh! Dr Soames says I need a little holiday, and Thomas says so too. He wants you to go with me. Do say you can. You haven't got another lodger yet, and Trudie could look after Muffin.'

'You're going to Monica's?' It would be lovely to go away from the dull little house and duller street. 'Yes, of course I'll come.'

'You will? You really won't mind? Thomas won't let me go alone...' She added quickly, 'And we're not going to Monica. We're going to Holland.'

Before Julia could speak, she added, 'Gerard has a little cottage near a lake. There's no one there, only his housekeeper. He says it's very quiet there, and the country's pretty and just what I need. Thomas wants me to go. He's got a couple of days due to him and he'll drive us there.'

'There won't be anyone else there? Only us?'

'Yes, you and I. Tom will stay one night and come and fetch us back—he won't know exactly when, but it will be a week or two. You're not having second thoughts?'

Which was exactly what Julia was having, but one look at her sister's still pale face sent them flying; Ruth needed to get away from London and a week in the country would get her back onto her feet again. Although early summer so far had been chilly and wet, there was always the chance that it would become warm and sunny. She said again, 'Of course I'll love to come. I'll fix things up with Trudie. When are we to go?'

'Well, Thomas can get Saturday and Sunday off—that's in three days' time. We shan't need many clothes, so you'll only need to bring a case—and I've enough money for both of us.'

'Oh, I've plenty of money,' said Julia, with such an air of conviction that she believed it herself.

'You have? Well, I suppose you have more time to work for the greetings card people now, and of course there's the rent from Trudie...'

Which was swallowed up almost before Julia had put it into her purse. But Ruth didn't have to know that, and she certainly wasn't going to tell anyone that she no longer had a market for her little verses. There would be another lodger soon, she told herself bracingly and she would find a part-time job; in the meantime she would enjoy her holiday.

The nagging thought that it was the Professor who had been the means of her having one rankled all the way home. For some reason she hated to be beholden to him.

She felt better about that when she came to the conclusion that he didn't know that she would be going; beyond offering the use of his house, he wouldn't be concerned with the details.⟿

The Professor, phoning instructions to his housekeeper in Holland, was very well aware that she would be going with Ruth; he had himself suggested it, with just the right amount of casualness. He wasn't sure why he had done so but he suspected that he had wanted her to feel beholden to him.

He was an aloof man by nature, and an unhappy love affair had left him with a poor opinion of women. There were exceptions: his own family, his devoted housekeeper, his elderly nanny, the nursing staff who worked for him, life-long friends, wives of men he had known for years. He had added Ruth to the list, so in love with her Thomas—and so different from her sharp-tongued sister. And yet—there was something about Julia...

No need to take a lot of clothes, Ruth had said. Julia foraged through her wardrobe and found a leaf-brown tweed jacket, so old that it was almost fashionable once again. There was a pleated skirt which went quite well with it, a handful of tops and a jersey dress. It was, after all, getting warmer each day. As it was country they would go walking, she supposed, so that meant comfortable shoes. She could travel in the new pair she had had for the weddings. She added undies, a scarf and a thin dressing gown, and then sat down to count her money. And that didn't take long! There would be a week's rent from Trudie to add, and when she got back there would be another lot waiting for her. She went in search of her lodger and enlisted her help.

Trudie was a quiet, unassuming girl, saving to get married, good-natured and trustworthy. She willingly agreed to look after Muffin and make sure that the house was locked up at night.

'You could do with a holiday. No doubt when you get back you'll have a house full of lodgers and not a moment to yourself.'

A prospect which should have pleased Julia but somehow didn't.

Three days later Thomas and Ruth came to fetch her. They were to go by the catamaran from Harwich, a fast sea route which would get them to their destination during the afternoon. Julia, who had received only a garbled version of where they were going, spent a great part of their journey studying a map—a large, detailed one which the Professor had thoughtfully provided.

Somewhere south of Amsterdam and not too far from Hilversum. And there were any number of lakes and no large towns until one reached Utrecht.

Ruth said over her shoulder, 'It's really country, Julia. Gerard says we don't need to go near a town unless we want to, although it's such a small country there are lots of rural areas with only tiny villages.'

It didn't seem very rural when they landed at the Hoek and took to the motorway, for small towns followed each other in quick succession, but then Thomas turned into a minor road and Julia saw the Holland she had always pictured. Wide landscapes, villages encircling churches much too large for them, farms with vast barns and water meadows where cows wandered. And the further they drove the more remote it became. The land was flat, but now there were small copses and glimpses of water. Julia looked around her and sighed with pleasure. Maybe there were large towns nearby, and main roads, but here there was an age-old peace and quiet.

Ruth, who had been chattering excitedly, had fallen silent and Thomas said, 'See that church spire beyond those trees? Unless I've read the map wrongly, we're here...'

# CHAPTER THREE

WHEN they reached the trees Thomas turned into a narrow brick lane between them which opened almost at once into a scattered circle of houses grouped around the church. Any of the houses would do, thought Julia, for they were really all cottages, some larger than others, all with pristine paintwork, their little windows sparkling. But Thomas encircled the church and went along a narrow lane, leading away from the road.

'Hope I'm right,' he said. 'The Prof said it was easy to find, but of course he lives here! Five hundred yards past the church on the right-hand side…'

They all chorused 'There it is,' a moment later. It was another cottage, but a good deal larger than those in the village, with a wide gate and a short drive leading to the front door.

It had a red-tiled roof, white walls and small windows arranged precisely on either side of its solid door, and it was set in a garden glowing with flowers, all crammed together in a glorious mass of colour. Julia, standing by the car, rotated slowly, taking it all in. She hadn't been sure what kind of a house the Professor would have—something dignified and austerely perfect, she had supposed, because that would have reflected him. But this little cottage—and not so little now that she had had a good look—was definitely cosy, its prettiness fit to grace the most sentimental of greetings cards. She tried to imagine him in his impeccable grey suiting, mowing the lawn…!

The door had been opened and a short, stout lady surged to meet them.

She was talking before she reached them. 'There you are—come on in. You must want a cup of tea, and I made some scones.'

She shook hands all round, beaming at them. 'Mrs Beckett, the housekeeper, and delighted to welcome you. Such a nice day you've had for travelling, and it's to be hoped that we'll get some fine weather. A bit of sun and fresh air will soon put you back on your feet, Mrs Scott.'

She had urged them indoors as she spoke. 'Now, just you make yourselves comfortable for a minute while I fetch the tea tray, then you can see your rooms. A pity Mr Scott can't stay longer, but there, you're a busy man like Mr Gerard. Always on the go, he is, pops in to see me whenever he can, bless him. He's so good to his old nanny.'

She paused for breath, said, 'Tea', and trotted out of the room.

Thomas sat Ruth down in one of the small armchairs and went to look out of the window. Ruth said, 'Oh, darling, isn't this heavenly? I'm going to love it here, only I'm going to miss you.'

Thomas went and sat beside her, and Julia wandered round inspecting the room. It was low-ceilinged, with rugs on the wooden floor, comfortable chairs and small tables scattered around a fireplace with a wood stove flanked by bookshelves bulging with books. Julia heaved a sigh of contentment and turned round as Mrs Beckett came in with the tea tray.

They were taken round the cottage presently—first to the kitchen, with its flagstone floor and scrubbed table and old-fashioned dresser, its rows of saucepans on either side of the Aga and comfortable Windsor chairs on either side of it. And on each chair a cat.

'Portly and Lofty,' said Mrs Beckett. 'Keep me company, they do. Mr Gerard brought them here years ago—kittens they were then; he'd found them.'

She led the way out of the kitchen. 'There's a cloakroom here, and that door is his study, and there's a garden room…'

Upstairs there were several bedrooms, and two bathrooms luxurious enough to grace the finest of houses.

'He does himself proud,' murmured Julia, leaning out of the window of the room which was to be hers.

They strolled round the garden presently, and then Julia went to her room again on the pretext of unpacking, but really so that Thomas and Ruth could be together. And later, after a delicious meal of asparagus, lamb cutlets, new potatoes and baby carrots, followed by caramel custard and all washed down by a crisp white wine, she excused herself from taking an evening stroll with the other two on the plea of tiredness. Not that she was in the least tired. She slept soundly, waking early to lie in bed examining the room.

It wasn't large, but whoever had chosen the furniture had known exactly what was right for it: there was a mahogany bed with a rose-patterned quilt and a plump pink eiderdown, pale rugs on the polished floor, a small dressing table under the window and a crinoline chair beside a small table. There were flowers on the table in a Delft bowl.

Like a fairy tale, decided Julia, and got up to lean out of the window.

Mrs Beckett's voice begging her to get back into bed and not catch cold sent her back under the eiderdown to drink the tea offered her.

Breakfast would be in half an hour, said Mrs Beckett, sounding just as an old-fashioned nanny would sound. 'Porridge and scrambled eggs, for I can see that Mrs Scott needs feeding up.' Her small twinkling eyes took in Julia's splendid shape. 'Women should look like women,' observed Mrs Beckett.

I shall get fat, thought Julia, buttering her third piece of toast. Not that it mattered. Now, if she were married to someone like Thomas she would go on a diet; men, so the TV advertisements proclaimed with such certainty, liked girls with wand-like shapes...

Declaring that she wanted postcards, she took herself off to the village and didn't get back until lunchtime. Thomas was to leave shortly and Ruth did most of the talking: clean shirts, and mind to remember to change his socks, and to wind the kitchen clock, and she hoped that she had stocked the fridge with enough food...

'I'll be back in just over a week, darling,' said Thomas.

When he had gone Mrs Beckett sent them to the village again, to buy rolls and croissants for breakfast, and they strolled back while

Ruth speculated as to Thomas's progress. Julia put in a sympathetic word here and there and ate one of the rolls, still warm from the bakery.

'You'll get fat,' said Ruth.

'Who cares?' The strong wish that someone would care kept her silent; it would be very nice if someone—someone who didn't even like her very much, like the Professor—would actually look at her and care enough to discourage her from eating rolls warm from the oven.

There was no reason why she should think of him, she told herself. It was because she was staying at his home, and it was difficult to forget that. I don't like him anyway, she reminded herself.

Between them, she and Mrs Beckett set about getting Ruth quite well again. It was surprising what a few days of good food, temptingly cooked, walks in the surrounding countryside and sound sleep did for her. After five days Ruth satisfied her two companions; she was now pink-cheeked and bright-eyed and, although she missed Thomas, she was willing to join in any plans Julia might suggest.

Another four or five days, thought Julia, getting up early because it was such a lovely morning, and we shall be going home again. But she wouldn't spoil the day by thinking about that. She skipped downstairs and out of the front door.

The Professor was sitting on the low stone wall beside the door. He didn't look like the Professor; the elderly trousers and a turtle-necked sweater had wiped years off him. He said, 'Hello, Julia,' and smiled.

She stood staring, and then said, 'How did you get here? It's not eight o'clock yet.' A sudden thought struck her. 'Is Thomas ill? Is something wrong?'

'So many questions and you haven't even wished me good morning. Thomas is in the best of health; nothing is wrong. I came to make sure that you were both comfortable here.'

'Comfortable? It's heaven! How did you get here?'

'I flew.''

'You flew? But how? I mean, do planes fly so early in the morning?'

'I have my own plane.'

'Your own plane?'

'This conversation is getting repetitive, Julia.'

'Yes, well, I'm surprised. Are you going to stay?'

'Don't worry, only for an hour or so.'

'And you'll fly back? You mean to say you've come just for an hour or so?' The Professor smiled, and she hopped onto the wall beside him. 'When we got here I was surprised—it didn't seem your kind of home. But now you're in slacks and a sweater I can see that it is. I just couldn't picture you in grey worsted and gold cufflinks being here...'

He didn't allow his amusement to show. 'You make me feel middle-aged.'

'Oh, no. Ruth told me that you're thirty-six or so, but you're remote, indifferent...' She paused to look at him. He was smiling again, but this time it was a nasty smile which sent her to her feet. 'I'll tell Ruth you're here.'

Indoors, flying up the stairs, her cheeks burning, she wondered what on earth had possessed her to talk to him like that. It was because he had seemed different, she supposed, but he wasn't, only his clothes. He was still a man she didn't like. She would make some excuse to go to the village after breakfast and stay there until he had gone again.

When, at the end of the meal, she stated her intentions, he told her carelessly to enjoy her walk, while Ruth said, 'Get me some more cards if you go to the shop, Julia.'

Mrs Beckett observed, 'You'd best say goodbye to Mr Gerard; he'll be gone before you get back.'

So Julia wished him goodbye, and he got up and opened the door for her—a courtesy which she was convinced was as false as his friendly, 'Goodbye, Julia.'

She spent a long time in the village—buying things she didn't need, going the long way back, loitering through the garden—for he might still be there.

He wasn't. 'How kind of him to come and make sure we were all right,' said Ruth. 'And he's arranging things so that Thomas can spend the night here before we go back next week. I've loved being here, but I do miss Tom…'

She glanced at Julia. 'You haven't been bored? We haven't gone anywhere or done anything or met anyone…'

Julia was replaiting her tawny hair. A pity she hadn't put it up properly with pins that morning; a pigtail over one shoulder lacked dignity.

'I've loved every minute of it,' Well, this morning was something best forgotten. It was obvious that the Professor had no intention of being friendly—something which she found upsetting and that considering she didn't like him in the least, was puzzling. All the same, just for a little while she had enjoyed sitting there on the wall beside him.

It had turned warm, warm enough to sit in the garden or potter around watching things grow. She would have liked to have weeded and raked and pulled the rhubarb and grubbed up radishes and lettuce from the kitchen garden at the back of the house, but the dour old man in charge wouldn't allow that. Whatever the language, it was obvious he objected strongly to anyone so much as laying a finger on a blade of grass.

Thomas phoned each day. The professor had arrived back safely, he told Ruth, and had gone straight to his late-afternoon clinic. News which Julia received without comment and an inward astonishment at the man's energy.

The week passed too quickly. Thomas would come on Saturday morning, so they must be ready to leave soon after breakfast. Julia, packing her few things, looked round her charming room with real regret; she was going to miss the comfort and unobtrusive luxury of the cottage, and still more she would miss Mrs Beckett's company. She was a contented soul, only wanting everyone else to be contented—

the kind of person one could confide in, reflected Julia, who had, in truth, told her a good
deal about her hopes and plans. And quite un-
wittingly revealed her uncertainty as to the future.

Mrs Beckett had listened with real sympathy
and some sound advice. It wouldn't be needed,
of course; if ever two people were made for
each other they were Julia and Mr Gerard. Of
course, they hadn't discovered that yet, but
time would tell, reflected Mrs Beckett comfortably.

The sun shone on Saturday morning, and the
garden had never looked so lovely. Julia,
dressed and ready to leave, had gone into the
garden to wish it goodbye. Ruth was in the
kitchen with Mrs Beckett, but Julia didn't want
to wish her goodbye until the very last minute.
She strolled round, sniffing at the flowers and
shrubs, and, coming upon a patch of white violets, got down on her knees to enjoy their
scent.

'My mother planted those,' said the
Professor from behind her.

Julia shot to her feet in shock and whirled round. 'Why are you here again?' she demanded.

'This is my home,' he said mildly.

Julia went red. 'I'm sorry, that was rude, but you took me by surprise.'

When he didn't speak she added, 'Have you come to stay? We are so grateful to you for inviting us to stay here. We've had a glorious time. You must be very happy living here; the garden is so beautiful too.'

'What a polite little speech.' The faint mockery in his voice brought the colour back into her cheeks once more. 'I'm glad that you have enjoyed your stay. Are you ready to leave? Mrs Beckett will have coffee waiting for us.'

She went into the house with him, not speaking, and Ruth came running to meet them.

'Julia, isn't it wonderful? Thomas can stay until tomorrow. We're going to fly back—we shall have a whole day together.' She put a hand on the Professor's sleeve. 'You've been so kind...'

'Thomas is due a couple of days off, and this has given me a good excuse to arrange things to suit all of us. I'm only sorry I can't stay longer.'

He took the mug of coffee Mrs Beckett offered him. 'I'll see Julia safely home.'

She was swallowing hot coffee...choked, and had to suffer the indignity of having her back patted and being mopped up. Then she said frostily, 'Is this something I should know about?'

Ruth laughed. 'Oh, didn't the Professor tell you? He's driving you back.' Before Julia could utter, he said, 'We need to leave in five minutes or so. I've patients to see later on to-day.'

Julia said childishly, 'But you've only just got here. I'm sure you must want to stay.'

'Indeed I do. As it is, I can't. So, if you would do whatever you still need to do, we'll be on our way.'

They were all looking at her and smiling; the Professor's smile was brief and amused and he turned away to stroll to the window and study the garden. She fetched her jacket, and was kissed and hugged and escorted to the Rolls with exclamations of delight at her good fortune at having such a comfortable journey.

Ruth poked her head through the window. 'I'll phone you when we get back. Trudie will be there, won't she? You won't be alone?'

'Who is Trudie?' asked the Professor as she settled back after a last wave.

'My lodger. Which way are you going back?'

'From Calais by hovercraft. That should get us back by the late afternoon.'

She must make an effort to be an agreeable companion—probably he didn't want her company anymore than she wanted his. 'A long drive,' she observed, striving for an easy friendliness.

It was at once doused by his casual, 'Yes—doze off if you want to, and you have no need to make polite small talk.'

Rude words bubbled and died on her lips; she couldn't utter them; he was giving her a lift, and she depended on him until she was back on her own doorstep. She sat silently seething, staring out at the countryside. But once they had reached the motorway there wasn't a great deal to look at, only the blue and white signposts at regular intervals. She watched them flash past.

'Why are we going to Amsterdam?' she wanted to know. 'You said we were going to Calais; you ought to be going south.'

He answered her in a patient voice which set her teeth on edge. 'We are going to Amsterdam because I need to. From there we will continue on our way to Calais. Don't worry, we are in plenty of time to catch the ferry.'

'I'm not worried.' Since there was nothing more to be said, she lapsed once more into silence.

But once they reached the city and had driven through its suburbs and reached the heart of it she forgot to be quiet. The old streets were lovely, the houses lining them much as they had been three hundred years earlier. 'Look at that canal,' she begged him, 'and those dear little bridges—and there's a barge simply loaded with flowers—and I can hear bells ringing...'

'Carillons. The barge is moored close to the street so that people can buy the flowers if they wish. There are bridges everywhere connecting up the streets. We are going over the one you see ahead of us.'

The street on the other side of it was narrow, brick-built and lined with large gabled houses on one side and a narrow canal on the other side.

Halfway down it the professor stopped the car, got out and opened her door.

'Would you rather I stayed in the car?' asked Julia. 'Perhaps...'

He opened the car door wider. 'Come along, I haven't time to waste.'

She got out huffily then, and went wordlessly with him up the double steps to the solid front door with its ornate transom. She was hating every minute of it, she told herself, while admitting to a longing to see inside the house. Friends of his, she wondered, or some kind of business to do with his work?

The rather bent elderly man who opened the door broke into voluble Dutch at the sight of them, which was of no help at all. It was obvious that he knew the Professor, and that the Professor held him in some regard, for he had clapped him gently on the back as they went in and addressed him at some length.

She allowed her gaze to wander around their surroundings and felt a surge of pleasure. They were in a long narrow hall with doors on either side and at its end a curving staircase. The walls were panelled, and it was all rather dark, but it was sombrely rich, she told herself, with a brass chandelier, undoubtedly old, a black and white tiled floor strewn with rugs of colours faded with age and a console table upon which someone had set a porcelain bowl of flowers.

The Professor's voice recalled her to her surroundings.

'This is Wim. He looks after the house and everyone in it.' When she offered a hand it was gently shaken and she was made welcome in his thin reedy voice.

The penny dropped then. 'This is your house?' said Julia.

'Yes. My home. We will have coffee and then I must ask you to excuse me while I deal with one or two matters. We must leave in half an hour or so.'

Wim was going ahead of them to open a door, into a long narrow room, panelled, like the hall, and furnished with comfortable chairs grouped round a vast fireplace. Its walls were lined with cabinets, a great long-case clock and a walnut bureau bookcase. There were small tables too, bearing gently shaded lamps, their glow enough, with the firelight, to bathe the room in soft light. And the room had an occupant, for a large dog came bounding to meet them, large and woolly with fearsome teeth.

'It's all right; he's only smiling,' said the professor, bracing himself to receive the delighted onslaught of the devoted beast.

'This is Jason, he's a Bouvier, a splendid chap who will guard those he loves with his life. Offer him a fist.'

Julia liked dogs, but she tried not to see the teeth as she did as she was told—to have her hand gently licked while small yellow eyes studied her face from under a tangle of hair. She said, 'I'm Julia,' and patted the woolly head.

'You must miss him,' she said, and sat down in the chair the Professor was offering.

'Yes, but I plan to spend more time here than in England. In the meantime, I snatch a few moments whenever I can.'

A casual remark which left her feeling vaguely disquiet.

Wim came in with coffee, and presently the Professor excused himself on the grounds of phone calls to make.

'We must leave in fifteen minutes. Wim will show you where you can tidy yourself.'

He went away, Jason at his heels, and Julia was left to finish her coffee before going slowly round the room, inspecting its treasures.

She supposed that it was the drawing room, but there were several other doors in the hall. It was a large house; if all its rooms were as splendidly furnished as this one then the Professor must live in some style.

'Ancestors going back for ever and ever,' said Julia, addressing a portrait of a forbidding gentleman in a wig, 'and loaded with money.'

She became aware of a wet tongue on her hand. Jason was standing silently beside her. She turned quickly; the Professor would have heard her… But apparently he hadn't; he was across the room, looking out of a window. She sighed with relief and said quickly, 'You want to go? If I could ask Wim…?'

'By the staircase. The door on the right. Don't be long.'

He sounded much the same as usual: polite, detached, faintly amused. She joined him after a few minutes with the polite remark that she hoped she hadn't kept him waiting, bade goodbye to Wim and was swept out to the car without any further delay. Jason, standing in the hall, had rumbled goodbye when she had bent to stroke him, and on impulse she had bent down and thrown her arms around his neck and hugged him.

'You mustn't mind,' she'd said softly. 'He'll be back soon.'

She had turned away then, not wanting to see the parting between master and dog.

The Professor drove through the city and onto the motorway, giving her little opportunity to look around her. She sat silently beside him, sensing that he didn't wish to talk. No doubt he had a great many important matters to think about. She settled down to watch the countryside. He was driving fast and she was enjoying the speed; it was a pity that the motorway bypassed the villages and towns, but there was plenty to hold her attention and she kept a sharp eye open for road signs—a map would have been handy...

'There's a map in the pocket beside you,' said the Professor. Was he a thought-reader or did he want to keep her occupied so that there was no need to talk? The latter, she decided, and opened the map.

South to Utrecht, on to Dordrecht and then Breda, where they stopped at a roadside café just outside the town. As they went in he said, 'Fifteen minutes. Coffee and a *Kaas broodje*?'

Julia had spied a door at the back of the cafe with Dames written above it in large letters, 'Anything,' she told him as she sped away.

The Professor got up and pulled out a chair for her when she returned to the table. The coffee was already there, so were the cheese rolls. Obviously this wasn't to be a social meal; they ate fast and silently and were away again with her mouth still full.

'Sorry to rush you,' said the Professor laconically.

To which she replied, 'Not at all, Professor.'

To tell the truth she was enjoying herself.

They bypassed Antwerp, took the road to Gent, bypassed Lille and flew on to Calais.

'Just nicely in time,' observed the Professor, going aboard the hovercraft with two minutes to spare.

He settled her at a small table by a window and said, 'Run along and do your hair; I'll order tea.'

It was early for tea, but the sight of the tea tray and a plate of scones gladdened her heart. The Professor, watching her pour second cups, thought how pretty she looked and how uncomplainingly she had sat beside him. The seat beside him might have been empty. Upon reflection he was glad that it hadn't been. A pity they couldn't like each other…!

They talked during the crossing, careful to talk about mundane things, and when he suggested that she might like to have a brief nap before they landed she closed her eyes at once, thinking that it was a polite way of ending their conversation. She wouldn't sleep, she told herself, but if she shut her eyes she wouldn't need to look at him…

A gentle tap on her shoulder woke her. 'Ten minutes before we land,' the professor told her. 'Run along before there's a queue.' He paused. 'And your hair's coming down.'

How was it, thought Julia, that her hair being untidy and going to the loo should seem so normal and unembarrassing between two people who didn't even like each other? She remembered with a shudder Oscar's coy references to powdering her nose, and the disapproving frown if she needed to stick a pin back into her hairdo.

There was no time to pursue the thought; they were going through Dover and speeding along the motorway to London without loss of time.

Saturday, she thought. She would have to race to the shops and get some food for the weekend. The idea of a cold house and an empty fridge didn't appeal, but of course a man wouldn't think of such things. No doubt, she reflected peevishly, the professor would go to wherever he lived when he had seen his patients and have a splendid meal set before him. She peeped at his calm profile; he appeared unhurried and relaxed but he certainly hadn't dallied on the way...

As they slowed through London's sprawling suburbs she began her rehearsed thank-you speech. 'It was very kind of you to give me a lift,' she began. 'I'm very grateful. I hope it hasn't held you up at all, me being with you.

If you want to drop me off at a bus stop or the Underground...'

'You live very close to the hospital; it will be easier to take you to your house. Stopping anywhere here will hold me up.'

So much for trying to be helpful. She held her tongue until he stopped before her door. The house looked forlorn, as did the whole street, but she said brightly, 'How nice to be home—and so quickly.'

A remark which needed no comment as he got out of the car, took her case from the boot, the key from her hand, opened the door and ushered her into the narrow hall.

'Don't wait—' and that was a silly thing to say '—and thank you again.'

'A pleasure. Goodbye, Julia.'

He drove away without a backward glance.

'He's a detestable man,' said Julia fiercely, standing on her doorstep. 'I hope I never meet him again. Rushing me back home just because he was in a hurry. Well, I hope he's late for whatever it is.' She added rather wildly, 'I hope it's a beautiful woman who will make him grovel!'

He would never grovel, of course, and she didn't mean a word of it, but it made her feel better.

She went indoors then, and into the kitchen to be greeted by Muffin, and a moment later by Trudie, coming downstairs to meet her.

'I knew you'd be back. The man who brought the box said you'd be here some time today.'

Julia went to fill the kettle. 'Box? What box?'

'It's from some super shop in Jermyn Street. It's on the table.'

They went to look at it together. It was a superior kind of box, very neatly packed under its lid; tea and coffee, sugar, milk, a bottle of wine, croissants, eggs, cold chicken in a plastic box, a salad in another plastic box, orange juice, smoked salmon…

Julia unpacked it slowly. 'There must be a mistake.'

Trudie shook her head. 'I asked to make sure. The delivery man said there was no mistake. A Professor van der Maes had ordered it by telephone late yesterday evening to be delivered this afternoon.'

'Oh, my goodness. He never said a word. He gave me a lift back so that my sister's husband could stay in Holland for a day. We had to hurry to get to Calais and we only stopped once on the way. He had to get back by the late afternoon.'

'Well, it's a gorgeous hamper,' said Trudie cheerfully.

'It's coals of fire,' said Julia.

'Well, I'm going out this evening,' Trudie went on. 'You'll be all right?'

'Me? I'm fine, and thank you for keeping an eye on Muffin and the house. No one called about a room?'

'No. You had a good time?'

'It was heaven. I'll tell you some time.'

Presently, alone in the house, she unpacked, fed Muffin and got her supper. The contents of the box might be coals of fire, but they made splendid eating.

Presently, in bed, she lay awake composing a letter to the Professor. Fulsome thanks would annoy him, considering the coolness between them, all the same he would need to be thanked. She slept at last, only to wake from time to time muttering snatches of suitable phrases.

The letter, when it was at last written, was exactly right. Neatly phrased, politely grateful— and it would have served as a model letter for a Victorian maiden to have written. The Professor read it and roared with laughter.

The house, after the charming little cottage, was something Julia would have to get used to. Ruth, back home, had phoned her, bubbling over with the day she had spent with Tom and happy to be back in her little house. Julia had assured her that she was fine, that there was the prospect of a lodger and that the garden was looking very pretty. None of which was true. She didn't feel fine. For some reason she felt depressed.

And I'll soon deal with that, Julia told herself, and went off to the newsagent's to put a To Let sign in his window, and then back to mow the small square of grass in the garden.

There were two applicants for the room the next day. A foxy faced middle-aged man who smelled strongly of beer and wanted to cook his meals in the kitchen, and a youngish woman, skilfully made up, with an opulent bosom and very high heels, who said coyly that she was expecting to get married and would Julia have any objection to her boy-friend calling from time to time?

She told them that the room was already let and watched them go with regret. The rent money would have been useful...

Something would turn up, she told herself, and in the meantime she got a temporary job delivering the local directory. It was dull business, for the neighbouring streets all looked alike, as did the houses, but she enlivened the tedium of it by memories of the cottage, and at the end of the week there was a little money in her pocket and she had written in reply to six vaguely wanting help with houses and small children—something she could surely do without any kind of training. And it wouldn't be for long, she told herself. If she could let a room—two rooms at a pinch—she could sleep in the box room.

She went to Ruth's for lunch on Sunday, and Thomas came over from the hospital for an hour or two. After the meal Ruth said, 'While you're here, Julia, would you look at that little chair I was going to cover? It's in the other bedroom and I've tried to do it, but it doesn't look right. You're so good at that kind of thing.'

So Julia went up the little stairs and into the second bedroom, which was small and unfurnished save for suitcases, a bookcase which was too large to go anywhere and the chair. It was a pretty little chair, and Ruth had pinned the velvet onto it in a haphazard fashion. Julia got down on the floor, undid it all to cut and fit, pinned and tacked, and sat back on her heels to study her work. It would do, but Ruth wanted a frill, she thought.

She was on the stairs when she heard Ruth's voice. The sitting room door was open and the house was small, with thin walls.

'Oh, Thomas, I can't ask Julia. Where would she go? But it would be wonderful. We'd have the money to start buying our own house, and Monica and George need central heating and a new bathroom—the house would sell for enough money for that?'

'Oh, yes, darling. Split three ways you would each get a very useful sum. But we mustn't think about it. If Julia marries you could suggest it then, but not before.'

Julia crept back into the room, closed the door quietly and sat down on the chair. Of course she had thought of it before, but had put it out of her mind. How could she have been so stupid? There was nothing remarkable about the house, but it had three bedrooms, and although the street was shabby it was quiet, and those who lived in it were law-abiding— striving to keep so. Moreover, there were buses

and the Underground into the City. It would
fetch a fair price—Ruth and Thomas could get
a house of their own; Monica could have her
central heating. As for herself…a small flat
somewhere, and the money to take a course in
something or other. She could think about that
later. She would have to wait for a few days
and then broach the subject…

Steps on the stairs sent her onto her knees,
fussing with the frill.

Ruth put her head round the door. 'You had
the door shut. You didn't hear me?'

'No. Were you calling? Look, do you want
a frill? I think it would be too much.' She got
to her feet. 'Has Thomas gone back? I'll come
down, shall I?'

# CHAPTER FOUR

THE opportunity to do something about the house came sooner than she had expected. Monica phoned to ask abut their stay in Holland, and when that subject had been exhausted she talked at length about George and the house and the village. 'I'm so happy, Julia…'

It seemed to be the right moment. Julia knew exactly what to say; she had rehearsed it carefully and now she made her suggestion with just the right amount of eagerness. 'I can't think why I haven't thought of it before. I haven't said anything to Ruth yet. Do you think it's a good idea? It's only an idea, anyway…'

She could hear the excitement in Monica's voice. 'But what about you?'

'I'd get a small flat and take a course in dressmaking. You know how I love making clothes.'

'Would we get enough from the house for all of us?'

'Yes, but perhaps Ruth wouldn't like the idea...'

'I'll talk to her and find out. Is this what you really want, Julia?'

'Oh, yes. Just think, I wouldn't have to depend on lodgers. I'd be free—have a holiday when I wanted to, come and go as I pleased and work at something I enjoy doing.'

She rang off presently, knowing that she had convinced Monica. Now she must wait and see what Ruth would decide, and let the news come from Monica.

She didn't have long to wait, Ruth phoned that evening. 'Monica rang and told me you'd suggested selling the house. But, Julia, what about you?'

So Julia repeated her carefully thought out words and added, 'Do you like the idea? It's only an idea...'

'You really want to? You'd be happier somewhere else? There would be enough money for you to feel secure?'

'I don't feel secure now,' said Julia. 'I need three lodgers to keep this house going and so far I've only got one; I didn't tell you that I got the sack from the greetings card people— but then I expected that; Oscar, you know. I could train as a dressmaker, live in a small flat...'

'Oh, my dear, I didn't know. I think it's a marvellous idea.' Ruth paused. 'As a matter of fact, Thomas and I have seen a house near the hospital—in a cul-de-sac, and so quiet. It's for sale...'

'You see,' said Julia bracingly. 'It's the hand of fate!'

Of course there was a good deal to discuss during the next few days. Julia, striking while the iron was hot, had the house valued, and the price the agent suggested clinched the matter. He had people on his books waiting for just such a house to come on the market. Ruth and Thomas, inspecting the house they so wanted to buy, had no doubts.

'A pity the Prof is away,' Thomas observed. 'By the time he gets back we'll probably have moved.'

'Will he be in Edinburgh much longer?'

'No, a few days more, but he's going straight to Vienna to give lectures and then a week or two in Holland.'

'He'll have a nice surprise. Oh, Thomas, I do hope the house sells quickly.'

Something Monica hoped too, with her writing desk awash with central heating brochures and magnificent bathroom catalogues.

As for Julia, unaware that the Professor was away, she went to see the solicitor who held the deeds of the house, bullied the house agent in the nicest possible way, explained everything to Trudie and hoped that the hand of fate she had been so sure about would point a finger at her. Now that they were selling the house she wanted to be gone quickly, to start a new life. That she woke in the night to worry about that was something she did her best to ignore.

The house sold within a week. Moreover, it was a cash sale, and the new owner wanted to move in as soon as Julia could move out. Monica and Ruth came, and, helped by a cheerfully co-operative Trudie, they all set to work to pack up the house.

It wasn't just the packing up. There was the furniture—what was left after they had each decided what they wanted to keep and, since Trudie hoped to marry soon, she had had her share—and then the removal men, the gas, the electricity, the telephone, the milkman—an unending stream of things which needed her attention.

With three days left before the new owners took over Julia found herself in an almost empty house. Trudie had moved in with the other teacher at the kindergarten, George had driven up in a borrowed van and taken the furniture Monica had chosen, and the local odd-job man had collected the tables and chairs and beds which Ruth wanted for her new home. Which left Julia with a bed, a number of suitcases, a box of books, the kitchen table and two chairs. The fridge and cooker had been sold with the house, so meals were no problem although lack of comfort was. Ruth had wanted her to go and stay with them, but to leave the house empty was risky. And it was only for two nights.

Tomorrow, thought Julia, getting into bed with Muffin for company, she would go in search of a room to rent. She knew what she was going to do: find a small flat in a quiet street in a better neighbourhood. Islington would be nice, if she could find something to suit her purse. Perhaps a basement flat with a bit of garden at the back—or Finsbury—somewhere not too far from Ruth and Thomas. She wished that she had someone to advise her.

The Professor's face flashed before her closed eyes and she said out loud, 'What nonsense. He's not even in the country, and in any case he hasn't the least interest.'

Ruth had said that he was away, and that they hadn't told him that they were moving. 'We're going to surprise him,' said Ruth happily. 'He'll be back soon.'

'Not before I've gone,' reflected Julia now. 'Disagreeable man.'

She went in search of a room the next day and returned home disappointed. She had been to several likely addresses, but most of them had proved to be top-floor attics which wouldn't do at all for Muffin. One or two had been grubby, and the only one which would have done at a pinch she'd been denied. 'Not cats!' the lady of the house had said. 'Nasty, dirty creatures.'

'We'll try again tomorrow,' she told Muffin, inspecting the fridge for their suppers.

She was just finishing breakfast the next morning when there was a thump on the door. And when she went to open it there was the Professor.

She was aware of delight at seeing him, and that was something she would have to think about later on. For now she stared up at him wordlessly. His 'Good morning Julia,' was coolly friendly.

Since he stood there, obviously expecting to be asked in, she said, 'Oh, do come in—has something happened to Ruth or Thomas?' She shut the door behind him with something of a snap. 'It's very early…'

'This has nothing to do with Ruth or Thomas. I wished to talk to you.'

He stood in the hall, looking around him at the empty place. 'Is there somewhere…?'

She led the way to the kitchen, angry that he should see its poverty stricken appearance: the milk bottle on the table, a loaf of bread beside it, her mug and plate with a slice of bread and butter half eaten…

'Do sit down,' she begged him in a voice of a polite hostess who must entertain an unwelcome guest, and when he had taken the other chair at the table she asked, 'Would you like a cup of tea? There's still some in the pot.'

His mouth twitched. 'Yes, please,' he responded as his eye fell on the loaf.

'Would you like some bread and butter?' she asked.

'Breakfast is always such a pleasant meal,' he observed, before he cut a slice and buttered it.

'There's no need to be sarcastic,' said Julia. 'Why have you come?'

'It must be obvious to you that this is not a social visit. Unfortunately it is the only time of day when I'm free...'

She interrupted him. 'Ruth said you weren't in England.'

'I got back yesterday evening. Tell me, Julia, have you any plans for your immediate future?'

'Why do you want to know?'

'If you will answer my question I will tell you.'

'I can't see why you should ask, but since you have, no.'

'You have somewhere to go tomorrow? A flat or rooms?'

'No. I intend to find something this morning.' She frowned. 'I don't see that it's any of your business—and we're not even friends...' She blushed scarlet the moment she had said it and mumbled, 'Well, you know what I mean.'

'I hardly think that friendship has anything to do with it, and it is my business in so far that I am asking for your help.'

'Me? Help you?'

'If you would refrain from interrupting, I will explain.'

He drank his tea and looked at her. She was untidy, for she had done some last-minute packing; her hair was in a plait over one shoulder, she had a shiny nose, and was wearing a cotton top faded from many washings. But she looked quite beautiful, he thought. Her sisters were beautiful too, but Julia was full of life, impulsive, refusing to admit that life wasn't quite what she had hoped for. She had a sharp tongue, and a temper too...

He said gently, 'Indeed you could help me if you would consider it. You haven't forgotten Mrs Beckett? I have been with her for a day or two. She is ill—pneumonia—and in hospital. It is a viral infection and she isn't so young. Would you consider going over to Holland and minding the cottage while she is away, and then staying for a while when she gets back until she is quite well and I can arrange some sort of help for her?'

It was so unexpected that she could only gape at him.

'Go to Holland?' said Julia at length. 'But does Mrs Beckett want me—and how long would I be there?'

'Mrs Beckett will be very happy to see you again,' said the Professor smoothly. 'I cannot say for certain how long your stay might be. But she will be in hospital for at least two weeks, and when she returns home she will need a good deal of cosseting.'

'She is in hospital now?'

'Yes, in Leiden. A colleague of mine is the consultant physician there. I have arranged for someone to look after her cats and the cottage but it is a temporary arrangement. I want someone with no other commitments so that I can be sure that both Mrs Beckett and the cats and cottage are in the hands of a person who is willing to remain until she is quite fit.'

'But why me?'

He ignored that. 'I am aware that this may interfere with whatever plans you have made.

You would, of course, receive a salary and any expenses.'

'Well, I haven't any real plans. I mean none that can't be put off for a few weeks. There is no reason why I shouldn't go. When do you want me to be there?'

It was impossible to tell whether he was pleased or not. 'Within the next day or so. I will arrange for you to fly over. You will be met and taken to the cottage. You will be kept informed as to Mrs Beckett's condition and taken to visit her if you wish.'

He got up and she, perforce, got up too. His goodbye was brief and he had gone before the dozen questions tumbling around in her head could be uttered.

She had been glad to see him, she couldn't deny that, and not having to decide about her future for another few weeks was a relief she didn't admit to. It was while she was going through her scanty wardrobe that she started to wonder how he had known that she was leaving the house. Had he been back in England earlier and had Ruth told him? Surely he hadn't made up his mind to ask her in the space of a few hours?

It wasn't until she was getting her lunch that her eye fell upon Muffin...

The phone hadn't been transferred yet, thank heaven; moreover, she was put through to the Professor at once.

'Muffin,' she began without preamble. 'I can't go to Holland—Ruth's far too busy moving house and he'll pine in the cattery.'

'No problem. My housekeeper in London will be delighted to look after him. I have arranged for you to fly over tomorrow afternoon. I will come for you at midday and we can leave Muffin with her as we go.'

And he had hung up without giving her a chance to say anything.

She addressed Muffin. 'I've been a fool. I have allowed Professor van der Maes to make use of me. I must be losing my wits.' Although, she reflected presently, it would be delightful to stay in that cottage again, and it would give her time to decide exactly what she intended to do next.

She was ready for him when he came; the new owners were moving in later that afternoon, everything was signed and sealed, the money was in Ruth's care, and her share would be waiting for her when she got back. In the meantime she had enough of her own to keep her going. The Professor had mentioned a salary, but probably it had just been a passing thought.

He greeted her in a businesslike manner and stowed Muffin on the back seat, her case in the boot and herself beside him without more ado. She didn't look back as he drove away. She and her sisters had lived in the house but it had never been home to any of them.

She sat without speaking as he drove through the busy streets. Presently he said, 'I shall have to drive straight to Heathrow.'

He had shown no signs of impatience at the slow progress they were making, but a glance at the clock told her that at the rate they were going they would never get to the airport on time. All she said was, 'Muffin?'

'I will take the cat to my house as soon as I have seen you on to the plane. I promise you that I will see that he is in safe hands.' He gave her a quick look. 'Trust me, Julia.'

'Yes,' said Julia, knowing that she meant it.

She was the last to board the plane; there had barely been time to bid Muffin goodbye before she was hurried away, told that she would be met at Schipol and would she telephone him that evening?

'The phone number is in the envelope with your ticket. Goodbye, Julia.'

Schipol was overflowing with people; Julia stood for a moment, wishing wholeheartedly that she hadn't come, then a short, thickset man, bearing her name on a placard he was holding before him, came to a halt in front of her.

'Miss Gracey? Sent by Professor van der Maes? I am Piet, to drive you to his house.' His English was strongly accented but fluent.

Julia held out a hand. 'How do you do? Is it a long drive?'

'No, I drive fast.' He picked up her case and led the way through the crowds, out to the car, which was an elderly Mercedes. Its appearance, she quickly discovered, was deceptive; it was capable of a fine turn of speed which, coupled with Piet's obvious wish to be a racing driver, took them at a hair-raising speed to the cottage.

As she got out Piet told her that he would call for her in the morning and take her to see Mrs Beckett at Leiden. He took her case into the cottage, gave her a broad grin and was gone.

There was someone in the cottage, waiting for her: a small woman with an old-fashioned hairdo, wearing a severe black dress. She smiled a welcome and broke into voluble speech, unfortunately in Dutch.

Julia smiled in return, offered a hand and mustered her few words of that language.

The woman was amused. 'I go. I come at morning, early.' She thought for a moment. 'Work, cook.'

'All day?'

'Mornings. Professor van der Maes tell.'

'I should hope so. How like a man,' said Julia crossly and her companion smiled and nodded. 'Nice man. Food ready. *Dag.*'

She trotted off in the direction of the village and Julia closed the door and found Mrs Beckett's cats staring at her.

'Well, at least I can talk to you,' said Julia, and at that moment the phone rang.

'You had a good journey?' enquired the professor. 'Mevrouw Steen was at the cottage?'

'Is that who she is? Why are you ringing me? You told me that I was to phone you this evening.'

'I thought that you might be anxious about Muffin. Why are you cross?'

'I am not cross.' She sounded peevish. 'I am in an empty house with two cats, I want a cup of tea, and *Mevrouw*'s English is as basic as my Dutch.'

'An excellent opportunity for you to improve your knowledge of the language.'

'I have no wish to do so,' said Julia haughtily. 'Is there anything you wanted to say to me? Because if there isn't I'm going to put the kettle on...'

He took no notice. 'Piet will take you to see Mrs Beckett tomorrow morning. Arrange with her or the doctor when you wish to visit her and let him know. Piet will drive you wherever you should wish to go and do any odd jobs or errands for you

She said stiffly, 'Thank you. Is Muffin all right?'

'Settled down very nicely. I hope you will do the same, Julia.' With which he rang off.

'Rude man,' said Julia.

She had every intention of wallowing in self-pity as she went into the kitchen, but the sight of the tea tray standing ready on the kitchen table made her hesitate. There wasn't only a pretty teacup and saucer and plate on it, matching the teapot, sugar bowl and milk jug, but also a plate of buttered scones and a little dish of jam, and when she opened the fridge door while the kettle boiled she found salmon, ready to eat, and salad and a bowl of potato straws. Moreover, there were strawberries and cream and a bottle of white wine.

She made the tea, carried the tray through to the sitting room and wondered uneasily if she had been a bit too off-hand with the Professor...

Her bedroom welcomed her: flowers on the dressing table, a pile of books and magazines on the bedside table, a carafe of water and a tin of biscuits, and in the bathroom towels and soaps and a delicious selection of oils for the bath. Somebody had been very thoughtful about her well-being, she reflected, going downstairs and taking the bottle of wine from the fridge. She didn't feel lonely or hard-done-by any more; it was as though she had been warmly welcomed even if there had been no one there to do that.

Presently she ate her supper, drank the rest of her glass of wine, fed the cats and, accompanied by them both, went upstairs to lie in the bath and then get into bed. Her two companions settled each side of her and she hoped that Muffin was being as well cared for. She would be all right, she decided sleepily; the Professor had said that he would look after her...

She woke to a splendid morning; hanging out of the window, she looked down at the garden, which was a riot of colour, and beyond it to the flat, peaceful countryside... She showered and dressed and skipped downstairs, intent on breakfast. She had fed the cats and was eating her boiled egg when Mevrouw Steen arrived.

She greeted Julia with a cheerful *'Dag'* and then added, 'Piet comes; I stay.'

So Julia gobbled down the rest of her breakfast, found her handbag, got into Piet's car and was driven to Leiden—a trip she would have enjoyed if she hadn't been so scared of the speed at which Piet drove. But he was a splendid driver, and of course the road ahead of them was flat as far as the eye could see. He put her down at the hospital, rather shaken and glad to feel solid ground beneath her feet. He would return in an hour, he told her, and wait until she came. She was not to hurry.

Mrs Beckett, looking half her normal size, was propped up against her pillows with an oxygen mask clamped over her nose. But she smiled and nodded to Julia and waved a languid hand.

'Don't talk,' said Julia urgently. 'I'm going to sit here and tell you all the news!'

Mrs Beckett listened, nodding from time to time, then asked, 'Portly and Lofty—how are they?'

'Both in splendid health; they slept on my bed. You don't mind?'

Mrs Beckett smiled. 'I'm glad. Mr Gerard has been to see me. He'll come again; he's so good to me.'

'He's organised everything,' Julia assured her. 'As soon as you're well again you are coming home, and I'll stay until you are perfectly fit.'

'You'll want to go home,' whispered Mrs Beckett. 'To your own home.'

'I haven't got one. We've sold it. I'll find somewhere to live when I get back. It's lovely being here again. The cottage looks lovely and

I'll look after everything.' She bent and kissed the pale cheek. 'I'm going now. I shall phone every day and come and see you again in a day or two. You are going to get well quickly; the Professor told me so.'

Which wasn't true, but a lie in a good cause...

'If he said so, then I shall.'

It was a relief but no surprise to find that the doctor she asked to see spoke English as good as hers. Mrs Beckett was making good progress, he assured her. She had been seriously ill—pneumonia in the elderly was not to be treated lightly—but she had responded well to treatment.

'You are a friend of Professor van der Maes?'

It would save a lot of explanations if she agreed...

'May I come at any time? Not every day, perhaps, but I will phone each morning and you will let me know at once if it's necessary.'

'Of course.'

He walked with her to the entrance, where Piet was waiting, and watched her getting into the car. A delightfully pretty girl, he reflected. Gerard had told him that she was a sensible young woman, very well able to look after herself and deal with any situation which might arise. And of course Gerard would come at once in an emergency....

After that first day Julia slipped into a gentle pattern of days. Visiting Mrs Beckett, even beginning to enjoy Piet's breakneck driving, cherishing Portly and Lofty, filling the cottage with flowers because she knew that Mrs Beckett would like that, weeding and tending the flowerbeds when the gardener allowed, practising her sparse Dutch on Mevrouw Steen and each evening listening eagerly for the phone to ring. The Professor never had much to say but his voice was reassuring.

She had been there for several days when he said, 'The question of your salary. I have arranged for my bank to send it to you each week in guilders.'

'I don't need any money,' said Julia.

'Money is something which everyone needs from time to time,' said the Professor, and hung up before she could utter another word.

When the postman brought it she sat at the kitchen table and counted it. There seemed to be a great deal, even when she did careful mental sums and changed it into pounds. 'For a month, I suppose,' she said and, feeling rich, went to the village and bought postcards, stamps and chocolate.

The following week the same amount arrived, so that evening when he phoned she pointed out to him that there had been a mistake; she already had her salary.

'Did I not make myself clear? Each week you will receive your money from my bank...'

'But it's too much.'

'I must beg you not to argue. When are you going to see Mrs Beckett?'

'Tomorrow, in the morning. Why?'

'If you will give me time to speak, I will tell you. She is so much better she will probably be able to come home within the next few days. She will need to convalesce in a leisurely fashion. I rely upon you to see that she does.'

'I'll take the greatest care of her. How will she come home? Shall I go with Piet and fetch her?'

'I will tell you in due course. In the meantime you will see her doctor tomorrow.'

'Very well.' Then she added, 'Don't you ever say goodbye?'

'Not to you, Julia.' And he hung up!

Mrs Beckett was sitting in a chair by her bed when Julia got to the hospital. She looked weary and far too pale, but Julia was pleased to see that she was taking an interest in life once more.

'I'm coming home soon,' she told Julia. 'I've missed it so…' Her eyes filled with tears.

'Won't it be fun? Lofty and Portly will be so glad to see you…the garden looks lovely, and so many people have asked me how you are. You have so many friends. They'll want to come and see you, but the doctor says you must be a bit quiet for a little longer.'

'I know. Mr Gerard told me. I'm to do what you say just for a time; he's promised that everything will be just as it always was.'

'Well, of course it will. And I promise you that I won't make you do anything that you don't want to do.'

She hugged Mrs Beckett because she looked so small and frail.

'If the weather is warm and fine, you shall sit in the garden and tell me what to do.'

Four days later Julia was awakened by a thunderous knocking on the door.

'Mrs Beckett—something's happened,' she told the cats as she tore down the stairs, tugging on her dressing gown as she went, her feet bare.

The professor was on the doorstep.

'I didn't use my key; I didn't want to disturb you…'

'But you have disturbed me. You've given me the fright of my life—I thought something had happened to Mrs Beckett. And why are you here?'

'If I might come in?' he asked meekly. 'This is my home!'

He sounded meek, but he gave her a mocking smile as she stood aside to let him pass.

'Oh, well—sorry,' said Julia. 'You could have phoned.'

He agreed blandly; he hadn't known until the very last minute that he could snatch twenty-four hours away from his work; too late to warn her of his intention.

'Tea? Breakfast?' Julia went ahead of him into the kitchen and turned to look at him. It was then she saw how tired he was…

'You've had no sleep. How did you come? When do you have to go back?'

'Tonight. I've come to bring Mrs Beckett home.'

'You'll have a cup of tea, then go and sleep for an hour or so while I get breakfast. What time do you plan to go to Leiden?'

'Shortly after midday.'

She had the kettle on, was setting out mugs, sugar and milk. 'Mevrouw Steen won't be here before eight o'clock.' She got the loaf and butter and cut him a generous slice. 'What a good thing I made the beds up yesterday…'

He sat at the table, watching her. Her hair was all over the place, her dressing gown had come untied, her feet were bare. She was, he decided, just what a man would want to see after a sleepless and tiring night.

Julia, far too busy to bother about appearances, put his tea before him, cut him more bread and butter and poured herself a mug. 'There's plenty of hot water,' she told him. 'Did you bring the car?'—

'Yes. I'll have a shower and a nap. Breakfast about nine o'clock?'

It was barely seven. 'Yes, would you like it in bed?'

He choked back a laugh. 'The last time I had breakfast in bed I was nine years old, suffering from the mumps.'

When she looked at him, he added, 'That was twenty-seven years ago.'

He smiled, and the smile made her suddenly aware of the flyaway dressing gown and no slippers. She said briskly, 'I will call you at nine o'clock.'

He went away then, and she saw to the cats, put everything ready for breakfast and went quietly upstairs. The bathroom door was open but the three bedroom doors were closed. She had a shower, dressed, then made her bed and went downstairs again. Just in time to say *dag* to Mevrouw Steen.

There was no need to tell her that the Professor was there; the car was before the door. Mevrouw Steen broke into voluble talk, smiling widely.

'Mrs Beckett is coming home today.' Julia thought for a moment and added in Dutch, 'This afternoon.'

Mevrouw Steen nodded. 'I clean house…'

She trotted off, but not before Julia had warned her not to go upstairs until the Professor was awake. 'No sleep,' she told her in her fractured Dutch. 'Driving all night.'

*Mevrouw* made sympathetic clucking noises, went into the sitting room and shut the door on the sound of the Hoover.

Julia began to get breakfast. Bacon and eggs, tomatoes, mushrooms, fried bread. There was no lack of food in the house. Toast and marmalade to follow, and tea or coffee. And while she was busy she considered lunch. Salad, and there was ham in the fridge, and in the evening before he went back she would cook him a meal. A Spanish omelette, potatoes in their jackets and a salad—a bread and butter pudding, perhaps, or a sponge pudding with custard…

The bacon was sizzling in the pan and it was nearly nine o'clock. Time to rouse him…

He came into the kitchen through the door leading to the garden.

'You're up,' said Julia, and frowned because that had been a silly thing to say.

'I wanted to have a quick look at the garden. Something smells delicious.'

He looked as though he had slept all night— shaved and immaculately turned out. Of course he would have clothes here, thought Julia, and, suddenly conscious that she had been staring at him, she blushed.

The Professor studied the blush with interest and decided that it made her even prettier than she already was.

'Can't I help?' He sounded casual.

'If you would make the toast?'

Mevrouw Steen came in then. She had a great deal to say and it was frustrating, for Julia only understood one word in a dozen. The dear soul paused for breath presently and Julia offered her a mug of coffee and she trotted off with it. She would go upstairs, she said, and clean.

'A good soul,' said the Professor as he speared a mushroom. 'When you leave here I must find some kind of help for Mrs Beckett. Mevrouw Steen's a splendid worker but she doesn't like responsibility.'

Julia looked down at her plate. 'I expect you would like me to go once Mrs Beckett is settled here.'

'Now, why should you think that? Mrs Beckett is going to need you for another three weeks at least. You wish to go home?'

'No, no. I love it here,' she burst out. 'I don't know how you can bear to live anywhere else. Well, I dare say that's not true, for you have your lovely house in Amsterdam.'

'You liked that too?'

'My goodness me, indeed I did.'

'Then we must find time to go there again.' He added casually, 'I am planning to do rather more work over here—go over to Scotland from time to time when necessary.'

'You mean you won't live in London?' The thought filled her with a dismay she couldn't understand.

The professor watched her face. 'From time to time,' he repeated gently. 'I'm going down to the village to see Piet. Shall we have lunch before we go to Leiden?'

'We? Wouldn't it be better if I stayed here and had everything ready—tea—and the cats waiting.' She looked at him. 'A welcome, if you see what I mean.'

He agreed readily, and presently she watched him walking along the lane. Even from the back he looked full of energy—a man who had had a good night's sleep and with not a care in the world.

# CHAPTER FIVE

THE Professor didn't come back until she was putting lunch on the table. 'Well,' said Julia to Portly, sitting beside her while she made a salad, 'I'm sure if he doesn't want my company I couldn't care less. After all, I'm only a kind of housekeeper.'

She wallowed in a comforting self-pity for a few minutes, and then forgot about it as the Professor came into the kitchen.

'Piet will come each day,' he told her without preamble. 'He'll do anything you want him to do and if you wish to leave the place he will stay with Mrs Beckett and Mevrouw Steen.'

'Thank you, but I'm happy to stay here. Will Mrs Beckett be able to sit outside for a while each day?'

'Dr de Groot—you saw him at Leiden—will come and see her in a day or so and let you know what he wants done.'

'I see. When will you go back?'

'Anxious for me to be gone, Julia?' He sounded amused. 'I'm going back this evening.'

'But you've only just got here. You've had no sleep; you'll be dead on your feet.'

'I'm going back from Harwich on the night ferry. I'll sleep then.'

He drove away after lunch and she tidied up, put the tea things ready and went up to her room. She wasn't a vain girl, but she had the sudden urge to make the most of herself. It would have to be the same blue denim skirt, because she hadn't another, but there was a newly washed and ironed cotton blouse, and she wasted a good deal of time trying out various ways of doing her hair, only to tug out the pins and bundle it up on the top of her head. 'He won't notice anyway,' she told Lofty, watching her from the bed.

Of course he noticed, the moment he got out of the car and saw her waiting on the porch. He lifted Mrs Beckett out of the car and carried her into the cottage, and as he passed Julia he observed, 'I like the hair. Is it in my honour?'

She went pink, going ahead of him to open the sitting room door as he bore his housekeeper in and settled her in the chair Julia had put ready. Mrs Beckett said in a wispy voice, 'My dear, how well you look—such lovely pink cheeks. I do hope I'm not going to be too much of a nuisance.'

Julia gave her a gentle hug. 'What nonsense. I love being here and I shall love looking after you. I'm going to get the tea; you must be dying for a cup.'

She got herself out of the room and Mrs Beckett settled back in her chair and nodded her head. 'A dear girl, don't you agree, Mr Gerard?'

He grinned at her. 'Don't fish, Nanny. When we've had tea you're going to bed, and mind you do exactly what Julia tells you. I must give her all the details of your treatment before I go.'

Tea was quickly over, which was a good thing for Julia could think of very little to say.

The Professor made gentle small talk, addressing her from time to time and staring at her in
a way which both annoyed and disturbed her.
His remark about her hair had shaken her
calm—perhaps she should have taken more
pains with it.

He'll be gone in a few hours, thought Julia,
and for some reason her spirits sank.

Getting Mrs Beckett to bed took time. There
were her things to unpack and put away and
frequent pauses while she discussed the hospital and her illness. When Julia finally went
downstairs she found the Professor in the
kitchen.

'I must leave in just over an hour,' he told
her. 'Come here and listen carefully to what I
have to say.'

'You must have a meal before you go. You
can still tell me while I'm cooking it.'

She had her nose in the fridge. 'A bacon
omelette? Asparagus? New potatoes?'

'Excellent. If you are as handy with the frying pan as you are with the needle I am indeed
a lucky man.'

'You have no reason to be sarcastic...'

'What do you intend to do when you get back to London, Julia?'

'Be a dressmaker. Only I must be taught properly first.'

'And where will you live?'

'Oh, somewhere...'

Since he didn't answer, and the silence got a bit lengthy, she added, 'Ruth and Thomas have found such a nice house; I expect you've seen it. And of course Monica and George have a lovely old vicarage...'

'And you, Julia—do you not wish for a home and a husband and children, or is the fashioning of garments the acme of your ambition?'

'I don't like you when you talk like this,' said Julia fiercely. 'Never mind me, and much you care anyway, just tell me what I must do to get Mrs Beckett on her feet again.'

He didn't speak for a moment, but looked at her with lifted eyebrows, and when he did speak he was Professor van der Maes, giving courteous instructions to a patient's attendant.

She listened carefully while she beat eggs and chopped bacon and mushrooms, and when he had finished said, 'Thank you, that's all quite clear, but please write her medicines down so that I can be quite sure.'

'And here is Dr de Groot's phone number. Don't hesitate to ring him if you feel the necessity.'

She set the potatoes to cook. 'Will you come again to see Mrs Beckett?'

'If it's possible. I have complete faith in de Groot. As for yourself, I think that Mrs Beckett will be fully recovered in three weeks. I shall arrange for suitable help before you return.' He wandered to the door. 'Will you let me know when my supper is ready? I'm going to sit with Nanny.'

It's my own silly fault, reflected Julia. Why can't we be friends? And why did he want me to come here if he dislikes me so much? Once I leave here I won't see him again; I'll find somewhere miles away.

Somewhere where—hopefully—she could make a living, find friends, perhaps meet a man who would want her for his wife. There must be any number of men around not in the least like Oscar, or, for that matter, the Professor. There was no one like him, she added…

She laid a place for him at the table, tossed the potatoes in butter and mint and had the pan hot ready for the omelette. She could hear the murmur of voices as she went into the hall when she called him and he came at once.

'There are strawberries and cream,' she told him, 'and I've made coffee.'

'Thank you. I've said goodbye to Nanny; she's a bit tearful, so I think a glass of claret might do her good before her supper. And you too, of course.'

He didn't talk much as he ate, and presently he went and got his bag.

She said awkwardly, 'I hope you have a safe journey and won't be too tired.' She had gone to the door with him. 'I promise I'll take good care of Mrs Beckett.'

He stood looking down at her. 'I'm sure of that. Look after yourself, Julia.'

He got into the car and drove away and she stood in the porch staring down the now empty lane. She felt empty too.

There were letters from Monica and Ruth in the morning; it was nice to know that selling the house had brought them so much happiness. And Monica wanted her to go and stay after she'd spent time at Ruth's, which solved the problem as to where she would go next. Somehow the future had seemed vague and far off, but the Professor had mentioned three weeks. In that time she must make up her mind what she intended to do.

Mrs Beckett was a model patient and, like a trusting child, did everything asked of her without question. Julia cooked her small tasty meals, helped her with the slow, tiring business of dressing and undressing, and after a few days led her carefully downstairs to sit and watch the TV or chat. Talking was something she enjoyed, and Julia was soon in possession of the professor's family history.

Old family, said Mrs Beckett, wealthy and respected. 'His father was a surgeon, you know. Retired now. His mother's a sweet lady. He has brothers and sisters too. A brother in Canada and two sisters in New Zealand. All married. His parents are visiting them and will be away for some months.'

'They live in Amsterdam?'

'No. No, dear. In den Haag. Mr Gerard took over the Amsterdam house when he came of age. Lovely old house too, but he needs a wife to run it…'

'I should have thought that the Professor would have had no difficulty in finding someone; he's rich and good-looking and well known in his profession.'

Mrs Beckett peered over her specs. 'Yes, dear, but Mr Gerard will never marry unless he finds his dream girl—he told me that a long time ago.' Before Julia could pursue the subject she added, 'I fancy a cup of tea. Make it in the brown pot, dear, it tastes so much better.'

It was in one of the numerous magazines Mrs Beckett had sent from England that Julia, idly leafing through its pages, saw the advertisement.

Skilful needlewomen were required to help in the repair of old fabrics and upholstery at a stately home in the north of England. Small salary and accommodation on the estate property. References would be required and full details as to the applicant's skill. Interviews would be held in London in one month's time.

Just what I'm looking for, reflected Julia, and miles away from London. Although why that should be so vital a need was something she didn't enlarge upon, even to herself. That evening she sat down and wrote a letter...

The weather was delightful and Mrs Beckett, spending quiet hours in the garden with Lofty and Portly in close attendance, began to look like her former plump self. As for Julia, cooking tasty meals, washing and ironing, pottering around the garden, she found life was a pleasure which she would have liked to continue for ever.

Mevrouw Steen and Piet smoothed her path, and if they found her Dutch inadequate and frequently laughable, they were too kind to say so. She had little time to herself, though, for Mrs Beckett liked to have company and was sometimes fretful at having to sit quietly and watch activity which she would normally have enjoyed herself. But as the days passed and she began to take up her normal life again Julia gradually handed over to her. In another week she would be back to her normal state of health.

The thought of leaving depressed Julia, although she told herself that it was time she went back to England and got on with her own life. After all she had money now, and soon she could decide what she wanted to do...

A problem solved for her for one morning, when a letter arrived for her. If she cared to present herself at a certain London hotel on a day three weeks from now, she would be interviewed with the possibility of being employed at the stately home. She should bring with her two references and a sample of her needlework. She would be good enough to acknowledge the letter...

Which she did, without saying anything to Mrs Beckett, trusting to luck that she wold be free by then. That done, she expressed a wish to do some embroidery. 'So that I can sit with you and not feel guilty while you knit,' she explained, and wished that she could take Mrs Beckett into her confidence.

Mrs Beckett was enthusiastic: there was a box in the attic, full of bits and pieces. Julia could rummage around and take whatever she fancied.

She found the ideal thing: a piece of patterned damask and a bundle of silks. She set to work, embroidering the pattern in a variety of stitches and various colours, and Mrs Beckett, examining it, declared that it was a lovely piece of embroidery.

'What a clever girl you are,' she observed. 'It's almost professional.' And she smiled so fondly at Julia that she almost told her of her plans. But she couldn't, of course, otherwise Mrs Beckett might feel that she was anxious to be gone—which thought was followed by another: if she told her companion what she hoped to do, the Professor might come to hear of it, and it seemed of the utmost importance that he should be unaware of her plans for the future.

He came a few days later, coming unhurriedly into the garden where they were having tea. Mrs Beckett saw him first.

'Mr Gerard—what a sight for sore eyes. And just in time for tea!'

He bent to kiss her. 'You're well again, Nanny. You look splendid...'

He nodded to Julia, half smiling. 'Julia has done a splendid job.'

'I'll get a cup and saucer and more tea,' she said, and took herself off indoors. So she was to go, and quite soon. And was he staying? Because if he was she would have to make a room ready and reorganise supper. She put the kettle on and warmed a teapot, found a cup and saucer and plate and a tray to put them on, and picked up a knife to cut the cake on the table.

It was taken from her and the Professor cut an enormous slice and began to eat it.

'Are you hungry?'

'For a home made cake? Always—don't you know that the way to a man's heart is through his stomach?'

She spooned tea into the pot. 'Are you staying?' Her voice sounded wooden in her own ears. Why, oh, why did she feel so awkward with him?

'For supper. I flew over; Piet will drive me back to the airfield later. I wanted to see how Nanny was getting on. She's fit again, but I have asked Dr de Groot to come tomorrow and give her a check-up. If he agrees with me, I'll be over in a few days with a nice middle-aged woman who will take over from you. You will be glad to go home, Julia?'

He had eaten the cake so she cut him another slice. 'Oh, yes, although I've been happy here, but Mrs Beckett wants to get back to her normal life. This lady who is coming—does Mrs Beckett know her?'

'Yes. She used to work for my mother. They were good friends and she will stay for as long as Nanny wants her to. I have told her and she's delighted.'

He picked up the tray and Julia followed him, the rest of the cake on a plate. She hoped that he would have time to tell her how Thomas and Ruth were and, more importantly, how she was to get back home. 'Home,' she muttered to herself. 'I haven't got a home...'

There was no talk of the return as they had tea, and it was Mrs Beckett who did most of the talking.

'I have never felt better,' she assured the Professor. 'This dear girl has looked after me as though she were my own daughter—all the delicious food she has cooked for me—I have grown quite plump. She chuckled. 'Julia says she has grown fat, but I tell her that she is just right—I like a woman to have a shape...'

Julia went pink and looked away, but not before the professor had caught her eye. 'You take the words out of my mouth, Nanny.'

Julia found his smile so disquieting that she jumped to her feet, declaring that she must see what there was for supper, and nipped smartly into the cottage. Safe in the kitchen, she shut the door, muttering to herself, and poked her head into the fridge, glad that she had something as prosaic as supper to take her mind off that smile.

She had made watercress soup earlier that day; there would be just enough for the three of them if she served it carefully. She had intended omelettes for the two of them, but now she took lamb chops from the fridge, scrubbed new potatoes, baby carrots and added to the broad beans. These on the Aga, she turned her attention to a pudding. Egg custards with plenty of cream...

That dealt with, she laid the table in the dining room. She and Mrs Beckett ate their meals in the kitchen, but for this evening Julia set the table as Mrs Beckett liked it, with flowers and a starched tablecloth, polished silver and the best glasses. It looked nice when she had finished it and it had been a good excuse to stay in the cottage. She went back to the kitchen, inspected the chops, and the Professor asked from the door. 'Can we talk now, or shall it be after supper?'

'Well, everything will be ready in ten minutes.'

'Ample time. You will want to know how you are to return home; it will take only a few minutes to tell you.'

So much for wanting the pleasure of her company, thought Julia, and clashed the saucepan lids with unnecessary noise.

She said, 'Well?' in an icy voice, and didn't look at him.

'If everything is as I hope it will be, I will come on Saturday—that's three days away. I shall bring with me Miss Thrisp, who has been here before and is already in possession of the facts of Nanny's illness. I want to leave after lunch. I shall have the car and we will go back by ferry.'

'Very well.' She added, 'Thank you.'

'Where will you go?'

'I'm staying with Ruth and Thomas for a while, and then Monica's asked me.'

'And after that?'

When she didn't answer he said carelessly, 'Oh, that isn't any of my business, is it? If supper's ready I'll pour us some sherry. When does Nanny have her glass of red wine?'

'With supper. Piet brought a case of claret; we've had some of that.'

'Good. I'll fetch Nanny in and bring you your sherry.'

Julia gave the potatoes a prod. 'Thank you.'

He came back presently with the sherry and put it on the table. 'You're as cross as two sticks,' he observed cheerfully. 'Was it because I admired your shape?'

Julia, her back to him, tossed back the sherry. 'Certainly not. I hope I'm not so childish…'

'Not childish, Julia, but very much a woman. Give me those dishes; I'll carry them to the table.'

It must be the sherry, decided Julia, making her feel peculiar. And she had every intention of forgetting what the Professor had said, or rather the manner in which he had said it. Had he been poking fun at her? Trying to annoy her? She found that hard to believe; he wasn't that kind of a man.

He left soon after their meal, thanking her pleasantly for his supper. He might annoy her but she had to admit that he had lovely manners. When he had gone she cleared away and settled Mrs Beckett in her chair, then sat and listened to that lady's reminiscences of the van der Maes family and the Professor in particular. 'Always knew what he wanted to do, yet he found the time to backpack round the world, spent his holidays working for them poor starving children in Africa, and a year or so ago he went with a team to Bosnia. Not a word to anyone, mind you.'

Mrs Beckett settled herself more comfortably in her chair. 'You'd never think it to look at him, would you? And he don't lack for social life, either. Could have married half a dozen times, and when I remind him—respectful, of course—that it is time he settled down with a wife and had children, all he says is he hasn't found his dream girl. Although goodness knows it wasn't lack of trying on the part of various young ladies.'

She peered at Julia over her specs. 'I dare say you've wondered about him, Julia?'

A truthful girl, Julia pondered her reply. 'Well, a bit, sometimes. But you see, Mrs Beckett, we don't know each other very well. Circumstances brought us together, but once I've left here I dare say I shan't see him again. You see, I have nothing to do with hospitals, and I don't know anyone he might know.'

'Such a pretty girl. I can't believe that you haven't had a boyfriend.'

'Well, hardly that...' She told her about Oscar then, and Mrs Beckett nodded her head when Julia explained why she had run away from the hotel. 'Quite right too, nasty man. How fortunate that Mr Gerard happened to be there.'

'Yes, he was very kind and helpful. Now, I'm going to get your hot milk and see you to your bed; it's been a busy day.'

'Yes, but a most interesting one,' said Mrs Beckett thoughtfully.

Lying cosily in her bed presently, Mrs Beckett reflected that the pair of them were ideally suited. It was to be hoped that they would discover that for themselves as soon as possible, though it seemed likely that Mr Gerard had already done that...

Ruth phoned in the morning. It would be lovely to have Julia to stay, and she was to make herself at home for as long as she wanted to. Thomas was busy at the hospital, but they could go shopping and there was such a lot of talking to do. 'And then Monica wants you to go and stay with them, so don't hurry to get yourself settled. I'm not sure when you'll arrive exactly, but I'll be home waiting for you.'

Julia should have felt happy and content that her future was arranging itself so pleasantly. First Ruth, then Monica, and then, if she was lucky, the job at the stately home.

'I'm free as air,' said Julia, and wished that she weren't.

Three days had never gone so fast. Julia and Mevrouw Steen got a room ready for Miss Thrisp, and while Mevrouw Steen polished and Hoovered Julia did the flowers, stocked the fridge with the food Piet went to buy for her and then did her own packing. That didn't take long, for she had had no chance to buy anything other than small necessities from the village. She would buy clothes when she got home; the money she had been sent each week was almost untouched. She allowed her mind to dwell on the pleasant prospect of buying the kind of clothes she hankered after. No more curtains, she promised herself. She would gather together an elegant wardrobe. It was a pity that the Professor would never see her in it…

There had been no word from him, but she hadn't expected it. Dr de Groot had seen Mrs Beckett, pronounced himself satisfied, observed that Julia had taken good care of his patient and gone again. Presumably the Professor didn't think it necessary to add to that.

She was up early, anxious to have everything just so before he and Miss Thrisp came; she organised fresh flowers, salad and cold meat in the fridge, strawberries and cream, plus a selection of cheeses; Miss Thrisp might not want to spend time in the kitchen after her journey. Julia had coffee ready too, and some of the little almond biscuits Mrs Beckett had shown her how to bake. As for that lady, Julia had made sure that she looked her best, sitting now in the sitting room, a good breakfast inside her, her hair just so…

Julia went to do her own hair then. There was too much of it, she thought impatiently, tugging it viciously. Perhaps she would have it cut really short. It was the fashion, and it would be nice to be fashionable.

The Rolls stopped without a whisper of sound and the professor got out and opened the car door for Miss Thrisp. Julia, who had conjured up several mental pictures of her, was pleased to see that she was exactly as anyone with a name like that would look, being tall, and thin, with a long face and a long thin nose, very dark eyes and a mouth which would stand no nonsense. But her smile was warm and friendly, and Julia thought that, despite the nose, she was rather nice. Well, she would be, she reflected, ushering the pair of them into the cottage, otherwise the Professor wouldn't have allowed her near Nanny.

And why should I be so sure of that? she wondered.

She left them in the sitting room after their brief introduction and a casual nod from the Professor, and went to the kitchen to fetch the coffee. She dawdled over that to give them time to exchange their first greetings, and presently, when she took the tray in, she found the two ladies sitting side by side, both happily talking their heads off. The Professor had gone to the open window and was looking at his garden.

He turned to face her as she put the tray down.

'We shall leave directly after lunch,' he told her. 'You're ready?'

She wondered what he would say if she said that no, she wasn't; he so clearly expected her to be waiting, case in hand.

She said, 'Yes. At what time do you want lunch?'

'Noon. So that there is ample time for good-byes.'

She said tartly, 'Will you come and sit down for your coffee?' Once everyone had coffee and biscuits, she sat down herself and joined in the ladies' conversation.

Miss Thrisp was shown to her room, then went to the kitchen with Julia to make sure she knew where everything was. Before she went back to the sitting room she put a bony hand on Julia's arm. 'You've taken such good care of Mrs Beckett; I couldn't have done better myself. I'd have come the moment the Professor told me she was needing someone, but I was getting over a nasty attack of flu myself and I was real bothered as to what would happen. But he was right, you're worth your weight in gold—he never makes mistakes about people. You look exactly as he described you.'

It would have been nice to have known just what that was, thought Julia.

Lunch was a cheerful meal, but they didn't linger over it. Julia helped Miss Thrisp clear the table and then, obedient to the Professor's look, fetched her case and made her goodbyes.

Mrs Beckett was inclined to be tearful. 'But of course you'll come again?' she asked hopefully, and Julia mumbled that perhaps she would, if and when she had got settled.

'You must get Mr Gerard to bring you over for a weekend.'

Julia mumbled again, shook Miss Thrisp's bony hand, and got into the car, to turn and wave to the two ladies and the cats as they drove away.

The Professor had had little to say, but he had been pleasant in a remote kind of way and there were several things that she wanted to know.

'Where does the ferry leave from and at what time?'

'The catamaran—it leaves tomorrow around two o'clock, and gets to Harwich in the early evening.'

'Tomorrow? You mean today?'

'I mean tomorrow. We are spending the night in Amsterdam.'

She sat up very straight. 'You may be Professor, but I'm going back today.'

'Why are you making a fuss? A few hours more or less can't make a difference to your plans, but it is a matter of urgency that I stay until tomorrow.'

'I should have been told; I could have made other arrangements. I have no wish to stay in Amsterdam. And where am I to go, pray?'

'To my house, of course. Where else? And don't worry; I shan't be there. Wim and my housekeeper will take care of you.'

'Why won't you be there?' she asked sharply.

'I shall be at the hospital, operating early this evening, and I shall be there all night until I judge my patient to be in a stable condition. I hope that satisfies you?'

She felt mean. 'I'm sorry I snapped, but if you'd told me that when I first asked I wouldn't have said anything more about it.'

He didn't answer, and she added cautiously, 'Won't you be too tired to travel tomorrow?'

His 'no' discouraged her from saying another word.

But presently she asked, 'Why do we quarrel?'

'I never quarrel, and nor, I think, do you. We strike sparks off each other, Julia.' He turned his head briefly and smiled at her, 'And that's as good a beginning as any.'

She was about to ask him what he meant, but then thought better of it, and they stayed silent as they neared Amsterdam, but it was a friendly silence.

The quiet street by the canal seemed remote from the bustling streets of the city, the old houses silent under the trees which bordered it.

It's like coming home, reflected Julia as Wim opened the door to them and greeted her as though he had known her all his life.

The Professor spoke to him quietly and he nodded and went away, to return with a solidly built elderly woman who listened to what the

Professor had to say, smiled at Julia and beckoned her to follow.

'This is Getske, my housekeeper,' the professor said. 'Go with her; she will show you to your room. We have time for tea before I have to go.'

Julia followed the housekeeper along the hall and up the staircase at its end. It opened onto a circular gallery with passages leading off it and any number of doors. Getske opened a door and stood aside for her to go into the room beyond. It wasn't a large room but was instantly welcoming, with its canopied bed, the dressing table to one side, a small upholstered chair with a table beside it under the long window and a soft carpet underfoot. Through a door in the far wall there was a bathroom, and leading from it a wardrobe fit to house more clothes than Julia would ever buy.

Alone, she prowled round, picking things up and putting them down again. Then, remembering that the Professor might want to leave, she tidied her person, stuck a few more pins in her hair, dabbed powder on her nose and went back downstairs.

He was waiting with well-concealed impatience in a little room leading from the hall. Really, the house was a rabbit warren, she thought, but a very luxurious one and very much to her taste.

Tea had been laid out on a small table between two chairs. The Professor got up from one as she went in and Jason pranced to meet her.

'He will keep you company this evening.' The professor drew up a chair for her. 'Will you be Mother?'

She sat down and picked up the silver teapot. She would miss this elegance, she reflected. It was something she had become accustomed to during the last few weeks. The thought saddened her.

The Professor had his tea, ate a slice of cake and got up to go.

'I'll see you tomorrow morning,' he told her. 'Wim will take you round the house if you would like that—ask for anything you want.'

He was standing in front of her, looking down at her upturned face.

'Oh, I should like that; it's a lovely old house.' She smiled at him, and he bent down and kissed her. It was a gentle kiss, so why did it arouse such strong feelings in her person? She wondered, watching the door close behind his vast back.

Wim's English was as sparse as her Dutch, but they contrived to understand each other well enough. He had been with the Professor's family, he told her, for fifty years or more, and they and the house were his life. With Jason at their heels, they went from room to room, taking their time, while he pointed out the plasterwork ceilings, the heavy brocade curtains at the tall windows, the bow-fronted display cabinets filled with porcelain and silver, the exquisite marquetry on a long-case clock. Julia looked at it all with delight, wishing that the Professor was there too, so that she could tell him what a splendid home he had.

The house was surprisingly large, with rooms opening from one to another until the final one opened onto a long narrow garden. Tomorrow, she promised herself, she would explore the garden early in the morning, before the professor got home.

Wim took her upstairs then, waiting patiently while she poked her nose round each door on each landing, until they reached the final narrow staircase to the attic. When Wim smiled and nodded she took a look, then climbed up to the small door and opened it. The attic was long and narrow, with small windows at each end and a steeply sloping roof. It wasn't empty, containing odds and ends of furniture, rolled up rugs, a row of ice skates hanging from hooks on the wall and a baby's cradle. In one corner there was a stack of framed pictures and old photographs. She bent to look and picked up the top one. A boy, a quite small boy. She didn't need to read the date and name on it. She put it down again, feeling as though she had pried into the Professor's private life. He was smiling in the photo and his smile hadn't changed…

She had dinner in the same small room where they had had tea: watercress soup, duckling in an orange sauce and *pofferjes* light as air and smothered with cream. There was a light white wine, and coffee to follow, and a beaming Wim to serve her.

It was a reward for looking after Mrs Beckett, she supposed; he had paid her wages, but he could hardly tip her...

She offered a morsel of the little sugary biscuit which had come with the coffee to Jason and allowed herself to daydream. But presently she sat up. She had allowed her thoughts to run away with her just because the professor had kissed her.

'I shall go to bed,' she told Jason, and did so.

She was awake after a dreamless sleep when a stolid young girl brought her tea. She showered and dressed and went down to the hall and found Wim. Breakfast would be in half an hour he told her; the Professor wasn't home.

So she went into the garden and walked with Jason up and down its narrow paths in the morning sun. It was full of old-fashioned flowers, with a circular rose bed and flowering shrubs against the brick wall at its end. She could have stayed there, sitting on the rustic seat, surrounded by honeysuckle and wisteria, but breakfast waited.

The Professor was standing by the window of the room leading to the garden. His good morning was pleasantly friendly, his enquiry as to whether she had had a good night uttered in the tones of a thoughtful host. He was immaculately dressed and one would have supposed that he had enjoyed a good night's sleep too, but Julia saw the tired lines in his face.

'Have you had any sleep?'

'Enough,' he told her, and smiled so that she remembered the little boy in the photo.

I must forget that, she told herself, and went with him to eat her breakfast. They ate in silence for a time until she asked, 'Was it successful? The operation? Or would you rather not talk about it?'

He didn't answer at once, and she said quickly, 'All right, you don't have to tell me. I'm not being curious, you know.'

He loaded butter onto toast. 'It was entirely successful. And I don't mind you asking, Julia.' He stared at her across the table. 'I think that I would have been disappointed if you had not done so.' He passed his coffee cup. 'A mutual interest is to be desired.'

'Oh, is it?' said Julia, bewildered. She had a feeling that things were moving too fast for her to understand, but she was aware of a pleasant excitement. And they had the rest of the day together.

# CHAPTER SIX

JULIA'S pleasant speculations about the morning were quickly cut short.

'We shall need to leave here after an early lunch,' said the Professor. 'I shall go back to the hospital presently, and I'll take Jason with me and give him a run. Perhaps you want to explore or go to the shops? I would be easier in my mind if you stayed here…'

She said brightly, 'I shall sit in the garden. I can do all the shopping I want when I get home.'

So he went away with Jason and she went into the garden again and sat down with the newspapers Wim had handed to her. She could so easily have gone with him, she thought; perhaps waited in the car while he was at the hospital, and then gone with him and Jason. He was deliberately avoiding her…

'I couldn't care less!' said Julia, and picked up the *Daily Telegraph* and read it from front to back page. She was none the wiser when she had. She tried the *Haagsche Post* next—she might as well improve her Dutch while she could—although it was a complete waste of time. She was puzzling out the small ads when the Professor joined her.

He said affably, 'Oh, splendid, you're improving your Dutch.'

'I have very little Dutch to improve,' said Julia coldly. 'I hope your patient is improving.'

He sat down beside her with Jason squeezed between them.

'Yes, I think he has a very good chance. I've left him in good hands.'

'Was he someone important?' She turned to look at him. 'Did they send for you specially?'

'Yes, and yes. Will you be sorry to leave Holland?'

'Oh, yes, although I've not seen anything of it. I'm sorry to leave the cottage and this splendid house, but they'll be lovely memories.'

'You would like to come back some time?'

'Perhaps.' She put an arm round Jason's woolly shoulders and he licked her hand gently. 'Jason is going to miss you.'

'Yes, and I shall miss him, but I shall be here again very shortly and he is used to my coming and going.'

He glanced at his watch. 'We had better have our lunch.'

The day which had seemed to stretch before her for hours of delight had telescoped into an all too short day. The professor might not like her, but that couldn't prevent her from enjoying his company. She supposed that she didn't like him either, but she was no longer quite sure about that. Of course, there was still the journey back to London...

Which was disappointing, in so far that the Professor, while thoughtful for her well-being, made only the most casual conversation, giving her no opportunity to get to know him better. On board, he excused himself smiling and began to study a case full of papers—first, however, making sure that she had something to read and a tray of tea.

She leafed through the magazines and wondered what he was thinking about.

She would have been astonished to know it was herself. Usually so sure of himself, the Professor found himself uncertain. That he had fallen in love with Julia and wanted her for his wife he now freely admitted, but she had shown no preference for his company; he thought that she liked him a good deal more than she was prepared to admit, but he wasn't prepared to rush her. Once back in London, he would have the opportunity to see her frequently. In the meantime, it was only by maintaining a casual disinterested manner that he was able to keep his hands off her...

They discussed the weather, the countryside and the state of the roads as he drove back to London. All safe subjects which lasted them nicely until he drew up before Thomas's and Ruth's new home.

They were warmly welcomed but the Professor didn't stay. He had a brief smiling chat with Ruth, observed that he would see Thomas at the hospital in the morning, and got back into the Rolls, brushing aside Julia's careful little speech of thanks.

He couldn't have been pleasanter, she thought, or more remote.

Mrs Potts, his housekeeper, and the two dogs were waiting for him. His housekeeper was middle-aged, brisk and devoted to him, and as for Wilf and Robbie, their welcome was estatic.

He took the car round to the mews at the back of the house, promised to be back for his dinner and took the little dogs for a run. The streets were quiet; London on a summer's evening could be delightful. He thought about the cottage—he would have to ring Nanny when he got back—and he wondered if Julia was thinking of it too. She had loved the house in Amsterdam; she would fit so easily into his life…

Despite his casual goodbye, Julia had expected to see him again while she was staying with

Ruth, but, beyond saying that he was working too hard, Thomas had nothing to say about him. Ruth wondered from time to time why he hadn't come to see them or at least phoned, but Julia's monosyllabic replies led her to a rather thoughtful silence. Julia looked splendid: full of fresh air, nicely tanned, apparently well pleased with life—and yet there was something wrong…

Ruth entered into the plans Julia had for an entire new wardrobe, and when she wasn't there phoned Monica. 'She looks marvellous, but there is something wrong. Do you suppose she met someone in Holland? She's coming to stay with you—try and find out.'

Getting ready for bed, Ruth asked Thomas, 'Has Gerard said anything about Julia?'

'Only that she has been a splendid help with Mrs Beckett. He's off to Glasgow tomorrow. He'll be gone for a couple of days.' Thomas gave her a sharp look. 'Why did you ask?'

'Oh, nothing, darling. They don't get on, do they?'

Thomas got into bed. 'Don't they? It isn't something I'd ask him—or Julia, for that matter.'

There were still ten days before her interview for the job. Beyond telling Ruth vaguely that she had heard of something, Julia had said nothing; instead she and Ruth went shopping.

With money in her purse Julia ignored the High Street chain stores and poked around boutiques, and, egged on by her sister, spent a good deal more than she had intended to. But the results were worth it; she bought well-cut jersey dresses, elegant tops and skirts, dresses for summer and a silk dress suitable for the evening. She thought that she might never wear it, that it would probably hang in the cupboard forgotten and regretted, but there was always the chance that she might need it—supposing the Professor should ask her to dine with him one evening?

It was highly unlikely—and even if he asked her she might refuse...

There were undies to buy too, shoes, a raincoat, a short jacket, a sensible outfit to wear if she got that job...

Afterwards she went to stay with Monica and George. She had a long weekend in which to explore their home and the village and listen to George preaching a splendid sermon. He had a good congregation too, said Monica proudly and she herself ran the Mothers' Union and Sunday School. Village life suited her, and now there was money to see to the plumbing and refurbish the vicarage. There was so much to see and talk about that no one noticed that Julia had almost nothing to say about her stay in Holland once she had given a brief account of it—and an even briefer reference to the professor.

Back with Ruth, she dressed in one of the jersey dresses and, for once very neat about the head, went to her appointment. It was to be held in one of the smaller hotels and, urged by the porter to take the first door on the left of the foyer, Julia did so. There were five or six other women there, all armed as she was with specimens of their handiwork. They paused in their talk to stare at her, answer her good morning with nods and then resume their chatting. There was one older woman who had smiled at her, but others were young, smartly dressed and discreetly made up. Julia decided that she had very little chance against their self-assurance. Probably they had all been to a needlework school and had diplomas and marvellous references.

They were called in, one after the other, and came out looking pleased with themselves. The older woman went in, looking anxious, and when she came out she said nothing, only smiled again as Julia opened the door in her turn.

There were three women sitting behind a table. They greeted her pleasantly, told her to sit down, and the one in the middle, middle-aged and looking how one would imagine a strict schoolteacher would look, asked her why she wanted the job.

This was unexpected; there was no time to prepare a speech. Julia said, 'I want to get away from London,' and then wished that she hadn't said it, so she added, 'And I like needlework and sewing and making things out of things.'

The three women looked at each other. 'Will you show us your work?'

So she unwrapped the tapestry, its pattern picked out with the silks Mrs Beckett had given her, and spread it out on the table and sat down again. It was passed from one hand to the other, looked at through magnifying glasses and held up to the light. She was asked which stitches she had used and why she had chosen to embroider the tapestry.

'I hadn't anything else. I was in the country with no shops for miles. So I used what I found in the attic.'

'You understand that this is temporary employment? A week's notice on either side. Tedious work, repairing very old curtains. Quite long hours and the remuneration is small. Bed and board is free, of course. We are prepared to employ you on those terms.'

Julia didn't give herself time to think. She said, 'Thank you; I should like the job.'

'It will be confirmed by letter and you will be given directions as to how to reach the estate. You will need to go to Carlisle and then to Haltwhistle, where you will be met. Are you free to travel within the next day or so?'

'Yes, I can be ready in two days' time.'

Back in the waiting room, she found the older woman still there.

She said hesitantly, 'I waited. I thought they might take you. I've got a job there.'

'You have? I'm glad—so have I. Perhaps we could travel up together. Do you know that part of the world?'

'I was born near the estate. I came to London with my husband. He died and I wanted to go back home.'

'I'm sorry about your husband. I just wanted to get away from London.'

They were standing on the pavement outside the hotel 'Do you have a phone number? Perhaps we could meet at the station?'

The woman nodded. 'My name's Woodstock—Jenny. It would be nice to travel together.'

*     *     *

It wasn't difficult to convince Ruth that the job was something which was exactly what she had hoped for. 'And,' she pointed out, 'it isn't a permanent one; I expect that once the repairs are made we shan't be needed. And while I'm there I can decide where I want to live and what I want to do.'

Ruth said, 'Yes, dear,' in an uncertain way. Something was wrong. Perhaps Julia *had* met someone in Holland? She was about to ask when Julia said casually, 'Ruth, don't let the Professor know where I am. Don't look like that. It's just that he has this way of turning up with some offer of a job or something…'

It sounded pretty feeble but Ruth, thinking her own thoughts, said at once, 'I won't say a word. It sounds rather fun, this job. It's a long way away, of course, but probably it will be a lovely old house full of treasures and you'll meet lots of people.'

The day before she was due to leave the Professor came. Ruth had gone to the hairdresser and Julia was in the kitchen getting lunch when he knocked on the door. She had opened it expecting the postman, and the sight of the Professor standing there, smiling a little, did things to her breath. She had wanted to see him just once more, for after she had gone from London she had every intention of forgetting him. On the other hand she would have liked to have gone away before he found out that she was no longer at Ruth's.

She said now, 'Oh, hello. Did you want Ruth? She's out...'

'I came to see you.'

There was nothing for it but to ask him in. 'I'm getting lunch,' she told him, and led the way to the kitchen. It would be easier to calm down if she had something to do. And why should she need to calm down? she wondered.

'You're glad to be back?' he asked.

She whisked eggs in a bowl and didn't look at him. 'Yes, yes, I am.'

'Will you have dinner with me tomorrow evening, Julia?'

It was so unexpected that she put the bowl of eggs down with something of a thump on the table. 'Tomorrow? No—no, thank you.'

She looked at him then, wishing with her whole heart that she wasn't going miles away, knowing suddenly that she loved him and that the thought of not seeing him again was unbearable.

She said carefully, 'I'm sorry, I can't...I wasn't going to tell you—I'm going away—tomorrow morning.'

Something in his quiet face made her add, 'I've got a most interesting job. I want to get away from London...'

'You were not going to tell me?' His voice was as quiet as his face.

'No—no, I wasn't.' She had spoken too loudly, and now added recklessly, 'Why should I?'

'Indeed, why should you?' He smiled gently. 'I hope that you will be very happy.'

'Of course I shall be happy,' said Julia in a cross voice, wishing that he would go so that she might burst into tears in peace.

Which was exactly what he did do, blandly wishing her goodbye, telling her cheerfully that he would see himself out.

She wept into the eggs then, and, since she couldn't see to do anything for a moment, sat down and buried her face in Muffin's furry body. Muffin, who loved her in his own cat fashion, bore with the damp fur and Julia's incoherent mutterings, but it was a relief when she settled him back in his chair. Feline instinct warned him that she was unhappy, that she was probably going away. But she would be back, and in the meantime he was quite comfortable with Ruth. He settled down for a nap and Julia went and washed her face, and then went back to the eggs.

Ruth, back home again, took a quick look at Julia. 'You don't have to go, dear. You know you can stay here as long as you like, and if you want to get away from London, Monica would love to have you.'

She went to the fridge and poured two glasses of white wine. 'Is that a soufflé? It looks delicious…'

Presently Julia said, 'The Professor came. I told him I was going away but he doesn't know where I'm going. Don't tell him, Ruth.'

'Of course not, love.' Ruth was brisk. 'Did he want to know?'

'No,' said Julia bleakly. She added, 'He didn't even say goodbye.'

Ruth forebore from pointing out that he was a man who never said anything he didn't mean. She began to talk instead about the morrow's journey.

Jenny Woodstock was at the station in the morning, mildly excited and happy at the thought of going back to her home. She talked in her quiet way about it during their journey and Julia was thankful for that, for it kept her own thoughts at bay. And she was glad to have someone with her who knew her way about once they reached Carlisle and, finally, Haltwhistle.

Even then their journey wasn't over. There was a middle-aged man, stocky, with a Land Rover waiting for them, and they drove for what seemed like hours through the wide countryside until he turned into a wide gateway and onto a long drive. They could see their destination now, an imposing mansion with a few trees around it. Even on a summer's day it looked bleak, but as they neared it Julia could see that it was lived in and that there were cars parked to one side of the house and people going in and out of the great entrance.

Mrs Woodstock enlightened her. 'They're open to the public twice a week.'

And the driver said over his shoulder, 'I'll drive you round to one of the side doors. The housekeeper will settle you in.'

A surly man, thought Julia. She hoped that the housekeeper would be more friendly.

Her hopes were realised. Mrs Bates was large and stout, with twinkling eyes and a wide smile. She offered tea and then led them out of the house and across a wide courtyard. 'Most of the sewing ladies come from the village,' she explained. 'I've put you here, Mrs Woodstock.' She opened a door in one of the outbuildings. 'It's a nice little room and there's a bathroom and a gas ring and so on, so's you can be cosy.' She looked at Julia. 'If you'll wait here, Miss…'

She was back in a few minutes. 'You're over here, up these steps.' She observed, 'The place is used for storage but you won't be disturbed.'

She surged up the steps and unlocked the door at the top, and Julia followed her. The room was quite large, with a low ceiling and a wide window. It was comfortably furnished—a divan bed, a table and two chairs, an easy chair and bookshelves. There was another door leading to a shower room and an alcove with a gas ring and cupboards.

'You'll eat over in the house but I'll see you have tea and milk so that you can have a drink in your own room. You'll be wanted in half an hour or so. Will you come back to me and I'll take you?'

Left alone, Julia took another look around her; it was nice to have a room of her own, away from the house, and once she had unpacked and put her small possessions round the place it would look more like home. She tidied herself and then went in search of Jenny.

Jenny was delighted. 'It's like a hotel,' she observed happily, 'and I'm only a few miles from where I was born.'

They followed the housekeeper through endless corridors until they reached a small staircase tucked away in a narrow passage. They climbed to the second floor before they were finally ushered into a vast attic with overhead lighting and a row of windows overlooking the front of the house. The severe woman who had interviewed them was waiting and they spent the next hour or so being led along the long tables where the repair work was being done. A cup of tea would have been nice, reflected Julia, being shown the wall tapestry she would be working on.

There wasn't much of the afternoon left. The half-dozen women around her began to pack up presently, and thankfully she and Jenny were shown the way to a room on the ground floor where tea was waiting. It was more than tea; there were eggs and ham, several kinds of bread, butter, pots of jam, a splendid cake and a great pot of tea. Julia, eating with a splendid appetite, wondered if this was the last meal of the day, for it was almost six o'clock.

As they got up from the table one of the women said in a friendly voice, 'You're new, aren't you? There's sandwiches and hot drinks about eight o'clock. Some of us live in the village but two of us live here in the house.'

It was going to be all right, Julia decided, going sleepily to her bed later that evening. Everyone was friendly, she had a pleasant room, good, wholesome food and she would be working at something she enjoyed doing. Nevertheless she cried herself to sleep, and her last thoughts were of Gerard. He would forget her, of course. Probably by the time she got back to London he would have gone back to Holland and got married into the bargain.

The Professor went about his work in his usual calm manner. For the moment there was nothing to be done; first he had to find out where Julia had gone. It was some days before he saw Ruth and enquired casually as to whether she had heard from Julia. And Ruth blushed because she was longing to tell him where Julia was, but a promise was a promise…

'She's very happy…'

'Splendid. What kind of a job is it?'

There would be no harm in telling him that. 'Repairing old tapestries.'

'And where is she?'

Ruth blushed again. 'She asked me not to tell you and I promised.'

'Then I won't bother you. I hope she will settle down and enjoy life. How fortunate that she heard of something so soon after coming back.'

'Oh, it wasn't sudden; she told me she'd applied for the job while she was still in Holland with Mrs Beckett—she saw it advertised in a magazine.'

Now he had one or two clues. He said casually, 'And how are Monica and George getting on? Will you be visiting them now that you're nicely settled in here?'

So Ruth told him all about the new bathrooms and the central heating in the vicarage, pleased that she had given nothing away about Julia.

It was the following day before the Professor had the leisure to phone Mrs Beckett. He listened patiently to her detailed account of her progress and when she paused for breath he asked, 'Nanny, which magazines do you read?'

'Now there's a funny question,' observed Mrs Beckett. 'English ones, of course, they get sent each week.' She named them and added, 'Why do you want to know, Mr Gerard?'

'Do any of them advertise jobs?'

'Not all of them. The *Lady* does—pages and pages of them.'

'Nanny, have you heard from Julia?'

Mrs Beckett looked out of the window and smiled. 'Well, yes, bless the dear child. Sent me a long letter but forgot the address. Got a lovely job, she says, embroidering and such-like. The post mark was Carlisle. Seems a long way from home, but I dare say she was visiting friends.'

His 'Probably' was non-committal, and she put down the phone with another smile. The path of true love never did run smooth, she informed a rather surprised Miss Thrisp.

True enough. But that wasn't going to deter the Professor from his own particular path. His secretary was bidden to obtain back copies of the *Lady* and he searched the advertisements until he found what he sought…

Life was very different for Julia now. The work was interesting and she enjoyed it; the other women were friendly and they were well looked after. There was a vast park to walk in when she had finished work in the evening, and an estate Land Rover took the staff to the village or Haltwhistle when they were free. All the same, she was lonely. It was a splendid job, she told herself. The country around was vast and lonely and very much to her liking, and although she didn't regret leaving London it was impossible to forget Gerard. She consoled herself with the thought that he would have forgotten her by now, but that couldn't stop her loving him.

She took to getting up early and walking in the park before breakfast. It was peaceful there: birds singing, distant sounds coming from the Home Farm, subdued noise from the great house waking to another day. It was such a vast place that she had only seen a little of it, and nothing of its owners.

She had been there for almost two weeks when a particularly splendid morning got her out of bed earlier than usual. She showered and dressed and drank her early-morning tea and let herself out of her room. There was no one about and she crossed the courtyard and went into the parkland beyond. Part of it was wooded, and there was a lake which dribbled into a small stream, and on such a morning it was a delight to the eye.

She wandered along and presently sat down on a tree stump, allowing her thoughts to wander too. She supposed that sooner or later she would go back to London, find herself a small flat and put her talents to good use. At least she would have a reference, and there were museums and art galleries and private houses who would employ her. And, although she might never see the Professor, she would be near him...

A cheerful 'Good morning' got her to her feet. A man was coming towards her, a young man with a pleasant rugged face. There were two dogs with him who crowded round her, tails wagging.

'You'll be one of the needlewomen,' said the man cheerfully. 'I heard Mother saying that there were one or two new ladies.' He held out a hand. 'Menton—Colin Menton.'

Julia smiled at him, warmed by his friendliness. 'Gracey,' she said in her turn. 'Julia. How do you do?'

They shook hands and he asked, 'Where are you from?'

'London.'

'You're a long way from home. Do you like it here? It is really rather different.'

'I didn't live in a very nice part of London; this seems like heaven.'

'It is.' They were strolling back towards the house. 'But it's not to everyone's taste—too quiet.'

'That's why it's heaven.' They had reached the courtyard. 'I must go.'

'Nice meeting you. Perhaps we shall see each other again. Do you go walking each morning?'

'Well, yes.'

'Then we'll meet again.'

She thought about him while she stitched patiently. It had been pleasant to talk to someone of her own age; the other needlewomen were really friendly, and she got on well with them, but they were twice her age and Jenny went to her home when she was free. Julia explored when she was free. Haltwhistle was near enough for her half-day expeditions. It was a small market town with a fine church, and she sent picture postcards to Ruth and Monica, quite forgetting that they might be shown to the Professor.

One day she got a lift to the small village of Greenhead. The road running through it was close to the Roman Wall and she walked for miles until she found a side road which took her back to Haltwhistle and eventually back to the estate. It was a long walk and she enjoyed every minute of it. She didn't feel lonely in the country and she had her thoughts of Gerard to keep her company.

She had done the right thing, she told herself; she had no intention of mooning after a man who hardly noticed her. Once or twice she had thought they could have been friends, but that had been a flash in the pan. And anyway there was always the possibility that Gerard would have gone back to Holland.

The thought of never seeing him again was unbearable, but she would have to learn to bear it and it would surely be easier as time passed. There was always the chance that they might meet... She would stay at the estate for as long as there was work for her, and then she would have to decide her future and what better place in which to do it than this remote countryside?

She wrote cheerful letters to Ruth and Monica, though both of them were mystified as to why she shouldn't want anyone to know where she was. But since she seemed so happy and content with the job, and they were both fully occupied with their own lives, they didn't pursue the matter further. Perhaps if the Professor had mentioned her on one of his infrequent visits they might have given it more thought…

A few days later Julia met Colin Menton again. The day's work was finished and she was crossing the courtyard to go to her room. It was late afternoon and still warm. She would go for a walk before supper and then write letters.

He met her halfway. 'Hello, finished work for the day? I don't suppose you feel like a walk? I'm going to the other end of the park to see if the trees we planted are doing well.' He smiled at her. 'Do say yes.'

Julia laughed. 'Well, all right, yes.'

The park was vast, merging now and again into fields of rough grass. Close to the house the gardens had been skilfully laid out, and there was a lake bordered by trees, but presently they followed a path into the trees on the edge of the park. It was pleasant walking and they found plenty to talk about. He begged her to call him Colin and told her that he'd been spending a month or two at his home before taking up a post abroad as an agricultural adviser. 'I shall be getting married before we go,' he confided.

Julia sensed a wish to talk about his fiancée. 'Is she pretty?' she asked.

The rest of their walk was taken up with a detailed description of his fiancée's perfections, and as they neared the house again he said awkwardly, 'Have I been boring you? Only I do like to talk about her.'

'Well, of course you do. She sounds a perfect dear, as well as being so pretty. I'm sure you'll both be very happy. How much longer will you be here?'

'Ten days. We're being married from her home in Wiltshire. We didn't want a big wedding, but you know what mothers are.'

They were standing in the courtyard. 'I enjoyed our walk. I suppose you wouldn't like

to drive over to Hexham? I have to see someone there but it shouldn't take too long. There
is a splendid abbey there that you might like
to visit if you're interested.'

'I should like that. I get two half-days in the
week—Tuesday and Thursday, both in the
morning.'

'Next Tuesday? It's no distance—fifteen
miles or so. If we left around nine o'clock we
could have coffee before I see this fellow. You
can look round and visit the abbey and I'll
meet you for lunch.'

'I have to be back at work by two o'clock.'

'Easily done. We can lunch early.'

Julia agreed; the prospect of an outing was
inviting and there might be time to do some
shopping.

Jenny, working beside her on the worn tapestry they were patiently repairing, gave her a
quick glance as they started to stitch.

'How are you getting on?' she wanted to
know. 'This is a grand job. If we ever get our
time off together you must come home with
me. You've no idea how marvellous it is to be

back with the family. You look perky. Have you made any friends?'

Julia nodded. 'And I walk miles—I love walking and the country is beautiful. I met Mr Menton one morning. He's offered me a lift to Hexham—I'd like to see the abbey and do some shopping.'

'Young Mr Menton? He's nice—getting married soon, did you know?'

'Yes, he told me about his fiancée and the job he's going to. He's leaving very shortly. Will the family go to the wedding? What happens here if they do? Will we still be open to the public?'

'I shouldn't think so. We'll be told, I suppose.' Jenny gave Julia an enquiring look. 'It's likely that there will be enough work for us until early next year. There are the curtains in the drawing room to mend and that wall tapestry in the hall. It'll be cold here after London. Will you stay?'

'Why not? Unless I have a good reason to go back to London. I have two married sisters;

they might have babies or need me for something or other.'

She spoke cheerfully but, much though she liked her surroundings, the prospect of being there for almost another six months was daunting. After all she had money now, enough to get a mortgage on a small flat—not necessarily in London—and find work. She choked back dismay at the prospect. She was letting herself drift; she who had never been faint-hearted in her life before.

That evening she borrowed an atlas. She mustn't be too far away from Ruth and Monica, but far away enough from London and Gerard. She made a list of likely towns and went to bed feeling that she had at last begun to organise her future.

And on Tuesday afternoon, bending over her stitching, she went over the trip to Hexham. It had been a success. She and Colin had fallen into an easy friendship and there had never been a lack of something to talk about during the short drive. They had had coffee before parting, and she had spent a happy morning looking round the abbey and then looking at the shops, buying some books and other small items on a list she had made. They had met at a pleasant old pub and had an early lunch before driving back. It had been a pleasant morning and she would miss his cheerful face and casual friendliness. He was leaving on Thursday, and she had said that she would say goodbye to him before she set off on a walk before starting work that afternoon.

He was to leave early, but she had breakfast before she went out to the yard. He had already said goodbye to his family and his car, an Aston Martin, was there, with him in the driving seat.

Julia lent over to shake his hand. 'Go carefully, and have a lovely wedding.'

'Oh, we will. I'm glad we met, Julia. I hope you will have a lovely wedding to some lucky chap one day.' He kissed her cheek just as the Professor drove the Rolls into the yard.

# CHAPTER SEVEN

JULIA straightened up with a laugh—and saw the Professor's car. The wild rush of delight at the sight of him turned at once to a mixture of panic and bad temper. Panic because he might have bad news of her sisters, and temper because she was wearing an old skirt and a cotton top, suitable for a walk in the country but not for meeting him of all people.

She waved in answer to Colin's wave, and watched the Professor get out of his car and come towards her. She would have liked to have run to meet him, but something in his leisurely approach stopped her. Yet when he reached her his, 'Hello, Julia,' was uttered in the mildest of voices.

She asked breathlessly, 'How did you know I was here?' She frowned. 'I asked Ruth…'

'Who told me nothing. But rest assured that I am quite capable of finding you if I wish to do so.'

'So why did you?'

'There would be no point in telling you that at the moment. I'm glad to see that you have found friends. Or should I say a friend.' His voice was silky.

'Colin?' She wanted to shake his calm. 'Oh, yes, we've had some pleasant walks. He is the son of the house.' She added, without much truth, 'We've seen quite a lot of the surrounding country—Hadrian's Wall...'

When he didn't speak she asked uneasily, 'Do you have friends in this part of the world?'

'Colleagues at the hospital in Carlisle.'

'Oh, you're doing something there?'

He didn't answer, only asked, 'When do you work?'

'From nine in the morning until five o'clock. We get breaks for meals and two half-days.' She added defiantly, 'I'm loving it.'

'And is this a half-day?'

She said Yes so reluctantly that he smiled.

'Then perhaps you will spend it with me? We could drive to Hadrian's Wall and have a walk and an early lunch. When must you start work?'

'Two o'clock.'

'An hour or two in the fresh air and a brisk walk will do you good.'

'I go walking each morning...'

He said smoothly, 'Ah, yes, but now that you will be walking alone it is never as inviting, is it? Go and do something to your hair. I'll wait here. Ten minutes?'

'I haven't said I would come...'

He smiled and her heart turned over. 'But you will!'

She went to her room then and got into a cotton jersey dress, and did her hair again and made up her face nicely, all the while telling herself that she was mad to be doing it. On the other hand, he would soon be gone again, back to London. Surely an hour or so in his company wouldn't make any difference to her resolve not to see him again. She wondered briefly how he had discovered where she was... She didn't waste time thinking about it; half-days were precious, and every minute of them had to be enjoyed. She hurried back to the yard and found the Professor leaning against his car, talking to Jenny, on her way to start her morning's work.

'Lucky you,' she called cheerfully. 'Don't forget the time, though in your shoes I would.'

Julia tried not to see the wink which accompanied the remark.

The Professor stowed her into the Rolls and drove away, embarking at the same time on a casual conversation which put her instantly at ease. She reflected that this unexpected meeting should have bothered her, but it hadn't. It seemed the most natural thing in the world that Gerard should have appeared out of the blue, as it were, and that they should be spending the morning together as if they were old friends. But, of course, it wasn't that at all; he had felt the need of company and had an hour or so to spare.

The Professor glanced at her puzzled face and smiled to himself. Just for once Julia had lost her tongue.

He took her to Brampton, not many miles away, gave her coffee at the hotel there, parked the car, booked a table for lunch and marched her off briskly. Hadrian's Wall was no distance, and when they reached it they walked beside it. It was quiet and the countryside was empty; the road was nearby but there was little traffic, and it was cool enough to make walking a pleasure. And they talked.

It was surprising how easy it was to talk to him, thought Julia, discussing her future, her doubts and problems until at a certain moment she stopped abruptly. She was a fool, telling him all this; he wouldn't be in the least interested. He might even be bored.

'Do you know this part of the world?' she wanted to know.

'Not well enough.' He had seen her sudden reluctance to talk about herself and so slipped easily into a casual discussion of the country around them. Presently she was lulled into the idea that he hadn't been listening, had shown no sign of interest. She had been a fool, telling him of her plans when she had made up her mind not to see him again. She supposed that being in love made one foolish...

Back at the hotel they had lunch in a delightful restaurant, its windows overlooking a well-kept garden. The place was half full and the service friendly. Julia, hungry after their walk, made a splendid meal. The food was well cooked and plentiful on the estate, but the food set before her now was something of a treat: game soup, a meal in itself, roast beef with Yorkshire pudding to dream of, roasted parsnips, crisp and golden brown, and a crème brulée which melted in the mouth.

'I'm not going to offer you wine,' said the Professor, 'or you'll droop over your curtains!' So they drank tonic water.

He drove her back afterwards, making casual small talk, and back in the court yard, when she would have uttered her carefully rehearsed thank-you speech, he said abruptly, 'I'm glad you enjoyed the morning. You must get Colin to take you again while the weather is good.'

Julia could think of nothing to say but, 'Yes', and watched him drive away while all she wanted to say crowded her tongue unuttered. Perhaps it was just as well, she thought unhappily. For a short time she had thought that perhaps he had sought her out because he had wanted to see her again, but that wasn't so; he had had a morning to spare and had used it to make sure that she was all right so that he could tell Ruth. It was a lowering thought…

The Professor drove himself back to London deep in thought. Julia had been glad to see him, he had seen the look on her face, but had the delight been at the sight of him or because he was someone from home? And this man, this young man, reflected Gerard, deeply aware that at thirty-six he could no longer be considered young. Though a man of no conceit, he was aware that he could make her fall in love with him—but he had no intention of doing that; she must learn to love him of her own free will. That they were meant for each other was something he never doubted.

He didn't think that she was happy; she liked her work and the surroundings in which she lived but she was sad about something. There was nothing he could do for the moment only have patience.

He phoned Ruth when he got back and gave her a reassuring account of Julia.

'I suppose he went to the Carlisle hospital,' she told Thomas, 'and discovered where she was.'

And Thomas, who knew better, agreed with her.

A week or two went by. The weather was unusually warm and dry, even in the north of the country, and sitting for long hours stitching was tiring. Julia, taking her solitary early morning walks, made plans for the future and then discarded them. There was a rumour that once the tapestry they were working on was finished they would be asked to work at the town-house the family owned in London. The local women wouldn't go, but Jenny and she might be offered work there. That wouldn't do.

Forgetting Gerard was harder than she had thought it would be. And how could she forget him when she loved him? The only thing to do was to go away, as far as possible...

She wrote cheerful letters to Ruth and Monica and scanned their replies for a mention of the Professor, but it was as though he had never existed. ✎

It was some time after four o'clock in the afternoon when the fire broke out. A sightseer, disregarding the 'No Smoking' notices, had lighted a cigarette and tossed the still burning match to one side. It had fallen onto the curtains shrouding the state dining room windows. Dry as dust, and fragile with age, they had smouldered unnoticed for some minutes and then suddenly burst into flames which had swept across the room and into an adjoining salon. From there it leapt from wall-panelling to tapestries, to chairs and tables, through the wide archway and into the music room beyond...

It was a large, rambling mansion, and there was no one in that wing when the fire started.

By the time the alarm was raised it had spread, burning the telephone cable and the fire alarm which connected it to the police station at Haltwhistle.

There was a certain amount of panic and great confusion, so that no one remembered that up on the fourth floor, under the roof, there were seven women, stitching…

Sounds from outside the house were muted in the attics; cars and coaches arriving with visitors were sounds so frequent that they were disregarded, as were the voices. The windows at the front of the house were kept shut on open days, since fumes from the cars might harm the delicate materials they were working upon, but that afternoon Julia's ear caught another sound: voices raised in alarm—more than alarm, terror: And seconds later she smelled the smoke. She went to a window and looked out and saw one wing of the house in flames, people getting into cars and buses and a confused mass of those who didn't know what to do…

By then the other women had left their work and joined her at the window.

'We'd better make haste and get out.' One of the women from the village, older than the rest, spoke urgently. 'We're quite safe if we go down the back stairs.' And indeed the fire was reassuringly distant from them.

But when they reached the second landing it was to find the staircase below already alight.

So far there had been no panic, they weren't women to do that, but now the sight of the smoke and the flames creeping around the staircase on the floor below shattered their calm. Someone screamed.

'The garden door at the back of the house— there's a small staircase…'

Someone told the screamer to be quiet, in a voice rendered hoarse by anger and fright, and they ran through the main part of the house along corridors and passages Julia had never seen before and found the staircase. It was still intact, but the floor below was well alight.

Julia caught one of the older women by the arm. 'If we go back to the attics we can break the windows—there's a narrow parapet, isn't there? Someone will see us; there will be a fire escape...'

The woman nodded. 'We're going back,' she shouted above the panicky voices. 'They'll get us off the roof.'

They went back the way they had come, and although there was a smell of burning and wisps of smoke and a great deal of noise the fire was out of sight. And once back in the attics they set about breaking the glass in the windows at the front of the house, shouting for help as they did so.

The fire had spread to the centre of the house by now, and there were a great many people running to and fro, but the noise of the fire carried away the voices of the women in the attic and no one saw them.

It was Julia who picked up a stool and hurled it over the parapet, and within seconds they were all tossing anything they could carry into the sweep below. And now they could see upturned faces, waving arms, people running and the heartening sight of the first of the fire engines belting up the drive. The third floor was alight now and the hoses were turned on to it. If the fire could be halted there, thought Julia, we'd have a good chance of getting out. She said so, loudly, and the little band of terrified women took heart.

It was five minutes—the longest five minutes of her life, reflected Julia later—before the fire rescue team arrived, and another five minutes saw the first of them being edged over the parapet and into the arms of the fireman perched on the end of the fire escape. In unspoken consent, the women who had children were the first to be rescued, then the two elderly ladies who were married to estate workers, and lastly Jenny and Julia.

And Julia, waiting alone in a blur of held-back terror, allowed herself to scream—for there was no one to hear above the roar of the flames below. She felt better once she had screamed; she had nothing to be frightened about now, the firemen would be back for her in a few minutes. Only she wished with her whole heart that Gerard was there beside her telling her not to worry…

The attic was filling with smoke when she was helped over the parapet.

The Professor was home early. He went to his study with Wilf and Robbie, closely followed by Mrs Potts and the tea tray, and sat down at his desk. He had a good deal of paperwork to do, and notes for a lecture to write. He drank his tea, gave his dogs the biscuits and turned to the pile of papers on his desk. But before picking up his pen, he turned on the radio.

Just in time for a news flash that an estate in the north of England was on fire. No casualties had been reported so far, said the voice, but it was feared that there might be people trapped in the house.

The Professor's instinct was to leap from his chair into his car and drive north within seconds. Instead he picked up the phone and dialled the hospital; Thomas was still on duty. He didn't waste words. 'I'm flying up within half an hour,' he told Thomas. 'Tell Ruth that I will bring Julia back here.'

'You're sure it's where Julia is?'

'They gave the name on the radio.'

The rush hour hadn't started. The Professor, as good as his word, left his house within minutes, outwardly calm, and made for the airport. He concentrated on flying, firmly keeping other thoughts at bay.

Almost at his journey's end, after picking up a hire car, he could see the glow of the fire ahead of him, and shortly after he turned into the drive leading to the house. He was stopped before he was halfway there.

'Sorry, sir, you can't go any further. Can I help?'

'Indeed you can. My future wife works here. She would have been on the top floor. I've come to take her back home.'

At the officer's look of enquiry, he said 'London. I've flown up. I'm a surgeon at one of the hospitals there.'

'Then you'd best find her. There's a rare old muddle checking everyone's out of the building, and quite a few have been taken off to hospital for a check-up or been taken home—local folk.' He nodded at the Professor. 'I'll phone through.'

The Professor drove on, parked the hire car and got out. The sweep in front of the house was crowded with people: firemen, police, estate workers and people from the village. The officer he spoke to was helpful; everyone had been got out and had been sent home, if they lived in the village, or into hospital at Carlisle… It was an elderly man standing near them who interrupted.

'Not all of 'em,' he said. 'There's one of the sewing ladies over at my place with the missus. Not from hereabouts, she isn't, and got nowhere to go.' He added, 'I'm the head gardener here.'

He glanced at the Professor. 'You'd best go and take a look. It's the end cottage, on its own.' He waved an arm. Tell the missus I sent you.'

The Professor thanked him and made his way through the throng, holding down his impatience and anxiety with a firm hand. When he reached the cottage he paused for a moment as an elderly woman came to the door. She was a sensible woman, who listened to his quick explanation and told him to go into the kitchen. 'If it's a girl called Julia, it's her,' she told him softly. 'She's not hurt, but she was the last to be rescued and it's shook her up badly.'

He thanked her quietly and pushed open the kitchen door. Julia was sitting in a chair by the old-fashioned stove, and when she looked up at him the Professor forgot that he was tired, hungry and thirsty. He would have flown ten times the distance he had to see that look on her face.

He spoke quickly, because he could see that she was struggling with tears.

'It's all right, my dear. We'll go home just as soon as I've let someone know that you are in safe hands.' He smiled down at her with the kindliness of an old family friend or elder brother.

She found her voice. 'Gerard, oh, Gerard. I've been so terrified and I didn't know what to do—and then you came...'

She gave him a lop-sided, watery small smile, and perhaps it was as well that the gardener's wife came in then.

'You could do with a cup of tea. You'll just have to see the police—the one who got the others sorted out is in that car with the blue light.' She turned to Julia. 'You do know this gentleman, miss?'

Julia nodded. 'Oh, yes, we're...' She stopped and added, 'He knows my family too; he'll take me home.'

'Then I'll boil the kettle, sir, and you come back as soon as you can. I dare say you've got a way to go.'

The Professor only smiled and went away, and Julia said, 'London.'

'You mean to say he's come up from London?'

'No, no. He sometimes comes to Carlisle, to the hospital—he's a surgeon.'

'Well, that's good fortune indeed. Here's your tea. Drink it hot; you're still all of a shake.'

Which was true enough. She had drunk half of it when the Professor came back. He drank his own tea, thanked the gardener's wife and walked Julia to the car. He had an arm around her and she was glad of it, for her legs felt like jelly. When they reached the car, he picked her up and popped her in, and fetched a rug from the boot and wrapped her in it. And all this with the air of an elder brother...

The car was warm and comfortable and she closed her eyes, only opening them when a police officer put his head through the open window.

'You're Miss Julia Gracey? I'm just checking that everything is OK.'

She managed a smile. 'Yes, that's me, and this is Professor van der Maes, who is a friend of my family.'

He nodded. 'There'll be someone round to see you at home, just to make sure that you are fit and well—get the record straight.' He

grinned at her. 'You had a lucky escape, miss.'
He turned to the professor. 'Safe journey, sir.'

Gerard got into the hire car and drove back
down the drive and on to the road. They would
have to stop on the way to the airport. He was
tired and hungry, and Julia, even if she slept,
would need a break and food. He glanced sideways at her, cocooned in the rug.

'We should be back in a couple of hours.
We will stop on the way for a hot drink and
something to eat. Are you all right?'

He sounded reassuringly normal. 'Yes,
thank you. Oh, Gerard, how fortunate that you
were here—I mean, at the hospital in Carlisle.'
When he didn't answer she said, 'You were
there, weren't you? I mean, how else could
you have come so quickly?'

'I heard the news when I got home…'

She peered at him over the rug. 'You came
all the way from London?' Her voice was an
unbelieving squeak.

'Yes. Now go to sleep, Julia.'

And, while she was still feeling indignant
about that, she did.

The professor looked at Julia's sleeping face. She was pale and smelled of smoke and her hair was in a tangle, but she was here, beside him, safe and sound. He kissed her grubby cheek and drove on.

At a service station he woke her gently. 'I'll get us tea and something to eat,' he told her. 'But first I'll walk you to the facilities.'

Julia, feeling better, was soon shovelled back into the car and told to stay awake.

The tea was hot and sweet and there were sandwiches, cut thick and filled with corned beef. They ate and drank in comfortable silence, the quiet dark around them.

Later, halfway through their short flight, Julia said, 'Would you mind if I went to sleep again for a little while? I'm tired.'

He had expected that, and had already tucked a rug round her. He held his own tiredness at bay while he considered plans and discarded them. Once Julia had recovered from her fright and shock she would probably disappear again; the last thing he wanted was for her to feel beholden to him.

In London, he had to stop once more. 'I'm going to be sick,' said Julia, suddenly awake. He stopped, hauled her briskly out of the car and held her while she heaved and choked and then burst into tears. He mopped her face, popped her back into the car, tucked her up once more and gave her a handful of paper tissues. 'You'll feel better now, try and rest again.'

She closed her eyes but she didn't sleep. She thought about him. He had been quick and gentle and matter-of-fact and impersonal, and she sensed a professional remoteness. And why should it be otherwise? she reflected sadly. The only times they met hadn't been because they had wanted to but by force of circumstances. *Why* had he come all the way from London? She was too sleepy to think about that, but just as she was dozing off she muttered, 'Ruth would have been worried— and he likes her and Thomas.'

The Professor smiled to himself. It was as good a reason as any.

It was late when he stopped before his house. He had phoned before they had left the estate and asked Mrs Potts to get a room ready for Julia. 'And go to bed,' he had told her, 'for we shall be back after midnight.'

Julia was awake again. He got out of the car and, with an arm round her, opened his front door. There was a wall lamp alight and as they went in Mrs Potts, cosily wrapped in a woolly dressing gown, came down the staircase.

'There you are,' she observed, 'and tired to death, I'll be bound, sir. Now, just you go to the kitchen and eat and drink what's there while I take miss upstairs. She'll have a nice warm bath and bed, and a glass of warm milk.' She nodded her head. 'And you'll go to bed too, sir.'

The Professor smiled at her. 'You're an angel, Mrs Potts. Have you had any sleep yourself?'

'Bless you, sir, I went to bed early, seeing as how things were.'

He picked up Julia and carried her upstairs and laid her on the bed in a small bedroom.

'Don't go,' said Julia, clutching his arm. 'I haven't thanked you.' She sounded meek and tearful, and later she would feel ashamed of herself for being so silly.

'We will talk in the morning,' said the Professor bracingly, and went away. Next she heard Mrs Potts's soft voice. 'Now, we'll have these clothes off you. You just sit there while I help you. Then a nice bath, and I'll wash your hair, and then bed and a good sound sleep. The Professor's going to bed too and you can both have a nice chat in the morning.'

So Julia was bathed and shampooed, and all the while Mrs Potts talked in a soothing voice and finally tucked her up in bed and told her to go to sleep. Which she did.

She woke to hear dogs barking and the muted sounds of a household getting ready for the day and, reassured, went back to sleep.

It was mid-morning when she sat up in bed, feeling perfectly well again, and found Mrs Potts standing by the bed with a breakfast tray.

'Oh, I could have got up for breakfast,' said Julia. 'I've given you so much trouble already and I feel fine…'

Mrs Potts arranged the tray on a bed table. 'Now just eat your breakfast, Miss Gracey. Your sister will be here with some clothes for you presently.'

'Ruth? How did she know that I was here?'

'Why, the Professor phoned her before he went to the hospital this morning. She's to stay for lunch.'

'Lunch? What's the time, Mrs Potts?'

'A little after ten o'clock.'

'The Professor said he'd see me in the morning. He's still here?'

'Lor' bless you, Miss, he's been gone these past two hours.' Mrs Potts shook her head. 'There's no stopping him. A couple of hours' sleep and he's off again. I'm to tell you he'll see you some time.'

Julia drank her tea and swallowed tears with it. 'Yes, of course. I've given him a lot of trouble. I'll go back with my sister after lunch. Is there somewhere I could write him a note?'

'I'll have pen and paper ready for you,' promised Mrs Potts, and left Julia to finish a breakfast which tasted of sawdust. He had gone to a great deal of trouble to rescue her, but now that was accomplished he would forget her—a momentary nuisance in his ordered life.

'But I'm not going to cry about it,' said Julia, and ate the breakfast she no longer wanted, then got up and showered. Wrapped in a voluminous dressing gown produced by Mrs Potts, she went downstairs, where she was shown into a small, cosily furnished room. There was a small writing desk with paper and pen set ready for her.

'Your sister will be here presently,' said Mrs Potts comfortably, and left her to write her note.

Not an easy thing to do, Julia discovered. She had to make several attempts before she was satisfied, but she hoped that her warm thanks coupled with the assumption that she was unlikely to see him—his work—her intention to leave London as soon as possible—would strike the right note. She had just sealed the envelope when Ruth arrived, bringing clothes and agog to hear exactly what had happened.

When Julia had finished telling her everything she said, 'I didn't know anything about it until Gerard phoned Thomas to say that he had found you and that you were safe...'

Julia said slowly, 'I thought he had come because you were worried about me?'

'No, no. Thomas told me that Gerard phoned him around half past four—he'd heard a newsflash about the fire. He was on the point of leaving.'

She saw the look on Julia's face and said quickly, 'You'll stay with us, of course, love, until you decide what you want to do.'

Julia said slowly, 'Would you mind if I went to Monica for a while?'

'No, of course not. It will be quiet there; you will have time to think.'

Something Julia didn't want to do, for she would only think of Gerard, who had rescued her and left a laconic message that he would see her some time. Well, that was something she could deal with. If she went to Monica he could forget her, something he must be wanting to do, only fate seemed intent on throwing her in his path.

They had their lunch, thanked Mrs Potts for her kindness and took a taxi to Ruth's home. Thomas was at the hospital and Julia seized the opportunity to phone Monica and invite herself to stay. 'Just for a week. I won't be in the way, but it would be nice to have a few days while I make up my mind what I'll do.'

'Come for as long as you like,' said Monica largely. 'No one will bother you. It must have been horrible, Julia, and so far away. You must have been glad to see Gerard.'

'Yes,' said Julia. 'I was. He's been very kind…'

'More than kind,' said Monica dryly. 'Come when you like, Julia; there's a room ready for you. The nearest station is Cullompton. George will meet you with the car.'

Thomas came home presently. He was glad to see her, and wanted to know about the fire—and never mentioned Gerard. She said in a carefully casual voice, 'I haven't seen Gerard since we got back here. I hope he wasn't too tired...'

'Gerard's never tired,' said Thomas. 'He's done a day's work and he's dining out this evening with the widow of one of his patients who has been angling for him for some time.'

Well, thought Julia peevishly, I don't need to waste any concern on the man. I hope she catches him and leads him a simply horrible life. She smiled brilliantly at her brother-in-law and wished she could go and shut herself somewhere dark and lonely and cry her heart out.

And Ruth made it worse by observing that Olivia Travis was one of the most beautiful women she had ever met. 'If I were a man I'd fall in love with her the moment I saw her.'

Thomas grunted, which could have meant anything.

Julia stayed for three days at Ruth's. She had to buy clothes and be interviewed by someone from the police, who assured her that they merely wished to be sure that she was quite unharmed and safe with her family. And each morning when she woke she wondered if she would see the Professor. But he didn't come. Nor did Thomas speak of him. She told herself that she was glad. He could at least have acknowledged her note, though. Perhaps he hadn't read it. His secretary might have put it with the junk mail and all the invitations which he didn't wish to accept.

On the third day she made arrangements to go to Monica. Ruth asked worriedly, 'Will you stay for a while, love? Come back here when you want to.'

'I'm being a worry for them,' Julia told herself as she got ready for bed. 'I must find something somewhere and settle down.'

Perhaps in some small town in the West Country. A small flat—she could rent one—or a shop. She had money enough; there was no reason why she shouldn't make a pleasant life for herself. She might even marry...

Out of the question, of course. She loved Gerard and no one else would do.

Up until the very last minute, until the train was leaving the station, she had the forlorn hope that she would see Gerard. But there was no sign of him. He'd be in Holland, thought Julia despairingly, and then, as the train swept past the suburbs and through green fields and trees, That's it, she told herself. You're going to forget him just as he's forgotten you. You're wasting your life hankering after a person who doesn't care a straw for you.

After which heartening speech she picked up the magazine she had bought and began to read it. It was full of artfully posed teenagers wearing what looked like fancy dress costumes, and they were all painfully bony, with sharp elbows and jutting collarbones. Julia felt fat and almost middle-aged just looking at them. She handed the magazine over to a young woman who had been peering at it from the opposite seat and then looked out of the window. The country looked lovely and she felt a sudden surge of interest in the future.

You never know what's round the corner, thought Julia.

# CHAPTER EIGHT

GEORGE, driving Julia away from Cullompton station, didn't bother her with questions. He thought that she looked tired and, despite her bright chatter, unhappy. He would leave the questions to Monica, he decided.

Monica was waiting for them with a string of questions and they had a cheerful lunch together.

'I'll take you over the house again, now that we've had the alterations done,' said Monica. 'It's far too large for us, of course, but we love it. And now we've got central heating and the plumbing works, it's easy to run.'

They had gone to Julia's bedroom after lunch and Monica was sitting on the bed while Julia unpacked.

'Is Ruth all right? And Thomas? And have you seen the Professor since you got back? What a man—going all that way to fetch you

235

home. I expect he must have seen how worried Ruth was, but it was a noble thing to do, especially as you don't like each other much.'

Julia had her head in a drawer. 'Yes, it was. I haven't seen him since, though, but I didn't expect to.'

'Ruth told me that there's a beautiful woman lurking!'

'Yes.' Julia emerged rather red in the face. 'I had a present for you, but of course I lost it in the fire. Perhaps we could find something to take its place. This really is a lovely old house, isn't it? Ruth's house is nice, too...'

Monica said concernedly, 'But you haven't a home, love. We do worry about you.'

Julia closed her case and put it tidily under the bed. 'Well, don't. I know exactly what I want to do. Leave London, for a start, and settle in a town between the two of you. I'll rent a flat to start with, and then find a small shop with living space. I shall sell everything to do with needlework and knitting and embroidery. While I'm here, if you don't mind, I shall take a look at some of the small towns round and about. I can hire a car. I know I haven't driven for years but I can't have forgotten how.'

Monica said suddenly, 'Do you ever wish that you'd married Oscar?'

Julia laughed. 'Monica, you must be joking! I'm happy as I am. ''Footloose and fancy-free''—isn't that what someone or other wrote?'

Monica laughed too, and didn't believe a word of it.

It was delightful living in the country. The village was a large one with a widespread parish, and Monica and George made her more than welcome, but after a few days she declared her intention of exploring the surrounding countryside with an eye to the future.

Honiton seemed as good a place to start as any. A small market town straddling the main road from London to the West, it was famous for its lace-making and antiques shops, but she discarded it reluctantly. It was too near Monica and too far from Ruth. It needed to be somewhere between her sisters and far enough away from both of them so as not to encroach on their lives. She pored over maps and guide-books and, sitting one morning with Monica in the garden asked, 'Where's Stourhead?'

'North of Yeovil. Not on a main road but easy to get at. It's a lovely place; we went there a month or so ago. Heavenly gardens and a Palladian house full of treasures.'

'There's an ad in your local newspaper. Guides for the house and people to repair and refurbish the furniture and the hangings. I know I want to start up on my own, but it looks rather inviting.'

She could see Monica's look of uncertainty and knew what she was thinking: that she was wasting time, drifting from one job to another, that she should settle down and make a secure future for herself—that was if she didn't marry, and that didn't seem likely.

Monica said worriedly, 'Yes, that might be a good idea. While you were there you might scout around and find a suitable shop in one of the small towns not too far away. There's Sherborne—the most likely, I should think. Yeovil is nearby, too, but that's quite large—

too large for the kind of shop you're thinking of, I imagine. There's Warminster and there's Gillingham and Shaftesbury, but I'm not sure if you could make much of a living with the kind of shop you're thinking of. I'd opt for Sherborne...'

So Julia went to Sherborne and liked what she saw there. It was an abbey town with a well-known public school and the right kind of shops. For the first time since she had returned from the north she felt enthusiastic about her future. She supposed that all this time she had been hoping that she would see Gerard again, that he might even discover that he liked her... But that wasn't going to be the case. Once and for all she would forget him.

Quite sure now that she knew what she wanted to do, she wasted no time. A visit to the town's estate agents left her with a handful of possible shops to buy or lease. She would strike while the iron was hot, she decided, viewing the future through rose-coloured spectacles. And phoned Monica to tell her that she was going to stay the night in Sherborne and inspect what was on offer.

'You haven't got anything with you,' Monica reminded her, so she went out and bought a cheap nightie and a toothbrush and booked in at a quiet hotel five minutes' walk from the town centre. It was already late afternoon, but it was a small town and she had no trouble finding the handful of addresses. The first three were no use at all, tucked away down side streets, but the fourth had possibilities; it was close to the abbey and the main shopping street, tucked in between an antiquarian book shop and a picture gallery. Its window was small, but it was in a good state of repair and the paintwork was fresh. She peered through the glass door. The shop was small too, with a tiny counter and a door behind it. The leaflet claimed that there were living quarters too.

She reached the estate agents as they were about to close and arranged to inspect the shop in the morning.

Momentarily inflated with a strong sense of purpose, she took herself off then to the hotel, had a splendid dinner and slept soundly.

The shop was small but it had possibilities. There was a little room behind it and a kitchen beyond that, and upstairs there was a bedroom and a shower and a toilet. She could, she decided, make it home without too much expense. And she could rent it on a year's lease which meant that she wouldn't need to dig too deep into her capital.

She said that she would rent it subject to a surveyor's report. 'I'll need a solicitor,' she said, 'and I'd like to take possession as soon as possible.'

She went back to Monica's that afternoon, her head full of plans and ideas. She would stay in Sherborne, get the place fit to live in, buy her stock and move in at her leisure.

Monica, told the news, nodded her head in approval. 'If that is what you want,' she said cautiously. 'I've no doubt you'll make a success of it, and you're bound to make friends— if that is what you want?'

Julia assured her that it was. Which wasn't quite true, of course. What she wanted was for Gerard to fall in love with her, marry her and live with her happily ever after, but, since that was something which wasn't going to happen, she must turn herself into a successful businesswoman.

'You'll probably meet a nice man,' said Monica.

There was no point in telling her that she already had.

'I'll have to go back to London to see the solicitor and the bank. May I stay here for a few more days while the agent gets organised at Sherborne? I'll have to sign papers and so on.'

'Stay as long as you like, love. You know you'll always be welcome here. You're not far away, and if you get a car... Could you afford that?'

'I think so. A small second-hand one.'

Several days later she went back to London and told herself that she felt relief to hear that the Professor was in Holland.

The solicitor was helpful in a cautious way; he hoped that she had thought about the drawbacks as well as the advantages of setting up a small business.

'A young lady on her own,' he said, shaking a grey head. He hadn't moved with the times, but she liked him for his fatherly concern. And the bank manager was cautious too. He would have liked her to have invested her money in something safe, so that she would have had a small steady income, and possibly lived with one or other of her sisters...

While she had been working on the estate she had picked up quite a lot of information about the wholesale firms which had supplied the materials for the work there, and it had given her some idea as to how to contact them; she intended to sell tapestries, knitting wools, embroidery silks and patterns as well as canvases and embroidery frames and anything else needful to the serious embroiderer. She would also knit herself, and sell what she knitted. She wouldn't allow herself any doubts; she had al-

244 AN INDEPENDENT WOMAN

ways been able to cope and this was a chal-
lenge…

She was in Ruth's sitting room, and making
yet another list, when the Professor opened the
door and walked in.

She sat back and gaped at him, unable to
think of anything to say.

'Close your mouth, my dear,' said the
Professor. 'Why are you so surprised?'

'I thought you were in Holland.' Mingled
with the delight of seeing him again was an-
noyance that he had sneaked in on her without
warning.

He sat down and stretched out his legs, the
picture of ease. 'So you're about to become a
businesswoman? No doubt you will be very
successful, make lots of money and fulfil whatever dreams you have…'

'Don't be sarcastic,' said Julia waspishly.
'and it's none of your business.'

'You're cross. Are you not pleased to see
me? I thought that we might have dinner together this evening. We could talk over old
times?'

She eyed him carefully. To spend an evening with him would be a dream come true, but on the other hand she had promised herself that she would forget him. The Professor, watching her face, said in just the right off-hand manner, 'I'm going back to Holland and you are leaving London.'

In that case, reflected Julia, there would be no harm done, would there? He was making it clear that they weren't likely to see each other again.

'All right. Though I'm sure we won't find anything to talk about.'

'No? The cottage? My home in Amsterdam? Mrs Beckett? I think we may be able to sustain some kind of conversation!' He got to his feet. 'I'll call for you at half past seven.'

'Shall I dress up?'

It was the kind of remark to make him fall in love with her all over again. One moment so haughty and the next as uncertain as a schoolgirl.

He said gently, 'Something short and pretty. We'll go to Claridge's.'

The moment he had gone she ran up to her room. There was a dress which might do. She hadn't meant to buy it but it had been so pretty: amber chiffon over a silk slip, plain, high-necked, and long-sleeved and elegant. She had bought it because it had seemed to her to stand for all the pretty clothes she had never been able to buy. Well, she would wear it— and even if she never wore it again it would be worth every penny of the money she had squandered on it.

Thomas and Ruth came in together and Julia said at once with a heightened colour, 'I've done the veg for supper and made a fruit pie. You won't mind if I go out? Gerard has asked me to dinner.'

Ruth gave Thomas an 'I told you so' look, and said, 'Oh, nice. Where's he taking you?'

'Claridge's.'

Ruth was on the point of saying, Lucky girl, but changed her mind. Having fallen in love with Thomas, just as he had fallen in love with her, without any doubts or complications, she found it hard to understand why two sensible people like the Professor and her sister could be so slow in discovering that they were meant for each other. She caught Thomas's eye and said instead, 'You could wear that amber chiffon dress…'

Studying herself in the dress later, Julia wondered if she would ever wear the dress again. She knew no one in Sherborne. It would take time to make friends, and they might not be the kind to take her anywhere as splendid as Claridge's. She would make the most of her evening, she promised herself.

She was glad that she was wearing the dress when the Professor came for her. In his sober, beautifully tailored suits he looked the epitome of the well-dressed man, but in a dinner jacket he looked magnificent.

He was standing in the hall talking to Thomas when she went down, but he turned and looked at her as she came down the stairs. 'Very pretty,' he observed, which left her doubtful as to whether he was referring to the dress or her person. She wrapped herself in the paisley shawl—the family heirloom she shared with her sisters—and bade him hello. She assured Ruth that she wouldn't be late back and went out to the car with him. She hoped that they would have the lovely time Ruth had wished them…

The streets were fairly free of traffic but their way took them through the heart of the city. Julia, mindful of good manners, made small talk from time to time, but since he replied in monosyllables she said coolly, 'You don't like me to talk?'

He glanced briefly at her. 'Why should you think that? You are determined to think the worst of me, Julia.'

Suddenly contrite, she said, 'I don't—really, I don't. You've helped me so often, even if you haven't meant to. I mean, circumstances…' She stopped. 'I've made a mess of saying that. I'm sorry. I would like us to part friends.'

'A most laudable notion. I hope that at last you are trying to overcome your initial dislike of me.'

Before she could think of an answer to that he had stopped before Claridge's entrance. And, after that, serious talk, even if she had wanted it, wasn't easy. She left the shawl in the hands of the haughty lady in charge of the cloakroom, rather deflated by the disparaging glance it was given, but her spirits were up-lifted by the warm appreciation in Gerard's eyes when she joined him.

They didn't dine immediately but had their drinks in a magnificent room where a small orchestra played gentle background music. The surroundings were of a kind to make even the most uncertain girl feel cherished and beauti-ful, so that by the time they were seated at a table Julia felt both. Moreover, she was sitting opposite the man she loved, even if it was for the very last time. Nothing must spoil this, their final meeting…

She might be head over heels in love, but it hadn't spoiled her appetite. They had water-cress soup, Dover Sole with lemon grass and tiny sautéed potatoes, and a lemon tart that was out of this world—and two glasses of champagne which gave her eyes a sparkle and her tongue a ready liveliness. She had, for the moment, quite forgotten that this was their last meeting...

The Professor, under no illusions as to that, led their talk from one thing to the other. He saw now that when Julia forgot that she didn't like him she was entirely happy in his company, so it was just a question of patience. He had no intention of forcing her hand, so he would let her have her shop for a while, and once the first flush of independence had worn off, she would turn to him. She was a darling, he reflected, but pig-headed, liable to be contrary. She must find out for herself...

So they had a delightful evening together, and it wasn't until they got back to Ruth's that Julia remembered that this really was their final meeting. All her good resolutions came tumbling back into her head, so that she said stiffly, 'Thank you for a lovely evening; I enjoyed it. I hope you will...' She began again. 'I expect you're glad to be going back to Holland. Please give my love to Mrs Beckett when you see her.' She couldn't help adding, 'Will you come back to England at all?'

'From time to time.' Indeed, he was going to Holland for a short time only, for consultations and hospital commitments there, but he had no intention of telling her that.

He got out of the car and helped her out and stood, her hand in his, looking down at her. 'A delightful evening, Julia, thank you for coming.'

She would never know what made her ask then, 'Are you going to get married?' She would have given a great deal to have unsaid her words, but they were spoken now, weren't they? And what did it matter, anyway?

The Professor studied her pink embarrassed face. He said evenly, 'Yes, that is my intention.' Idle curiosity? He wondered. Or could it be more than that?

Julia recovered herself. 'Well, I hope you'll be very happy,' she told him.

'And you, Julia?'

'Oh, I can't wait to do something I've wanted to do for so long…'

'And what is that?'

'Be independent.' How easy it was to tell fibs, she reflected, when one was desperate.

'Ah, yes, of course. I must wish you every success.' He bent his head and kissed her then. A kiss to drive all thoughts of independence out of her head. But he didn't wait for that. He pushed her gently through the door and closed it behind her, and she stood in the hall, listening to the gentle purring of the Rolls as he drove away.

She wasn't going to cry, she told herself, creeping silently to her room to hang up the pretty dress she supposed she would never wear again before getting into bed to weep silently all over Muffin, who had crept up with her. He was Ruth's cat now, but he had a strong affection for Julia and bore patiently with her snuffles and sighs.

Thomas had already left for the hospital by the time she got down to breakfast. Ruth took one look at her face and turned her back to make the toast.

'Did you have a lovely evening? We didn't hear you come in. Was the food good? I suppose it was all rather grand?'

'Well, it was, but you didn't notice it, if you see what I mean. It's a beautiful restaurant and the food was marvellous. It was a lovely evening.'

A remark which Ruth took with a pinch of salt, although she said nothing.

'Monica phoned yesterday evening. I'm to tell you that you're to go there if there is any kind of hitch at Sherborne. You have got everything fixed up?'

'Yes, I'll stay at a bed and breakfast place while I get the shop ready and buy some furniture. That ought not to take too long.'

She had been to a wholesaler and ordered her stock, packed her bags once more and there was nothing to keep her in London. And the Professor had gone back to Holland. The sooner she started her new life the better.

It was raining and chilly when she reached Sherborne, and she was glad that the estate agent had been kind enough to recommend a place where she could stay. She had arranged to go there for a week, but probably it would be longer than that…

The house was in the centre of the town, one of a row of stone-built cottages of a fair size, and when the taxi stopped before its door Julia thought how cosy it looked. But the lady who answered the door didn't look cosy; she was immaculately dressed, not a hair out of place, a no longer youthful face carefully made up. Mrs Legge-Boulter welcomed Julia with chilly courtesy and within five minutes had made it clear that only most unfortunate circumstances had forced her to take in guests.

'It is not at all what I've been used to,' she observed, 'but beggars cannot be choosers, can they?' She laughed, but since she didn't look in the least amused Julia murmured in a noncommittal manner as she was led upstairs to her room.

'I serve breakfast at half past eight,' said Mrs Legge-Boulter, 'and my guests are expected to be out of the house by ten o'clock. You may return after six o'clock. At the moment you are the only guest, so you may use the bathroom between nine and ten o'clock in the evening.'

'You don't offer evening meals?' said Julia hopefully.

Her landlady looked affronted. 'My dear Miss Gracey, you can have no idea of the work entailed in providing a room and breakfast for my guests. I am totally exhausted at the end of my day.'

Left alone, Julia examined her room. It was furnished with everything necessary for a bedroom, but the colour scheme was a beige and brown mixture unrelieved by ornaments or pictures. A place to sleep, decided Julia, and hoped that breakfast would be substantial. The sooner she could move into her little shop the better.

She unpacked her things and, since it was mid-afternoon, went into the town. She had tea and then went to take another look at her future home. Tomorrow she would see the estate agent and ask if he would let her have the key. She had signed the papers and paid over the money for the lease and the first month's rent. She sat over tea, making a list of all the things which had to be done, and then she wandered round the shops, looking for second-hand furniture and the mundane household equipment she would need. She earmarked several items, and then went in search of somewhere she could get her supper.

She found a small café near the abbey, serving light meals until eight o'clock, and she sat over a mushroom omelette and French fries and a pot of coffee until closing time and then returned to Mrs Legge-Boulter's house.

That lady opened the door to her with a thin smile, a request that she should wipe her feet and a reminder that breakfast was at half past eight. 'I must ask you to be punctual; I have my day to organise.'

Not only her day, reflected Julia, mounting the stairs, but the day of any unfortunate soul lodging with her. She had a bath and, mindful of the notice on the door, cleaned it and went to bed. She had a good deal to think about; the next few days were going to be fully occupied.

But when she finally closed her eyes she allowed herself to think of Gerard. Even though she never intended to see him again, there was no reason why she shouldn't dream a little of what might have been...

She was tired, so that she slept well, and when she woke her only thoughts were concerned with getting down to breakfast. It was a frugal meal, served by Mrs Legge-Boulter with disdain, as though offering a boiled egg and two slices of toast was an affront to her social status. A miserable meal, decided Julia, gobbling everything in sight and shocking her landlady by asking for more hot water. The tea was already weak...

She left the house before ten o'clock, saw the estate agent, got the shop key and, fortified by coffee and a bun, let herself into what was now, for the moment, her property.

Not a great deal needed doing, she decided. A carpenter for the shop fittings, carpeting for the living room, and a good clean everywhere. So she went to the shops and returned presently with a bucket, broom, dusters and cleaning materials and set to. She paused for lunch and then went in search of a carpenter and a carpet shop.

It took a good deal of the afternoon but she found a carpenter who would come in the morning and also someone who would come and measure the floors. She went back to the café for a meal and then made her way back to Mrs Legge-Boulter's house, where she received the same tepid welcome as before. Really, thought Julia, lying in a hot bath and eating potato crisps, one wondered why her landlady chose to have lodgers when she obviously disliked them so much.

Breakfast was a boiled egg again. At least I shall get slim, thought Julia, and wondered if Gerard might like her better if she wasn't so curvy. A stupid thought, she told herself; he didn't like her whatever shape she was. She might be deeply in love, but it had made no difference to her appetite; she was still hungry when she left the house, and went along to the shop armed with a bag of currant buns, still warm from the oven at the bakers. Munching them, she went round the little place again, quite clear in her head as to what needed doing, so that by the time the carpenter arrived no time was lost. The floors measured, she took herself off to choose carpets, persuading everyone that everything had to be done as quickly as possible. A good morning's work, she decided, eating a splendid lunch in a friendly pub.

Buying a sewing machine and material for curtains took up her afternoon; tomorrow she would get them made and go in search of furniture. Hopefully she would be able to move in by the end of a week...

She had been busy all day, so that it had been fairly easy to forget Gerard. But now, back in her unwelcoming room, she forgot all about the shop and thought only of him. It wouldn't do, she told herself, sitting up in bed making yet another list. The sooner she got the shop open and had her hands full, the better. All the same, before she slept, in her mind's eye she roamed through the house in Amsterdam, remembering its age-old beauty and the endless quiet. She supposed that she would never forget them. She allowed herself a moment to wonder what Gerard was doing before she slept.

He was sitting in his magnificent drawing room and his mother was sitting opposite him, drinking after-dinner coffee by the small fire, for the evenings were cool.

Mevrouw van der Maes was a tall, imposing woman, elegantly dressed, not showing her age save for her white hair, worn in a French pleat. She had good looks still, and bright blue eyes. She sipped her coffee.

'This is delightful, Gerard; I see you so seldom. That can't be helped, I know. Den Haag is only half an hour's drive away, but that's too far if you've had a long day at the hospital. But I wish I saw more of you.'

'I'm thinking of cutting down on my work in England—not the London hospital but some of the provincial ones.'

'That means that you will make your home base here?' his mother asked, and added, 'You are thinking of getting married at last?'

He smiled. 'I've taken my time, haven't I? But, yes, that is my intention.'

'Do I know her? Oh, my dear, I shall be so happy…'

'An English girl; you may remember I mentioned her coming over here to look after Mrs Beckett?'

'And Nanny loved her, as I'm sure I shall. You will bring her to see me?'

'In a while, I hope.'

Something in his voice made her ask, 'She knows that you want to marry her?'

'No. When we first met it was hardly on the best of terms, and she has been at great pains to let me know that she is indifferent to me. At times she has allowed me to think that she likes me at least, but I think that has been due to circumstances…'

Mevrouw van der Maes asked quietly, 'You have told her that you love her?'

'No, and I've been careful not to show my feelings.'

His mother sighed silently. She loved Gerard deeply, and she was proud of him, his brilliant career, his good looks, his complete lack of pride in his success—and yet despite all those he was behaving like an uncertain youth in love for the first time. Men are so tiresome at times, reflected Mevrouw van der Maes.

There were a great many questions she wanted to ask him, but they must wait. When he had anything to tell her he would do so. Instead she began to talk about family matters.

The Professor, in Holland for a number of consultations, lectures and meetings with colleagues, found time to visit Mrs Beckett. He found her quite her old self again.

'Well, now,' said Nanny, offering a cheek for his kiss, 'how nice to see you, Mr Gerard. Miss Thrisp has been away for a week and I'm ripe for a gossip.'

So he told her all the news and gossip he knew that she enjoyed.

'And what's this I hear about Julia? She writes to me, bless her, but never a word about herself until this very day.' Mrs Beckett got out her specs. 'I had a letter this morning. Dear knows what the girl is doing—opening a shop, if you please. Full of plans, as bright as a button—and such nonsense. Why, she should be getting herself a husband instead of setting up on her own...'

The Professor asked casually, 'And where is this shop to be?'

'Sherborne—that's a small town in Dorset.' She took the letter from a pocket and re-read it. 'She's going to sell wools and embroidery and suchlike, and do a bit of dressmaking if there's a chance.'

Nanny turned the page. 'Here's a bit I missed. What does it say?'

She read it and looked worriedly at the Professor. 'She says not to tell anyone where she is—and now I've told you, Mr Gerard.'

He said placidly, 'Don't worry, Nanny, I won't tell a soul. I'm glad she still writes to you and that she appears to have such a bright future.'

'Future?' said Mrs Beckett pettishly. 'Nonsense. A lovely girl like her, selling wool to old ladies...' She added, 'And I thought you were taken with her...'

She looked at him, sitting at his ease, Jason at his feet, and saw his grin. And then she smiled herself while thoughts crowded into her elderly head: a wedding, babies and small children coming to stay with old Nanny.

But all she said was, 'Well, you've taken your time, Mr Gerard.'

# CHAPTER NINE

SPURRED on by Julia, the carpenter made shelves and did some small repairs while two men laid a carpet in the living room; two more came to install a small gas stove and a gas fire. The little place was wired for a telephone and she had been promised that she would be connected as soon as possible. Everything was going smoothly, she thought with satisfaction, and took herself off to buy furniture.

She has already found a second-hand furniture shop down a small street, and she spent almost an hour there, searching out a nice small round table and two straight-backed chairs, a bookcase and a rather battered oak stand to hold a table lamp. She chose a chest of drawers too, and an old-fashioned mirror to go with it, and another little table which would do for a bedside stand with a lamp. Pleased with her purchases, she went back into the main street and bought a small easy chair. It cost rather more than she had expected, as did the padded stool for the bedroom and the bed, but she reminded herself that she could afford it.

She stopped for lunch presently, and then went in search of bed linen, towels and table-cloths, pots and pans, cutlery and all the small odds and ends which make up a home. She was tired by the evening, but she was getting everything done so far without a hitch; she slept like a proverbial log in her unwelcoming room and went downstairs in the morning to eat the inevitable egg, her head full of what still had to be done.

The little shop was ready to receive its contents; the first consignment of wool arrived that afternoon and she spent a long time arranging it on the shelves the carpenter had made. And some of the furniture had been delivered.

She saw Mrs Legge-Boulter, who, told that Julia would be leaving the next day, said with an unkind little titter, 'Well, I hope you won't regret opening a shop. I'm sure there isn't much call for wools and embroidery and so on, and that's not in the best shopping area.'

Julia, tired and to tell the truth a bit frightened of the future, said airily, 'I dare say I shall make more of a success of it than you with your bed and breakfast trade.'

To which Mrs Legge-Boulter took thin-lipped exception. 'Not a *trade*, Miss Gracey,' she explained coldly. 'A perfectly genteel way in which gentlefolk may add to their income.'

'Well, you're not adding much, are you?' observed Julia tartly. 'You'd do much better to put a few flowers in the rooms and offer some bacon for breakfast.'

She took herself off to bed and spent the next hour feeling ashamed of herself. She would apologise in the morning.

Which she did, for she was a kind-hearted girl even if her temper was a little out of hand at times. Her landlady ignored the apology, reminded her that she must be out of the house by ten o'clock and offered a boiled egg, not quite cold and rock-solid, and toast burnt at the edges.

There was no sign of her when Julia left the house. She had presented the bill at breakfast, waited while Julia paid, and then gone out of the room without a word.

A bad start to the day, thought Julia, although it had its funny side too. Only there was no one to laugh with her about it—the Professor for preference…

But once in the little room behind the shop she felt better. The odds and ends of furniture and the cheerful carpet and curtains made it quite cosy. She went into the tiny kitchen and arranged her few saucepans on the wall shelf and put the kettle on for a cup of coffee. There was no room for a table, only a worktop over the two small cupboards. Later, she promised herself, she would give the walls a coat of cheerful paint. She went through the shower room and loo and opened the back door. The patch of garden outside was neglected but the fences were sound and there was plenty of room for a wash-line.

The day went quickly; by the time she had made her bed and unpacked her things it was noon. She stocked her cupboard after lunch, made a cup of tea and sat by the gas fire drinking it. Tomorrow she would arrange the window, and then she would open the shop.

She phoned Ruth and Monica in the morning, after a sound night's sleep in her new bed, and warned them that until she had the phone connected they weren't to worry if she didn't ring for a day or two. The nearest phone box wasn't far away, but it would mean locking up the shop to go to it and she didn't want to miss the chance of a customer.

The window looked attractive, she thought: a small display of knitting wools, embroidery silks and patterns, tapestry for canvas work, a little pyramid of coloured sewing thread… She sat behind the counter and watched people passing. Some stopped to look in but no one came into the shop. 'Well,' said Julia, 'I didn't expect anyone on the first day.'

Ruth and Monica had sent cards of good wishes, and Mrs Beckett had sent her a letter. The Professor, apprised of the opening date by

Nanny, had restrained himself from rushing out and ordering six dozen red roses.

Julia had her first customer on the following day; an elderly woman came in and, after deliberation, bought a reel of sewing thread.

Her first customer and hopefully the start of many more.

Julia closed her little shop for the day and had tea and crumpets round the fire. The days were drawing in and the evenings were chilly; the housewives of Sherborne would be thinking of quiet evenings with their knitting or embroidery...

She hadn't expected instant success, but as the days went by with a mere trickle of customers her initial euphoria gave way to doubts which she did her best to keep at bay. Perhaps the ladies of Sherborne didn't knit? Perhaps they needed a little encouragement? She dressed the little window in a different fashion, with half-finished knitting arranged with careful carelessness in the corner, an almost complete tapestry opposite, and between them a basket filled with everything a knitter or nee-

dlewoman might need. And that brought customers—not many, not nearly enough!—but it
was early days yet, she told herself.

Monica and George drove over to see her,
and she led them round the shop and house,
assuring them that everything was fine and that
she was happier than she had been for years.

'So why does she look like that?' demanded
Monica of her George as they drove back
home. 'As though her world has come to an
end? Oh, I know she was laughing and talking
nineteen to the dozen, but that's not like her.'
She frowned. 'Do you suppose…?'

George said, 'I agree that she isn't happy,
but since she was at such pains to conceal that
from us I feel that we should respect that.'

'She's in love,' said Monica, to which
George said nothing. He was fond of his sister-
in-law but she was a fiercely independent
young woman. Any efforts to alter that, he
considered, weren't for him or her sisters.

Monica, on the phone to Ruth, voiced her
concern. 'And George says we mustn't interfere,' she added, with which Ruth agreed.

She wouldn't interfere, but she might drop a hint. She couldn't help but notice that whenever she saw the Professor he never once mentioned Julia. Ruth, sharing Mevrouw van der Maes' opinion that the best of men could be tiresome at times, bided her time.

A senior consultant at the hospital was retiring and she and Thomas had been invited to attend his farewell party—a sober affair, with sherry and morsels of this and that handed round on trays. Once the speeches had been made there was ample opportunity to mingle and chat. It took a little while to get the Professor to herself, and she wasted no time.

One or two remarks about the retiring consultant, a brief enquiry as to when Gerard would be going to Holland again, and then Ruth came to the point in what she hoped was a roundabout manner.

'So you're going to Holland...?'

She glanced up at him. He loomed over her, the picture of ease and she added, 'I expect you will go to your dear little cottage. That was a lovely holiday; Julia loved it too. She's quite settled, you know.'

'Sherborne is a charming little town, I'm told. I hear she has set up shop.'

Ruth gaped at him. 'You know? Who told you? She made us promise not to tell...'

He smiled down at her worried face. 'I thought that might be the case. It wasn't too difficult to discover where she was living.'

'Why do you want to know? I mean, you're not—that is, I didn't think that you liked each other much, even though you were always there when she needed someone.' She touched his sleeve. 'I'm sorry—I shouldn't have said anything. Only she's my sister and I love her very much.'

Two dignified members of the hospital committee were about to join them. 'So do I,' said the Professor gravely, and he turned to greet them.

She had no chance to speak to him again, and when a few days later she asked Thomas in a purposely vague manner if he had gone to Holland, Thomas answered just as vaguely that he was still at the hospital. 'Catching up on his work,' he added, but didn't mention that his chief was busy because he was planning a few days off.

Monica, at the other end of the phone, agreed that there was nothing to be done. 'Julia can be as stubborn as a mule; if she got even a hint of all this she'd shut the shop and disappear. And as for Gerard, he'll sort everything out in his own good time. When you think about it, it's inevitable, isn't it? Only they've been at cross purposes ever since they met, haven't they? And they are so obviously suited to each other...'

A week later, on a fine, bright and chilly morning, the Professor bade Mrs Potts goodbye and, with Wilf and Robbie curled up in the back of the car, drove away from London going west.

Julia, totting up the week's takings, had to admit that business was slow. There had been several customers but none of them had bought more than a skein of wool or some embroidery silks. Even her simple arithmetic told her that she was running at a loss... And she had been open for three weeks now.

She rearranged the window display and added a notice that garments could be knitted, telling herself that it might be several months before she was established, then she made herself a cup of coffee, determined not to be downhearted.

She was rewarded not half an hour later by a customer who bought three ounces of wool and some knitting needles, and she was followed by a cross-looking woman who wanted a knitting pattern. She spent a long time sifting through the little pile Julia offered her, choosing with as much care as someone spending hundreds of pounds on a purchase. She still hadn't made up her mind when the shop door opened again and the Professor walked in.

Julia gave a gasp and the woman looked round and then back at the patterns. None of them, she told Julia, were what she wanted. She would do better if she went to a larger shop. And she swept out of the door.

The Professor eased his bulk from the door to the counter, his head bowed to prevent it coming in contact with the ceiling, and the little place was all at once overcrowded.

He said blandly, 'I hope that the rest of your customers are more profitable than that one!'

Julia glared at him. Her heart had turned over and leapt into her throat and she had only just managed to get it back where it belonged. She supposed that being in love made one feel giddy. But she was cross too; walking in like that without so much as a 'hello'—and if he hadn't then the woman might have bought something.

He leaned on the counter, disarranging the pile of patterns.

He said, 'You ran away...'

'I did no such thing. I have always wanted to own a shop and be independent...'

He leaned over the counter, opened the till drawer and looked at the handful of small change in it. 'Well,' he observed genially. 'You own a shop, but are you independent? Is that today's takings?'

It was a temptation to fib, but somehow she couldn't lie to him even if it was about something trivial. She said, 'The week's.'

He closed the drawer. 'It's a lovely day; will you have lunch with me?' And when she hesitated he asked, 'Have you ever been to Stourhead? There's a splendid lake there, with ducks and magnificent trees and all the peace in the world.'

He smiled slowly. 'Just for an hour or two? You must close for lunch; an extra hour won't make too much difference.'

'Well, it would be nice, but I must be back for the afternoon.'

She came from behind the counter and turned 'Open' to 'Closed' on the door, and asked, with her back to him, 'Are you on holiday?'

'Yes, for a day or two.'

'You aren't going to Holland?'

'Yes, but not immediately.'

She said, 'I won't be long—I must get a jacket.' She opened the door to the living room. 'If you'll wait here…'

She left him there and went up to her room, found a jacket and sensible shoes, poked at her hair and added lipstick and went downstairs. She was out of her mind, she told herself, seeing him sitting in the armchair, looking as though he belonged there. She wondered why he had come and how he had known where she was. Perhaps he intended to tell her that he was going back to Holland for good, to marry and live in his lovely old house in Amsterdam.

Doubtless she would be told over their lunch.

He had parked the car at the end of the little street and she was surprised and pleased to see Wilf and Robbie side by side in the back of the Rolls.

The Professor popped her into the car and got in beside her.

'We'll go to Stourhead; these two need a good walk.' He drove out of the town carrying on the kind of conversation which needed no deep thought and few replies. Their way took them through a quiet countryside with few villages and only the small town of Wincanton halfway. It was a bright day, and autumn had coloured the trees and hedges. The approach to the estate, with tantalising glimpses of its magnificent trees and shrubs over the high stone wall bordering the narrow road, was like a great tunnel, opening into a narrow lane leading to the gates.

There was a pub on one side, and a house or two on the other, and Gerard turned into the car park by the pub.

'We can lunch here. Shall we have coffee and then take the dogs for a walk? There's plenty of time.'

'Yes, please, I'd like that. Will Wilf and Robbie be allowed inside?' She looked down at the two whiskered faces and said, 'I never imagined that you would have dogs like these two.' And then went red because she had spoken her thoughts out loud and they had sounded rude.

He smiled a little. 'Neither did I; sometimes things happen whether one wants them or not.

I wouldn't part with them now for a small fortune.'

They were walking to the pub entrance. 'And they're company for Mrs Potts when you're in Holland. Will you take them with you when you leave England?'

'They will go where I go,' he told her, and opened the pub door.

There was no one in the bar, but the cheerful man who was stacking glasses wished them good day and had no objection to Wilf and Robbie—and certainly, he told them cheerfully, they could have coffee.

I shouldn't be here, reflected Julia. I ought not to have come. But she knew that nothing would have stopped her; she felt as though she had left her mundane life behind and had gone through a door into a world where there was no one but Gerard. And this really is the last time, she told herself, forgetting how many times she had already said that.

The Professor, watching her thoughts showing so clearly on her face, had his own thoughts, but all he said was, 'Shall we go? If we walk all round the lake it will take an hour or so.'

There was a church by the pub, small and old, and while Gerard got their tickets from the kiosk at the gate she wandered up the path between the ancient tombstones and peered through its open door. It was beautiful inside, quiet with the quietness of centuries, and there were flowers everywhere. Presently she felt the weight of Gerard's arm on her shoulders and they stood together without speaking, then turned and went down the path together.

The dogs were waiting patiently, so they each took a lead and started along the path round the lake, not hurrying; there was too much to see—towering trees, bushes and shrubs, ducks on the water and, hidden away from the path, Grecian temples and presently a waterfall, and a wooden bridge under which there were shoals of small fish. They didn't talk much, but every now and then Julia clutched Gerard's arm to point out something she wanted him to see.

There weren't many people there and it was quiet save for the birds. They found the grotto presently, at the bottom of narrow steps, and then walked the short distance back to the gates.

There were a few people in the pub now, but they found a table in a window and Wilf and Robbie, refreshed with water and a biscuit, curled up at their feet while they ate a Ploughman's lunch and emptied a pot of coffee. And Julia, munching warm bread and cheese, didn't think of the past or the future, only the happy present.

She looked up and caught his eye. 'I feel happy,' she told him seriously, a remark which brought a gleam to his eye.

He drove her back to Sherborne presently, talking easily about their walk, and discussing what they had seen. When they got to the shop, he got out and unlocked the door for her, listened to her thanks, assured her that he had enjoyed himself as much as she had and then bade her a cheerful goodbye.

She watched him drive away and went through the shop and sat down in the living room. She wanted very much to have a good cry, but a customer might come. No one came. She locked the door at half past five and made herself a pot of tea. She wasn't hungry, and the memory of the Ploughman's lunch, eaten so contentedly in the Professor's company, would serve for her supper.

Of course she didn't sleep; she lay awake thinking of him driving back to London. He had had a free day and, having discovered where she was, had made her the purpose of a drive into the country. He had wished her goodbye in a most casual manner; now he had seen for himself where she was he would lose all interest—if he'd had any in the first place. But he had been kind to her on several occasions; perhaps he felt under an obligation to Thomas…

She dropped off to sleep at last and woke with a start. The shop doorbell was ringing— the postman must be getting impatient. She got into her dressing gown and slippers and hurried to the door, not stopping to pull up the blind.

Wilf and Robbie trotted in, and hard on their heels was the Professor. He shut the door behind him, turned the key in the lock and then stood for a moment, looking down at her sleepy face and tangled mane of hair. He had had a sleepless night too, but there was no sign of that in his quiet face.

He gathered her into his arms. 'Tell me truly,' he begged. 'Are you happy here?'

She shook her head against his chest.

'Then would you consider marrying me? I have waited patiently for you to make a career for yourself, for it seemed to me that that was what you wanted more than anything else. But there is a limit to a man's patience and I am at the end of mine. But you have only to say, Go away, and I will go.'

Julia sniffed back tears as she mumbled, 'Don't go. Please don't go.' And then, 'You shouldn't be here; its seven o'clock in the morning. And if you love me, why didn't you say so? And I don't want to be independent.

Only there wasn't anything else and I thought you didn't like me.'

'My darling,' said the Professor soothingly. 'Let us get one thing straight. I fell in love with you when we first met, although perhaps I didn't realise that at once. I have never stopped loving you and I never shall.'

'Really?' She looked up into his face and smiled at what she saw there.

'Really,' said the Professor, and bent to kiss her.

It was quite a while before she went upstairs to dress, leaving Gerard to put the kettle on and let the dogs into the little back garden. Her head was a jumble of thoughts: they would marry just as soon as possible; she would go back to London with him that morning; she was not to worry about the shop, he would deal with that; they would live in his lovely old house in Amsterdam. But none of these were important. The one thought which filled her head was that he loved her. She bundled up her hair, dashed powder on her nose and ran downstairs to tell him once again that she loved him too.

# MILLS & BOON® PUBLISH EIGHT LARGE PRINT TITLES A MONTH. THESE ARE THE EIGHT TITLES FOR SEPTEMBER 2001

## THE MARRIAGE ARRANGEMENT
Helen Bianchin

## SAVAGE INNOCENCE
Anne Mather

## A CONVENIENT HUSBAND
Kim Lawrence

## HIS MIRACLE BABY
Kate Walker

## MISTRESS ON HIS TERMS
Catherine Spencer

## WIFE BY ARRANGEMENT
Lucy Gordon

## HUSBAND FOR A YEAR
Rebecca Winters

## AN INDEPENDENT WOMAN
Betty Neels

MILLS & BOON®

*Makes any time special*™

# MILLS & BOON® PUBLISH EIGHT LARGE PRINT TITLES A MONTH. THESE ARE THE EIGHT TITLES FOR OCTOBER 2001

---

## A PERFECT NIGHT
Penny Jordan

## THE SWEETEST REVENGE
Emma Darcy

## TO MAKE A MARRIAGE
Carole Mortimer

## THE BOSS'S SECRET MISTRESS
Alison Fraser

## HUSBAND BY NECESSITY
Lucy Gordon

## THE IMPETUOUS BRIDE
Caroline Anderson

## TWINS INCLUDED!
Grace Green

## THEIR BABY BARGAIN
Marion Lennox

MILLS & BOON®

*Makes any time special*™